THE SACRIFICE
OF THE
SHANNON

BY
W. ALBERT HICKMAN

INTRODUCTION BY
IAN JOHNSTON

Formac Publishing Company Limited
Halifax

Formac Publishing Company Limited acknowledges the support of the cultural affairs section, Nova Scotia Department of Tourism and Culture. We acknowledge the financial support of the Government of Canada through the Book Publishing Industry Development Program (BPIDP) for our publishing activities. We acknowledge the support of the Canada Council for the Arts for our publishing program.

Cover illustration: *Holy Lock*, J.H. Wilson, Scotland (n.d.)

Series Editor: Gwendolyn Davies

National Library of Canada Cataloguing in Publication Data
Hickman, Albert, 1877-1957
The sacrifice of the Shannon

(Formac fiction treasures)
ISBN 0-88780-542-6

1. Ice-breaking vessels—Nova Scotia—History—Fiction. I. Title. II. Series.

PS8465.I325S3 2001   C813'.52   C2001-903027-4
PR9199.3.H465S2 2001

First published in 1903 by Frederick A. Stokes Company, New York

Formac Publishing Company Limited
5502 Atlantic Street
Halifax, Nova Scotia B3H 1G4
www.formac.ca

Printed and bound in Canada

Presenting Formac Fiction Treasures

Series Editor: Gwendolyn Davies

A taste for reading popular fiction expanded in the nineteenth century with the mass marketing of books and magazines. People read rousing adventure stories aloud at night around the fireside; they bought entertaining romances to read while travelling on trains and curled up with the latest serial novel in their leisure moments. Novelists were important cultural figures, with devotees who eagerly awaited their next work.

Among the many successful popular English language novelists of the late 19th and early 20th centuries were a group of Maritimers who found in their own education, travel and sense of history events and characters capable of entertaining readers on both sides of the Atlantic. They emerged from well-established communities which valued education and culture, for women as well as for men. Faced with limited publishing opportunities in the Maritimes, successful writers sought magazine and book publishers in the major cultural centres: New York, Boston, Philadelphia, London, and sometimes Montreal and Toronto. They often enjoyed much success with readers 'at home' but the best of these writers found large audiences across Canada and in the United States and Great Britain.

The Formac Fiction Treasures series is aimed at offering contemporary readers access to books that were successful, often huge bestsellers in their time, but which are now little known and often hard to find. The authors and titles selected are chosen first of all as enjoyable to read, and secondly for the light they shine on historical events and on attitudes and views of the culture from which they emerged. These complete original texts reflect values which are sometimes in conflict with those of today: for example, racism is often evident, and bluntly expressed. This collection of novels is offered as a step towards rediscovering a surprisingly diverse and not nearly well enough known popular cultural heritage of the Maritime provinces and of Canada.

INTRODUCTION
by Ian Johnston

The Sacrifice of the Shannon, William Albert Hickman's only full-length novel, was first published in 1903. Both a romance and a marine adventure, it closely mirrors actual events, settings and characters that were familiar to the author. The town of Pictou, for example, is renamed Caribou, and a real-life rescue on the ice-fields of the Gulf of St. Lawrence that took place in the winter of 1901-02 partially fits the rescue mission depicted in the novel.

Hickman was born into a shipbuilding family in Dorchester, New Brunswick, in 1877; after his father's death, when he was still a young child, his mother moved to Pictou County and married entrepreneur D.H. Purves. Hickman was educated at Pictou Academy and entered Harvard University in 1896 where he earned a BS in Marine Engineering. A talented and, in many ways, remarkable young man, he took up sculling. When he was in England, a few years after graduation, he was proud to report that he participated in the Diamond Sculls at Henley-on-Thames, where he was defeated by none other than Harry Blackstaffe, Olympic champion for Great Britain in 1908.

The novel is dedicated to the Hon. Clarence

Primrose, Member of the Senate of Canada — the author's relative. Family connections were important to young men like Albert Hickman, and in 1899, aged 21 and fresh out of Harvard, he was appointed Commissioner for the Province of New Brunswick. Stationed in London, he wrote articles and gave illustrated lectures to stimulate interest in immigration to the province, especially for the purposes of farming. His success at this work led to a similar appointment from the federal government, which took him into parts of central and western Canada to observe the areas being opened up for farming in Manitoba and Ontario.

Hickman's interests and lifestyle were entirely appropriate for a nineteenth-century gentleman with a twentieth-century mindset: he was a sportsman who enjoyed hunting and fishing; he played tennis and was mostly likely proficient at winter sports. When travelling he stayed in the best hotels, and in Montreal, New York and London he belonged to suitable social and athletic clubs. He had a keen interest in natural sciences — botany and zoology — and a fascination of engines. He experimented with cutting-edge technology in marine craft, developing the Viper speedboat in 1906. He developed cigar-shaped, high-speed motor boats and a motorized sea-sled that rode on the water using a surface, not a submerged, propeller. In 1914 he tried to interest the British Admiralty in the sea-sled's application for carrying and discharging torpedoes. He did not make any breakthrough until late in the war, and at the same time, the United States navy adopted the sea-sled for aircraft tenders. In 1920 he moved to the States and established two firms for design and construction of motorboats, and set world speed records racing sea-sleds on the Great Lakes.

Coming from a privileged, wealthy family meant that as a young man Hickman moved around quite freely, spending time in Montreal and in the fashionable resort of St. Agathe-des-Monts, returning to Pictou periodically, as well as to Saint John and Dorchester, New Brunswick. In most of these places he visited relatives and family friends. He took up writing as a profession during a two-year period of convalescence that began in 1903. For subject matter he took places and people that were familiar — Pictou and the ship-owning and shipbuilding elite.

In the late eighteenth century Pictou was settled by Scottish immigrants whose is still evident in granite houses, like those described in the novel. In fact, the architecture of these houses is closely copied from homes in western Scotland.

Shipbuilding and forestry were the area's economic mainstays until well into the twentieth century. By the early 1900s traditional wooden shipbuilding and the lucrative export trade were in decline, but accumulated wealth from these exploits was still very evident. The surrounding area was a prosperous industrial centre; in nearby Stellarton and New Glasgow mining, steel

foundries, mills and other enterprises had helped build
flourishing communities, equal to towns and small
cities elsewhere in eastern North America. At the
same time, farming, a mainstay of the rural economy,
benefitted from the ever-expanding urban markets.
The rich fishing grounds of the Northumberland
Strait attracted boats from Nova Scotia and Prince
Edward Island. In these days the Strait and, indeed
all of the Gulf of St. Lawrence, was busy with coastal
trade, especially during the summer and fall.
Communities were dependant on ships for transportation of people and goods, and it was ships, not
railways or roads, that had determined where
European settlement would first occur. Sheltered harbours such as Pictou were prime choices.

Where once such harbours were filled with masts,
around the turn of the century iron and steel was
quickly transforming the foundations of the local
economy. In *The Sacrifice of the Shannon*, the shipowner
MacMichael, like his real-life model Carmichael of
New Glasgow, has had the foresight to sell his fleet of
wooden ships and invest in iron steamers. He intends
to compete with his rival, the Northumberland
Steamship Company, by purchasing icebreakers. In
reality, the ice-crushing service provided by federal
government boats in the Strait was not successful in
keeping shipping lanes open. It was prudent for
coastal shippers to find their own ways to break up
the ice.

At this time, icebreaking technology was in its infancy, spurred on by the desire to extend trade into areas that were ice-bound in winter and spring. In *The Sacrifice of the Shannon*, both Ashburn, the narrator, and Wilson design an icebreaker that will surpass all previous models; they submit the design to the Northumberland Steamship Company, which commissions two vessels in succession, the *Shannon* and the *Liffey*. The test of the their design occurs when one of MacMichael's ships, with the owner himself aboard, becomes trapped in the ice-fields of the Gulf. The rescue attempt closely follows events that took place during the winter of 1902 when the Canadian government icebreaker *Minto* came to the rescue of its fellow vessel, the *Stanley*, which had become frozen in the centre of an ice pan and was drifting for sixty-six days. In the preface to the first edition, Hickman says that he wrote portions of this novel when he was aboard the *Minto* in February of 1902. Photographs taken by the young author were included in the first edition.

The sacrifice of the *Shannon*, the second ship to be lost in the novel, is the point at which the story parts company with factual events. Historically, the *Minto* lost its propellers and was eventually towed ashore when the *Stanley* broke free from the ice. The recounting of the *Shannon*'s demise, however, provides the reader with an intensified awareness of the great dangers faced by men in these conditions and the courage required to persevere and save lives. Apparently well protected from the elements in their steel ships, the situation could quickly change. Ice could crush the supposedly strong steel plates, and the power of two ice-fields could lift a ship out of the water onto the ice.

The *Stanley* was the first steel ferry on the Prince Edward Island-Nova Scotia crossing; it began service in 1888. A pioneer ice-breaker with a deep stem and a shallow bow, it could climb the ice floes and break them with its weight. It had the same icebreaking design as the *Shannon*, and more horsepower than any previous vessel on the Strait crossing; it was capable of travelling at fifteen knots. Although Hickman accurately describes the unpredictability of the ice conditions, his description of the effectiveness of icebreaking steamers at that time is somewhat exaggerated. In spite of its unique design, the *Stanley*, like other early steamers, frequently got stuck in the ice. The ice often proved to be too thick, and the ship was unable to crush it. In the early 1900s, winter ferry service between Prince Edward Island and the mainland was often interrupted. Delays of up to three weeks and sometimes longer were fairly common.

For example, in the winter of 1902-03, ice boats were called into service when the ferries were incapacitated; they transported 246 passengers and more than a hundred thousand pounds of mail. A crew of strong men either rowed or dragged these sturdy whalers across the icy Strait, using a route between

Cape Traverse on the Island and Cape Tormentine on the mainland. Transportation delays caused by ice became less and less frequent during the twentieth century. Before the opening of the Confederation Bridge in 1997, car ferries such as the *Abegweit* and *John Hamilton Gray* rarely operated behind schedule because of ice. However, ice still causes problems with shipping in the Gulf of St. Lawrence and on the coastal waters of Quebec, Newfoundland and Labrador. Heroic rescue attempts still occur, although they are usually performed by helicopters and other search-and-rescue vessels.

Courage and fortitude are requisite qualities for an adventurer such as Hickman's David Wilson — "the type of chap that doesn't seem to be common enough these days." Tall, tanned and exceptionally strong, he is quiet and alert and shows "an inborn aptitude for things in general that no training could ever give." He is a naturalist, an inventor and a world traveller — in short, a gentleman through and through, except for one contradiction. He appears to have no steady income, yet he seems free as a bird. As shipowner MacMichael tells Ashburn, "A man of his [Wilson's] ability should know that, no matter how much brains you may have, you've got to have some little money to be altogether a success."

Wilson's foil is "Captain The Honourable Frederic Ashburn," as the narrator calls himself. Slightly older and more experienced than Wilson, he bears the lovelorn scars of having been refused by an Irish girl. Ashburn shares many of Wilson's talents and interests, especially ships and technology. He deeply admires both Wilson and young Gertrude MacMichael, whom he describes, respectively, as a "jewel" and a "living wonder"; neither are afraid of dispensing with society's conventions. Wilson befriends the Indians in the wilderness; Gertrude is a first-class skipper on her own yacht. And yet they are completely at home in the social milieu of the Caribou elite.

This is the milieu that Hickman loved: at dinner parties and afternoon teas, men like David Wilson who rose to meet life's challenges were revered. Their achievements were undoubtedly frequent topics of conversation, and young men were groomed to emulate their example. But Hickman's heroes also reflect a progressive attitude: they are absorbed by technology, machinery, ships and inventions.

In a 25th anniversary Harvard alumnus report Hickman lists his occupations as "Literature, Manufacturing." In spite of the popularity of his novel, his literary life did not develop and grow with the same impetus from which it started. He published short novels and magazine articles, and contributed fiction and marine sport articles to the *Century* and the *American Magazine*. Two of his stories appeared in the *Canadian Magazine* and others appeared in *Scribners*. In 1914, a single volume entitled *Canadian Nights* appeared which comprised three short novels and four short stories. Both "An Unofficial Love Story" and "The Cockawee" illustrate Hickman's innovation in bringing technology into fiction.

Hickman died in Massachusetts in 1957. He was survived by his mother who was 103 years old at the time. His marine legacy, especially the sea-sled design, has endured and developed over the century. In this reprint of his only full-length novel, his literary candle has been relit.

AUTHOR'S PREFACE.

To anyone who knows Eastern Canada I suppose it would be useless to deny the identity of the " Caribou " of this story with Pictou in Nova Scotia. It is, however, little more than an identity on natural conditions—of physiography—though I have borrowed one or two minor incidents from the wealth of characteristic stories that belong to this beautiful little Gulf of St. Lawrence town.

" Donald's " dialect is a Nova Scotia product, and was studied from life in a number of individuals who exhibited no predilection toward specialising in either Highland or Lowland Scotch peculiarities, but who seemed to be in every case impartial, and to add to the fusion an indescribable something that recalled Vickers-Maxim and Barrow-in-Furness.

Once or twice, in the circumscribed type of language I have allowed myself, I have tried to bring to the reader some conception of the tremendous impression made on the mind by the wonderful silence and by the sense of the resistless power of the northern ice. How thoroughly inadequate any description must ever be can only be realised by the comparatively few who have seen for themselves.

A portion of this story was written aboard the Canadian Government ice-crusher *Minto*—the steamer which served me in part as a model for the *Liffey*—in the ice of the Strait of Northumberland, in February, 1902. To Captain Allan Finlayson, the captain of the *Minto,* and to Mr. Ferguson, her chief engineer, are due my most sincere thanks for facilitating my efforts to be accurate.

W. ALBERT HICKMAN.

THE SACRIFICE
OF THE SHANNON

I'M ASHBURN, who was captain of the old *Shannon*. I should like to tell you this story for half a dozen reasons. One is that the man is a jewel, and whether you're man or woman, if you've any of the right kind of feeling you'd love him if you knew him. Yes! I said "love him;" not necessarily as a woman would, though if you're a woman you might love him any way, and I'd never blame you. I love him, though some of them say I'm a bit of a crank, so that needn't be any criterion. I've been through enough to make a shipload of cranks—or men. The particular reason I have for thinking as much of him as I do is that he's the type of chap that doesn't seem to be common enough these days. His name is Wilson, and I shall tell you more about him in a minute or two.

Another reason I want to tell you the story is that the girl is a wonder, a living wonder, and I know you'll be interested in her. No man or woman could help being interested in her, though some women have expressed their interest in queer ways which were not always intended to be complimentary. If you analyzed them you usually found that they were complimentary if they were anything, no matter what they were intended to be. I've called the girl a wonder because, though, if you take the average girl as your criterion she is far away from it, still, from a cool, unbiased, critical point of view, she is normal,—thoroughly normal. Kindly remember that " normal " is not " average." She's got a circulation that swings a crimson flush in under her sun-tanned cheeks. She walks like a tiger, and looks at a thing or a person, not for the effect of her eyes, but to see. Incidentally she gets the effect a thousand times better than if she tried for it.

I've seen her come over the crest of a snow-drift, going forty miles an hour, on a pair of ski, and, after sailing through the air for fifty feet, light with a thud that would make even a Norwegian's hair stand on end, and, with her lips set and eyes flashing, go on careering down a drifted slope until, in a blinding cloud of snow, she had to throw herself to keep from running into a bunch of alders at the bottom. I've seen her get dumped out of a canoe in a rapid, and laugh while she hung on to a rotten log while they were trying to get a rope to her from the shore. I've carried parcels for her and gone into a house where everybody was sick and everything had gone wrong and nobody had any temper left. I've seen her wheedle the whole family into good humor apparently merely by presupposing that things must come right, and when we had left everyone would be smiling just as she had been doing throughout. Then I've seen her in a ballroom, enjoying herself like an irresponsible schoolgirl; combining the frankness and unconventionality of such a young lady with the carriage of a princess. All the time she was breaking hearts as——well, as the old *Shannon* used to break ice. Not that she intended it in the least, for I think she was rather vaguely sorry she did. Besides these little traits, she knew things,—actually knew things; and most of them—or a good many, any way—were things that the majority of girls didn't know, and don't yet. I don't say she could argue. Few women can: perhaps none. But then—she didn't have to. She got at the bottom of most things without trying, and then she acted. Intuition they call it; and when you find a girl with spunk enough to act on the result of her intuition you've found a wonder, and you've got to keep your eye to windward for white squalls.

Perhaps you don't think all this is normal. Well, it's all-round development, any way. Gertrude MacMichael—that's her name—is a thoroughbred, and that's being normal from my point of view.

Your point of view! you say? Yes, my point of view. Simply because I choose to have been the captain of the *Shannon* doesn't necessitate my always having been the captain of the *Shannon*. I used to be Captain The Honourable Frederic Ashburn, which, by the way, I still am, though nobody knows it in this part of the world, or at least very few do. I know most of the nooks and corners in a good many noblemen's houses from Carlton House Terrace west to South Kensington, and from Sussex Gardens to South Pimlico. I can hum most of the tunes that the orchestra used to play in the days when the old St. James loomed up in the restaurant world, before the time of Prince's and the Carlton. There are some boxes in Drury Lane, the Adelphi, and the Lyceum in which I have fairly worn out the upholstery, and this instant I can catch the scent of a spray of crimson roses that clung to the heaving front of a white-silk bodice, and hear the rippling melody of " Patience " at the old Savoy :—

> "If I can wheedle a knife or a needle,
> Why not a silver churn ?"

Where am I? Oh! I am merely telling you this to let you see that I know when a girl is a thoroughbred and when she isn't. I've seen about all the kinds this world turns out——and loved one or two of them——and Gertrude Mac-Michael's far and away above them all.

This all reminds me that there is just one thing in which she was not normal; she didn't seem to know how to get in love.

Well! Well! Imagine an old chap with his hair getting iron grey going off into a burst like that about any living woman. In love with her? No, most decidedly. No! A more disinterested admiration for a woman—a girl—a man never had.

There are plenty of other reasons why I want to tell you the story. It's nice, for instance, to be able to tell of a man being unselfish, and nobody in the world knowing about it, and yet to find that the man got his reward in this life. You always do, you know. Then it's nice to be able to tell of infallible people being mistaken—sometimes.

Perhaps—in fact it's very likely—you've never seen the Gulf of St. Lawrence in a northeast gale in winter, with the ice-floes smashing each other into lolly and grinding the tops off the reefs. It's something to be able to tell you of human beings venturing into that for duty, and in one case for love.

James MacMichael, the father of the girl I've been telling you of, is known pretty well by everyone who ever had anything to do with eastern Nova Scotia. His parents came out from Scotland, and landed at Caribou, on the shore of Northumberland Strait. MacMichael went into shipping, as did everybody in those days, and before James had much more than learned his Shorter Catechism he started in with his father as part-owner of a two-hundred-ton brig, and from that he went on. When wooden shipping began to take the path that was to drag down half the industries of the Maritime Provinces of Canada, James MacMichael, keen as steel, was the first to see the change. He sold out his fleet before it was too late, and went in for iron steamers,—potbellied traders, tramps.

Everybody knows the MacMichael boats. They trade pretty well everywhere. If there's a little war on,—say between two South American republics,—they always seem to be mixed up in it, and usually get captured for a time, for which the Government that charters them has to pay sundry charges to MacMichael & Co.; meanwhile the men of the captured steamers do as most prisoners of war in like circumstances, enjoy themselves, and put in spare time with chipping and painting.

The engineers have time to overhaul things down below, and the officers see something of the life of the port, and ruminate on the astuteness of " the old man " at home. Then something happens; peace is reëstablished; and the *Duncannon* or the *Duncansby*, or whichever it may be, goes on her way to carry cotton, or iron, or deal, or what not, from anywhere to anywhere between the equator and the polar oceans. So the Mac-Michael boats pay twenty per cent., and James MacMichael is rich.

Up in the Gulf, through the long days in summer, when everything is rippling blue and sunshine,—for nowhere in the world is there summer weather like that of the Gulf of St. Lawrence,—if you see a black smudge on the horizon it's a fifty-per-cent. chance it's a MacMichael boat. Perhaps it's the *Duncrieff* bound up to Cape Tormentine for deals, or the *Dundalk* with coal from Sydney to Montreal. Perhaps, as she comes hull up, you may see the four masts of the big *Dungeness*, the one that old Donald McDonald, when he was chief in her, used to drive at twelve knots, though no one to this day knows how he did it. A good many of them manage to get into Caribou, where MacMichael lives, once in the season.

When January comes round and the harbour freezes, while the bay ice makes outside, and the big fields of queer-shaped clumpets and bergs

come down from the northeast and fill the whole
Gulf, then the MacMichael boats have to clear
out.   If they want to come to a Nova Scotia port
they have to try Halifax or somewhere else on the
south coast.

Now Prince Edward Island—Canada's smallest
province—well deserves its pet name, "The Garden of the Gulf,"—for a garden it is.   Time was—
and not so very long ago either—when there was
no chance of carrying to the mainland of New
Brunswick and Nova Scotia in winter any of its
traditional products,—potatoes, oats, and servant-
girls.   There was a great demand for all three on
the mainland as well as for the thousand-and-one
other things "The Island" turned out, and consequently there was a great stroke of business
to be done by the man who could devise a means
of carrying them across through the ice-floes that
crowd the Strait of Northumberland from January
to April.   The result of all this was that the soul
of MacMichael was troubled.   It was not only that
there was money to be made—though that was
always a consideration; but MacMichael was and
is a philanthropist,—and especially a commercial
philanthropist,—and, still more especially, a commercial philanthropist near home.

Up between Cape Tormentine and Cape Traverse the mails and a few passengers were carried
across the Strait by the ice-boats.   These were

practically small whale-boats with runners on their bottoms, manned by crews of strong experienced men who rowed their boats over open water and dragged them over floes and clumpets from Cape to Cape and back again the season through. The ice-boat service bred plenty of heroes, but even heroes don't always give commercial satisfaction.

At last a new power came into being and undertook to solve the problem, and finally the problem collapsed. Then MacMichael, more or less behind for the first time in his life, decided to come into violent collision with the new power. The result was more far-reaching than he or any one else — but one — could have dreamed. It's this that I want especially to tell you about.

Now, first I must give you an idea of this chap Wilson. He stood a neat six feet, and he was as light on his feet as an Indian. His complexion wasn't dark, though the sun in summer and the March wind had had their say, and he looked as wholesome as a ten-year-old boy. His father, an old country doctor, had come out from the north of Ireland, somewhere near Loughbrichland in County Down, to Nova Scotia. His practice went over three counties and his fame over three provinces, and where his fame went there he was loved. He attended two brothers,—one rich and the other poor,—during a long winter season. Both got well. The rich one got a bill for four

hundred dollars, which he paid. The poor one
got two hundred of those same dollars, which he
needed, besides unlimited barrels of flour and Bay
of Fundy shad, which he and his family ate. And
so things went. Some of his patients died—some
people will; but the majority of them lived, for
the time being, for his skill was marvellous. Some
of his patients got bills, and paid them; but most
of them seemed to get other things, and blessed
him for them, though he didn't give them for the
sake of the blessings. When the old Doctor died
not only the whole county but the whole country
turned out to the funeral, and, because they didn't
want to look up, walked with bowed heads to the
cemetery, and wept real tears. I never knew the
Doctor, but those who did have told me that
though his voice could be as soft as a girl's he
had a will like nickel steel. Young Wilson in-
herited this peculiarity as fully as he did some
others.

I'll remember the day I met him as long as I
do my own name. It was a little after I'd let
everything slip in England. Before that I was
in the navy. I think I'd been lucky, and things
looked pretty bright. I——well, I had a fairly
good time, and used to distribute myself pretty
well as far as women were concerned. I quite
realized that some chaps—most of them, in fact
—were really seriously affected by love, and knew,

from what I remembered of my boyhood's experiences, that there was something in it which would affect weak or undeveloped men. Yes, I was funny those days. I used to reason that way, and took myself a good deal in earnest. Then that Irish girl came along,—Kathleen—Kitty Tyrrell; God bless her! I collapsed. She didn't. That's a terse way of putting it at this distance, though there's more blood and sweat in the words than I care to think about.

I decided that there were plenty of lieutenants that wanted a step up, and that Her Majesty's Navy could struggle along without me if it had to. My friends said a good many hard things, but I got on a tramp outward bound for deals, and was landed at St. John, New Brunswick.

It was about the 1st of September, and I got a canoe and an Indian and went up the Tobique River hunting, and tried to forget things. Perhaps you know what sort of a success you make of that in the woods. In the daytime, out of the rapids in the Big Serpentine, I'd hear a rich voice with a laugh in it. At night, when the only sound was the ripple of the river, the moon would throw the shadows of the spruces down on the tent, and as I'd roll over in my sleeping-bag and look up I'd see those shadows trace the form of a beautiful stately blue-eyed girl. Then Plymouth would come up, and the deck of the *Centaur:* then

Ilfracombe: then London: then Portrush, and the great white sweep of the Ladies' Wishing Arch, where I saw her last.   Then—perhaps—I'd sleep.

We'd worked along up to Nictor Lake at the head of the Tobique.   It's beautiful if ever a lake was.   It winds around through wooden mountains with the Sagamook itself rising on the south twenty-four hundred feet from its edge.   We were going to camp on an island near its head, but as we paddled up we saw the smoke of a camp-fire. When we got nearer a man came down and beckoned us ashore.   We were eighty miles from a house and hadn't seen a human being but each other for two weeks.   The Indian rushed the canoe ahead with short quick strokes that made the water hiss under the bow.

"Das Meesta Weelson," he grunted; "you lak'm heem.   He very good t' Injun.   Sposem he's jus' com' up de Pisiquit.   Goin' down Tobique. He try t' fin' out 'bout som' leetle bird or mebbe 'bout som' fish.   He wan't t' fin' out 'n' he chase'm from here t' Labrador."   From which I inferred that Mr. Wilson was a naturalist, whatever else he might be.

We ran into a little cove under some big spruces, climbed out, and pulled the canoe up on the pebbly beach beside a beautiful little clinker-built cedar belonging to the stranger.   The man the Indian called Mr. Wilson walked over to meet us.   He

nodded at the Indian and said: " *Wal-a-gis-kut,*
Tom," and then went off into a stream of *kngs*
and *ahahys* and *ttcs* that make up the burden and
mystery of the Malicete language. The *Wal-a-
gis-kut* I got to know meant " It's a fine day," or
something equivalent, but beyond that I never
got.

While he was speaking to the Indian I had
time to take him in casually. He stood about a
neat six feet, as I've told you. He was dressed
in a dark neutral-grey gaberdine suit, light oil-
tanned moccasins, and was hatless. His hands
and face, from constant exposure to the sun and
wind, were almost as brown as those of the Indian
beside him. But what I noticed especially was
the great breadth and apparently enormous
strength of his shoulders and back, and the depth
of his chest. He came over and shook hands.

" I'm very glad to meet you," he said, in a
peculiarly soft, low, even voice, enunciating each
word as clearly as ever an elocutionist did, but
naturally and without effort. " Your Indian, who
is an old friend of mine,"—and he smiled at Tom,
who grinned back complacently,—" tells me that
you have been having a couple of weeks' shooting.
Won't you come up and have supper with me?   I
don't know whether I intuitively knew that I was
to be honoured with your company or not, but
I've got an unusually large bill of fare, including

trout and caribou and grouse and buckwheat pan-
cakes and marmalade and coffee. If you think
that is tempting enough I should be very glad to
have you come."

I accepted, and while the Indian was putting
up my tent I went over by the fire and talked to
my host. When I was a boy I used to visit an
uncle up about the north of Scotland near Duncansby Head, and there I got fond of studying
birds, so we had at least one bond of interest.

Wilson—David Wilson was his name—impressed me more and more strongly and more and
more favourably every minute I saw him. He
was big, as I have told you, but so long had he
been accustomed to outdoor life with all its health-
fulness that he moved with a step as springy and
light as a fawn's. His hair was brown and wavy.
His blue eye was always bright and *alert,* and his
hand was quick and precise in whatever it did.
Both showed the training of a scientist, and, still
better, an inborn aptitude for things in general
that no training could ever give. Without apparent effort he canted a thirty-foot cedar log out
of the way of my tent door, when the Indian could
hardly move it, and when I proceeded to marvel
he smiled in an amused way and went on talking
as if he had been handling a cordwood stick. He
spoke with a peculiar impressive quietness, and
his voice was very low. Perhaps what impressed

me most then is the same peculiarity that has
impressed me ever since. This was his faculty
for doing things on which the majority of men
would centre their every attention, with little or
no apparent effort. He cut three six-foot lengths
out of a fir log as additions to his fire-back, and
carried them over and placed them. The next
instant he ran his eyes over a bunch of young
birches, selected one that suited him, and with a
swing of his belt-axe cut it out. He trimmed it
and rammed it in the ground by the fire for a
chiplaquagan. Then his eye lighted on some of-
fending young spruces, and, seizing them, he tore
them up with half a cartload of earth and leaf-
mould. Nearly all the time he was looking either
at me or out on the lake, the calm surface of which
was reflecting the mountains and a grand sunset,
and talking in the same quiet way, his voice now
sincere, now with a laugh in it, as he lightened
some bit of description with an epigram or a
quaint simile.

In the twenty minutes while he was cooking
that supper and preparing for the night he captured me as I've never been captured by a man
before or since. He'd had all sorts of experiences
and been in many places; yet he was young, perhaps not more than twenty-eight. He knew London almost as well as I did myself, and Paris and
New York and Fr'isco a great deal better. He

had seen the bad as well as the good. He had kept out of it—much better than I had—and yet he knew it all.

"It was a good deal for my own sake," he said, laughing, "and a good deal for the sake of the girl I'll marry some day."

"Have you discovered her yet?" I asked, laughing also.

He smiled with a most peculiar half-amused, half-reminiscent expression. He looked out over the lake for a second or two, then casually around him until his eye lighted on the last spruce-bush remaining in front of the tent. It wasn't particularly in the way and was very much larger than the others. However, it seemed to be a satisfactory size for him to vent his feelings on, and he did it in what I afterwards learned was a characteristic way. I chuckled to myself as he walked over, bent down, and without a change of expression—except perhaps that his lips tightened up a little—dragged it out of the ground with a great tearing of roots and flying of earth, and heaved it hissing into the lake. He looked down somewhat triumphantly into the hole, tramped the moss down around it, and walked back to where he had been standing. Then, looking at the top of the Sagamook, he answered my question: "Hmm! I'm sorry, but I'm afraid I hardly know."

I whistled beneath my breath and let the subject drop. "More fool she!" I thought. "Another case like my own; but then——she couldn't
be like Kitty!" Things afterwards proved that
they had at least one point in common.

I don't know why it was. Perhaps it was because we were in the woods and alone. Perhaps
it was because that girl had pounded me into
jelly and I was particularly plastic. Any way, I
made friends with Wilson more quickly than I
ever had with a man before. In fact I made
friends as I never had with any man. After all,
it was probably just because he made friends with
every one on sight,—yes, and every dog and horse
too. I know a beautiful English countess. When
she meets you for the first time she impresses on
you—without saying so—that you are the one
man she has been looking for all her life. Then
you succumb. She is a diplomatist and not always
in earnest. Wilson had almost the same effect
on me, with the exception that I knew he was in
earnest from the start.

He was a typical Canadian, and I was a typical
enough Englishman, though since that a good
many of my Englishisms have gone down under
Nova Scotia influence. I had a good bit of money
—have yet; but I didn't know where to turn to
get away from myself, so when Wilson told me
that he was going to do some scientific work on

tides and ice and birds and fishes in the Gulf of St. Lawrence, and that he'd be glad to have me go along, I jumped at the chance. It was a love for adventure that took me into the navy, so the prospect was well to my taste.

We hunted and fished for a few days on the lake. One night Wilson was paddling me back to camp. We had been talking everything from Russian politics to the vagaries of tropical cyclones; from Gloucester fishermen to London music-halls. The old feelings came back with a rush, and I told him all my troubles. He was as sympathetic as a woman, and do you know, a couple of tears rolled down my cheeks. I, Frederic Ashburn, once captain of Her Majesty's Ship *Centaur;* I, whose pride it was that I could lick every man and officer in my crew with gloves or bare hands,—I actually shed tears, a thing I hadn't done since my mother died. Good Lord! think what sickening pain a girl like that must give a man like me to wring tears from him,—and they seem to know it so little. Of course he didn't see it.

"Why did you give it up?" he asked ingenuously.

"What could I do? She didn't love me and told me so, and—more—told me she never could. Unless you impress a girl at first there is not much chance of impressing her afterwards!"

"Oh! there isn't, eh! How did you obtain that astonishing piece of information?" This half laughingly. Then a silence, while the canoe hissed and boiled ahead like a destroyer on a trial trip.

"Under similar conditions," he continued with a funny emphasis, "I'm inclined to think I'd try; yes"—slowly—"I'm inclined to think I'd try— a little." I had an idea what "a little" meant.

Then I cursed myself for lacking pluck, a thing I'd never had to do before.

The next morning Tom Bernard, the Indian, packed both tents and the dunnage into my canoe, crowned the load with a couple of caribou heads we had got, and we started down the Tobique. I was with Wilson. On the way down he talked a good deal to the Indian in Malicete, in which language he seemed to be as fluent as in English, and when we at last reached Tom's camp I learned another phase of his character. All the Indians knew him, and he visited all the camps. Many of the squaws had beaded belts and moccasins as presents for him, and he went around to every family, distributing money enough to buy them all sorts of little luxuries for the winter. Afterwards I found that he was doing things of this sort constantly.

We left in his canoe and started down river. A few moments afterwards he stopped paddling.

"I hope you won't mind my asking you a favour, Captain Ashburn," he said. "I shall be able to tell you the reason later on. Now, you mustn't think it peculiar, but sometimes you may see things that would lead you to infer that I have a good deal of money. As he had probably surmised, I already thought as much from his rather lavish generosity to the Indians. "If you should infer this—and it's not at all impossible—please don't say so to any one. I know you will understand. I only dare say this to you because you have not known me before and might suppose that some knowledge of my affairs was common property."

"My dear boy"—he was ten years younger than I—"if you wish it I shall be most careful in keeping whatever thoughts I may have to myself. But I sometimes think that if a man chooses to do good it is not always well to hide it too thoroughly."

"Perhaps not," he answered, "but I'm afraid I'm not unselfish enough to make that a motive. There are other reasons." Though I wondered at the time, with that I had to be satisfied.

Well, we went down to St. John, and there I got together all my traps and went with him to Caribou by the Intercolonial Railway. There is no more beautiful little town in all the world than Caribou. It lies on the sloping north side of a grand harbour, and is all beauty and repose and climate. Wilson moved there with his mother, he told me, after his father's death, partly because he had friends there, but chiefly because the place made a convenient centre for his scientific work.   Near at hand Caribou has great coal-fields, and, as I have told you, is the home of the MacMichael boats and of MacMichael.

I wanted to go to a hotel, but Wilson wouldn't have it.   He made me go with him to his home, a beautiful little stone place perched on a hill top two hundred feet above the sea.   His mother, a sweet-faced woman of fifty, showed me where her son had got part of his character at least, and taught me for the first time the wonderful way strangers are welcomed in Canadian homes.

After tea was over, Wilson asked me to go with him to see a friend of his.

" He's a lawyer named Henderson," he said, " and we've shot and fished a good deal together.   He's not overburdened with wealth and can't get away as much as he would like.   He's a crank on boat-racing, as, for that matter, am I.   Are you fond of it ? "

" Yes ! " I answered, " though ' fond of it ' hardly gives a fair idea of my liking for it.   I think I can sail a boat better than I can do any other one thing, and I expect you might call me a crank too."   Then I told him about some races I'd sailed in the Solent and in the North Sea.

When we reached Henderson's house, a big wooden place half buried in vines and hedges, we were ushered into a room that might have been the model-room of a yacht club. Everywhere there were models, and boats, and pictures of boats. Then there were stuffed trout and a salmon, and in a corner a couple of rods and a landing-net. Another corner held rifles and shot-guns and a couple of deer head and an ugly looking Canada lynx. They told me the story of that lynx that night. Sometime I'll tell it to you.

Henderson had been writing, and got up as we went in. He was a medium-sized, rather slight man, dark and with a black silky moustache. He was wiry and moved quickly. He shook hands with Wilson in a way that showed in an instant how much he was attached to him.

" Dave, I can't tell you how glad I am to see you," he said.

" I'm glad to see you, too, Will; I've brought a friend with me,—Captain Ashburn, Mr. Henderson. Captain Ashburn is as fond of boats and sailing as you and I are."

Henderson shook my hand. " You're in luck, then," he said warmly, " we've got a regatta coming off to-morrow, and we expect to get some fun out of it."

" What regatta's that? " asked Wilson.

" Why, the Caribou Annual."

" So it is. I've been forgetting. This is the best regatta of the year here, Captain." Then, turning to Henderson again, " Are there many entries? "

" More than ever before.   There will be fifty lobster-fishermen in if there's one, and in the twenty-one
foot water-line yacht class there are some new boats.
Only two days ago a perfect beauty, finished in
natural wood and covered with yacht jewellery,
came in from Montreal for MacMichael.   From
what I've seen of her I think she's likely to prove
the fastest in these waters.   She's entered: Miss
MacMichael came down and entered her herself, and
I shouldn't be surprised if she sailed her herself,
too.   She can do it better than any man in the Gulf.
There's only one boat I've ever seen that would have
any chance of holding her, Dave, and that's your old
Glooscap."

Wilson smiled in a way I had seen him smile but
once before.   It was when he pulled the big spruce-
bush out of the ground on the island in Nictor Lake.
He bent down and picked up a round stick of poplar
from the wood-basket by the fireplace.   It was a
good two inches through, but he broke it across his
knee and tossed the splintered pieces into the fire.
That smile always seemed to be the precursor of
some feat of strength.   The exertion seemed to be
necessary as an outlet for the energy of which the
smile seemed to be one of the indications.   What
was the train of thought which brought up the
smile?   The last time, I had asked him if he had
discovered the girl he was going to marry.   He had

said that he hardly knew. This time we had been talking of boat-racing and of a Miss MacMichael. Perhaps Miss MacMichael——well, for my own satisfaction I'd keep my eyes open.

When finally he spoke I couldn't detect any change in his voice or manner except that perhaps he spoke a little more quietly than usual :—

" The *Glooscap,* bless her old heart, she hasn't been out three times this season.   But I think I'll sail her to-morrow.   Yes, I'll sail her to-morrow.   Will you come with me as part of a crew, Captain Ashburn? "   I was glad enough to get the chance, and accepted.

Wilson asked about the MacMichaels generally, and then we discussed some overhauling he had to do before the *Glooscap* would be ready for work.

Just as we were leaving Henderson turned to Wilson.

" You'll be glad to hear, Dave," he said, " that the *Aurora* and the *Walrus* have been doing splendidly. The summer's work has been really good, and with last winter we shall be able to pay in this one year fifty per cent on all the capital invested.   That should please the Northumberland Steamship Company, shouldn't it ! "

" Yes ! " was the answer, " I think the company should be satisfied with that.   They probably are."

On the way home Wilson explained.

" You know that these harbours and bays in the

Gulf freeze in winter, and the drift-ice comes down from the north and helps to fill the whole of Northumberland Strait. Up to within a few years ago there was no way of crossing the Strait except between the Capes in small ice-boats, and the great trade between Prince Edward Island and the mainland was killed from January to April. Then the Northumberland Steamship Company, with headquarters in London, put on the *Aurora,* a steamer of peculiar and tremendously heavy build, to run between this port and the Island. She pounded her way across through the ice and was a success, so much so that the company put on another boat, the *Walrus,* last year. The boats work in the coastal trade in the summer. In winter they have a monopoly, and, as you have heard from Henderson, have been paying heavily. Henderson knew the Company very well, and was appointed by them to have full control of the boats. It's been a considerable help to him. The Company also gives me employment while I am here, and as it pays me fairly well I am glad to have it."

Besides the money he made through his scientific work, which couldn't be much, it was apparent, then, that Wilson had no other source of income than that he derived from the Northumberland Steamship Company. I wondered what he could have meant when he asked me not to say anything which would indicate that he had considerable money. Later I wondered still more.

CHAPTER II.

WELL, the next morning we turned out before dawn to overhaul the *Glooscap*. We had breakfast by lamplight, after which, from a canvas bag, Wilson produced a big brand-new spinnaker of white silk—which must have cost something—and from the same bag a pennant of heavy crimson corded silk with the tomahawk and arrow of the mighty *Glooscap* embroidered in gold.

" She sails dressed to-day," he laughed, " for she sails for supremacy, or, in any case, for all she's worth. She carries a balanced lug-sail and consequently a short mast, and I've got a bamboo mast and boom for that spinnaker. I've just had it made. I've never had a spinnaker on her yet, but from what Henderson says she'll probably need it to-day." A few minutes afterward, with the spinnaker and the two bamboo sticks on our shoulders, we were on our way to the boat-house.

It was between dawn and sunrise, and as we passed the long market wharf we could see a small forest of boats' masts; and out beyond, boats of all sorts coming in under clouds of white duck. Every fisherman has his suit of racing-sails, and they're usually half as large again as he should have on a boat of the size: but in the Gulf they race with unlimited sail area. Length of water-line is the only thing that counts. It's inclined to be risky in some winds with some kinds of men, but it gives good races. *" Win, or drive her under "* has been the motto with some fishermen, and not infrequently they didn't win.

The *Glooscap* was in the boat-house. I liked her the instant I set eyes on her. She was an able-looking convex-bowed long-countered boat with a big bilge, easy entrance and retreat, little dead-rise, and a walloping big steel centreboard. She was on rollers, and we passed a line to a windlass and eased her down the skids. She rode the water like a duck.

" Where did you get the design? " I asked.

" Oh! made it," was the answer. " They said her bilge was too big to sail fast, but she's beaten them all for four years. One of Mr. MacMichael's engineers designed a boat for him, and she succumbed like the rest. Later Miss MacMichael told me she was going to get a Montreal man to design and build one for her, that would leave the *Glooscap* somewhere on the horizon. The new arrival is probably the boat."

We tested and overhauled everything from masthead to centreboard, bent the new spinnaker on, and lashed it beside the cockpit ready for work. The

crimson pennant was fastened to the peak, and the
Glooscap was ready for the gun.

The third member of our crew, a Swede who accompanied Wilson on many of his winter trips,
Hans Brun by name, turned up about an hour before the first race, that of the lobster-boats. He in-
formed us:

" Der vas yoost 'bout feefty lobster-boat. T'vas
goin' to be a mighty beeg race. De yachts dey don't
know Mr. Vilson's home. Don't tink der *Glooscap* 'll be out. [The boat-house was in behind a
pier and not visible from the course.] Mees Mac-
Michael's got old Donald McDonald und Captain
Irland and von of dose tam offitsers vom Halifax
for a crew."

Wilson looked at me and smiled. " Irland is the
captain of the *Amphitrite,* the flagship of the revenue
cruisers in the Gulf," he said, " and the other is probably young Billings, a midshipman. Anything in
the shape of a naval officer rubs Hans the wrong
way, like most coastal fishermen. We've got more
to fear from old Donald, who is as keen as steel
and absolutely fearless, and from Gertrude Mac-
Michael herself, who is just as fearless as Donald,
and, if possible, a better sailor. As the yachts'
crews don't know we are going to sail, we'll stay
where we are and give them a bit of a surprise."

We went out on the end of the pier and watched
the race of the fishing-boats. The wind was north-

west, and increasing. It was one of those wonderful clear bracing days such as seem to exist nowhere else but in eastern Canada. There were hundreds of people on the market wharf and on the other wharves near the start.

In a couple of hours the lobster-boats had all staggered home across the line, and the judge's boat prepared for the yacht race. More people came down, and launches, tugs, and passenger steamers were crowded. The northwest breeze was still blowing heavily, and still increasing. The yachts came out one by one and went rushing around with bones in their teeth and lists that would test their standing rigging.

Wilson was watching the boats through a pair of stereoscopic binoculars and speaking half to himself. "The *Kelpie;* let's see, that's the *Pirate;* there's the *Siren.* Oh! there's her pennant!"— and he pointed to a smart-looking boat, with a sliding-gunter mainsail and a big jib, flying a blue-and-white pennant.

"Is that Miss MacMichael's boat?" I asked.

"Yes, and she seems to be a beauty, too. She's got a perfect suit of sails, and she's sailing her well. Come along, let's get ready for business." I thought he displayed a good deal of enthusiasm— for him.

"Don't you think," I said, "that you'd really rather be in that boat than in the *Glooscap.*"

He looked at me and laughed. "Captain," he said, "you're a deep thinker."

When we got back to the boat Hans had everything in readiness. A gun was to be fired precisely ten minutes before the race started, and as this would give us plenty of time to get down to the line, Wilson decided not to hoist the sail until the first gun. He held a stop-watch in his hand, and when at last we heard the *boom* behind the pier Hans and he ran up the big sail while I cast off and took the tiller. The *Glooscap* was under way.

It was a fine sight when we rounded the head of the pier. The steamers had come far up back of the line to be out of the way of the boats. Down beyond them, off the crowded wharves, were twenty-odd sail of yachts manœuvering for a start. I saw at a glance that the *Glooscap* was the only boat with a balanced lug-sail, so we would be easily recognized.

Wilson came aft and took the tiller. He steered for the centre of the little fleet of steamers. Now that we were out of the shelter of the pier we realized how hard it was blowing. The *Glooscap* listed to starboard and rushed ahead, with the crimson and gold pennant blowing out straight abeam.

The people on the steamers were so much taken up with the boats near the start that they never saw us until we were right among them. Then they all seemed to yell at once, a few hundred handkerchiefs fluttered, and the whistles of every boat tooted and spluttered until the crowd on the market wharf turned to see what the noise was about.   Evidently the *Glooscap* and her owner were favourites.

The yachts, with one exception, were working up and down behind the line, fighting for position. That exception was the boat with the blue-and-white pennant, and she was working back toward us. Her skipper evidently knew her business.   She was on the starboard tack and to windward just far enough for her mainsail to hide us from the eyes of her crew as we came out from behind the steamers. She came roaring up close-hauled, throwing a boiling smother of foam from her bow and with the green water hissing along her washboard clear back to her counter.

We were running pretty free, and luffed a little as the distance between the two boats shortened. Then we ran straight for the lee bow of the new boat, and as we rushed together Wilson swung the *Glooscap* off when a few seconds more would have sent us both to the bottom.   Our rival hissed past to windward, a picture of polished oak, red cedar, and white canvas.   While Hans and I trimmed the mainsail home Wilson jammed down the tiller for a second and we swung close to the wind.   We rounded her stern so close that her long boom swept over our washboard.

"Look out!" yelled a voice, and its owner, the

midshipman Wilson spoke of, stood paralysed at the apparition of a hitherto unseen boat within twenty feet.

Then a girl's voice, clear as a bell, rang sharp as a drill-sergeant's:—"Hard a-port! Watch that jib-sheet, Donald. There. That's good." I had a vision of a lithe, hatless, dark-haired girl as she jumped and forced the long tiller hard over and held it with her leg as she pulled in a soaking main-sheet, hand over hand, like a Gloucesterman pulling a mackerel-line. The big mainsail flapped viciously. She shifted the sheet to another cleat, and in a few seconds more had filled away on the port tack and was directly astern of us.

This was my introduction to Miss Gertrude Mac-Michael. It had taken Wilson a few minutes to capture me, but this girl had made a conquest in as many seconds and without even speaking. And remember, I'm not impressed with people very readily, either.

In a moment she was standing on the counter of her boat, steering with one foot and holding the loose end of the main-sheet. She put her hand to her lips:

"*Glooscap* ahoy!" she shouted. "Awfully glad to see you. You got ahead of me that time—a little—but wait: I'll catch you yet."

Wilson laughed. "I'll be glad to have you try. Your new boat is a beauty; what do you call her?"

" The *Osprey!* don't you like it? "

" Oh yes! A very pretty name, but she's not fast enough. If you wanted her to catch the *Glooscap* you should have called her the *Duck-Hawk.*"

" Perhaps it won't be necessary," came the laughing reply; then, pointing to our spinnaker, " What's that you've got rolled up there? "

" Just a little spare sail in case of accidents," said Wilson.

" Yes! big spinnaker I expect. If I'm fortunate enough to be near you, and that's likely to be well ahead,"—I saw Wilson smile with pleasure at the ring of poorly hidden admiration in the words,— " I'll make you use every rag you've got. I've got Donald sworn to help me ' win or drive her under,' and when Donald swears you know he's a dangerous man." We could see Donald smile.

The conversation was interrupted by a cheer that drifted across the water from the market wharf. We had been working to windward and down toward the line, of which the wharf, with its crowd of people, formed the windward end. I found afterward that so often had the *Glooscap* saved some coveted cup from being carried off by some slippery craft from Charlottetown or somewhere else, that she had become a general favourite, and now, when the big lug-sail loomed up unexpectedly, with the crimson-and-gold pennant, the crowd cheered itself red in the face. Miss MacMichael heard the cheer and changed in an instant. Her lips tightened; she trimmed her mainsail a bit closer and watched for every shade of advantage. Evidently she had plenty of ambition to win and didn't propose being beaten if she could help it.

Time was pretty nearly up. We worked a little further to windward, and then with two minutes to spare eased off and started for the line with the *Glooscap* still in the windward position. We got there together and crossed just as the gun fired. One powerful-looking boat from Charlottetown, the *Enchantress,* had worked further to windward than the *Glooscap* and gave us some trouble up to the first buoy. She blanketed us, and as a result the *Osprey* got around perhaps half a minute ahead. The next leg was a beat, and the *Osprey* began to have her little troubles with a couple of smooth-looking boats from Antigonish. They worked together, and Miss MacMichael was forced about more than once.

At last she began to draw ahead of them, and about the same time we got well clear of the *Enchantress.* The course home saw the *Osprey* and *Glooscap* well in the lead, with the *Osprey* a good three lengths ahead. That way we passed the market wharf on the first round, and the crowd yelled enthusiastically.

Then it began to blow. Not that it hadn't been blowing, but it blew harder. The race was three times round the buoys, and so far we had had no chance to use the spinnaker. We were free of the other boats now and began to pick up on the *Osprey*.

" She's a good boat! " I said.

" She is," said Wilson. " Hans, come a little further aft. That's better." When we reached home the second time round we were almost on even terms, and the best of the rest of them were not far behind.

Now, I've sailed in nearly everything in the shape of a boat from a Bay of Fundy shad-boat to a Malay flying proa, but I've never had such a sail as the third time round those buoys in Caribou harbour. The wind had been blowing half a gale from the west-northwest before, but now it backed into the southwest, came down smoky, and blew great guns. Most of the boats behind shook up and took in a reef or two. The *Osprey* showed a wall of red-cedar topsides and bilge, and the water hissed green and white along our washboard.

" Are you going to reef? " I asked.

" After Miss MacMichael," said Wilson, and he scanned the *Osprey* with perhaps a shade more of anxiety in his eye than one usually wastes on boats one is racing with. The girl had ordered her crew on to the washboard, and they were stretched out hanging to the gunwale. There were some heavy puffs that made both boats bear down until the water ran along the cockpit coaming, but as far as

I could see she never eased her main-sheet an inch. She was grit, clear grit all through. Then came a puff that made the *Glooscap's* yard bend, and brought three or four buckets of water in over the lee coaming. The blue-and-white pennant went so low that some of the seas seemed to wash up to its level, and we could see Donald climb down and start to bail out the cockpit.

Hans pointed back. " Look at der *Pirate*. I'll be dam' eff she's not bre'k her main boom," he chuckled.

Sure enough, the black boat, with the skull and crossbones on her pennant, was wound up in a bunch of splinters, topping-lift, and torn duck. Our old rival the *Enchantress* had smashed her throat halyard, and a boat from Georgetown came struggling along with her topmast swinging from her masthead, and a man aloft with a hatchet trying to cut away the wire rigging. A fine-looking clinker-built knockabout, burying herself in a smother of foam, was ahead of them all, and with a single reef was making a fine fight to hold her own with us.

We——well, we were flying, and so was the *Osprey*. Yet it wasn't any too safe. There was a nasty lop of a sea running, and if your boat went from under you and left you with a life-preserver or an oar to hang on to you'd get very wet before you got ashore or before you got picked up. I could see that Wilson was going to beat the *Osprey* if he could. It would never do to let a girl like that beat you,—that is, if you wanted a chance of winning the girl. It was funny to see the expression of mixed anxiety and admiration on his face when he looked to leeward.

Miss MacMichael was sailing her boat beautifully. She kept an eye on everything, and all down that leg she was gaining on us slowly. The first buoy was not more than two hundred feet from the head of an old wharf on the side of the harbour opposite the start. She jibed around the buoy four or five lengths ahead of us, and for a second I thought she'd go over in that jibe.

"Oh! the cub, look!" said Wilson. I looked. Young Billings had gone overboard and was swimming for the wharf. Miss MacMichael swung to leeward and then prepared to come about to pick him up.

Wilson handed the tiller to me and jumped forward. "Go ahead!" he roared.

The girl heard him, looked for a few seconds at Billings, who was making good progress toward smooth water, then turned, smiled, and waved her hand as she started to beat up to the next buoy.

"Did he fall over?" I asked, as Wilson came back.

"No. Rounding that buoy was too much for him. He had enough, so he decided to roll out

and swim ashore while the shore was near enough
to swim to. Look at him climbing out on that
wharf. Can you imagine a chap—whoa! look out!
H'm! that was a pretty stiff one!" This when a
howling puff came down that tore the tops off the
seas and sent the spray over our peak. The *Glooscap* stood the strain like a fishing-boat.

Wilson reached down, pulled a couple of life-
preservers out of a locker under the rear deck, and
held them between his feet. Then he glanced at
the *Osprey* as the squall struck her, and his mouth
set for a moment. Over she went until we could
see the swirl of her fin keel, and then her jib-sheet
was let go, but only for a few seconds. She righted up, and we could see Donald sheet the jib home
again. Then she bounced into some short seas, and
the spray flew over her as it does over the bow of
a despatch-boat in the Channel. Miss MacMichael
put on an oilskin coat and changed her yachting cap
for a sou-wester.

That beat from the first to the second buoy was
a great race in itself. The sea was running heavy
and everything was white. Every boat except the
Osprey and *Glooscap* was reefed down. Both the
latter were in a smother of spray all the time, and
through it I could see that girl with the ends of two
sheets in one hand and the tiller in the other. Her
feet were braced against the lee cockpit coaming and
she always had an eye to windward.

The wind was dead southwest now, and still heavier. It began to look as if somebody would have to reef pretty soon, but Miss MacMichael evidently decided to try to get to the second buoy without. If she could do that with the wind as it was she could run home before it, with the advantage of her extra spread of sail. The *Glooscap's* balanced lug set as flat as a board, and good as the *Osprey* was we caught her at last. We were both sailing in the teeth of the wind, and I could see the girl shifting old Donald and Captain Irland round, evidently to get the boat in the best trim possible on every tack. Then she tried to blanket us and failed. We passed her and went sloping down on the buoy a good three lengths ahead.

Both boats were now just able to stagger under their sail. At last we spun round the flag and squared away for home. The *Osprey* hissed and roared around a few seconds after us, and her long main boom swung out.

It was blowing a living gale. The tugs, launches, and passenger steamers had come down to accompany us home and were just ahead. The crowd cheered as we turned, a cheer we could hear above the wind and the hiss of the sea. It was evidently heard on board the *Osprey*, too, for Hans, who, after raising the centreboard, had been sitting on the centreboard trunk descanting in mixed Swedish and English on the merits of Miss MacMichael as a boat-sailor, suddenly stood up, and, bringing his big fist down on his thigh, said " Yesus! "—his largest oath—" Dam' if she's not pootin' on der spinniker."

Now, you can say what you like, but you didn't see the day, and you didn't see the water, green and white—mostly white. Yes, you can say what you like, but I don't think any other woman or girl on earth would have thought of putting a spinnaker on a boat on such a day, even if she were losing all the things she liked in the world instead of a mere yacht race. Wilson didn't think of it, and I didn't think of it. The wind wasn't dead astern, and the heavy sea bothered both the boats as it was. But we had hardly time to realize it before the big white sail ran up and bellied out like a balloon.

Honestly, for a second or two the bow of the *Osprey* was fairly buried. Then she came on, throwing a wall of foam and spray like the poor old *Viper* doing her thirty-seven knots.

Wilson glanced up at the tip of the *Glooscap's* yard, where the crimson-and-gold pennant was being blown to ribbons. Then he looked to the westward at the little steamers, bounding up and down on the white seas, as if he were trying to calculate the speed of the wind from their smoke as it blew ashore low over the foam. As the *Glooscap* swung from side to side and rushed ahead, now in the hollow of a sea, and now on the crest, with two great white waves roaring out from under her chain-plates and six feet of her bow out of water, he steadied himself against the coaming and looked back for a few seconds at the *Osprey*. Then he looked at me and laughed.

"She seems to be thoroughbred!" I said—meaning the girl—"Look, she's gaining every second. Are you going to put the spinnaker on now?"

"Yes! she's a thoroughbred," he mused, and he smiled again in that same peculiar way I had seen before. He turned and watched the flying boat behind.

"We'll have to put the spinnaker on or she'll beat us, and that would never do. We can't be slow either. Hold the tiller, Ashburn. Here! Hans, cast that spinnaker loose. Bring that halyard aft!" In an instant Hans and he were working like beavers, and a few seconds afterward the big Swede was trying to hold down a rustling pile of white silk while Wilson was bending on the halyard. Then, while Wilson held down the sail, Hans went forward to make fast the luff.

In the meantime the *Osprey* had been coming up on us like a duck-hawk on a flock of golden-eyes. Wilson was bending on a sheet, and Hans was working with a snatch-block. The snatch-block wouldn't open, and the Swede reached for a marlinspike and looked back despairingly at the long glistening bow now not ten yards astern on the port side.   Then he twisted and pryed at the block.   He couldn't move it, and the *Osprey* came on.

Wilson glanced now at the boat, now at the Swede.

"Let me have the block.   Good!   Throw the marlinspike too."   He caught the flying iron, held the block in his hand, and with a few blows smashed the patent lock into chippings, though not without cutting his hand in half a dozen places.   He tossed the open block back to Hans, who grinned complacently, while even above the wind I could hear him muttering something about "breaking rocks mit—fist" as he rove the rope he was handling as deftly as a girl at South Kensington handles her silk.

The *Glooscap* was swinging in the heavy seas and I was having my own little troubles, and all the time the *Osprey* was coming up.   It takes a while to get a new spinnaker on, especially unexpectedly and in a gale of wind, and before we were ready Miss MacMichael had her boat alongside of us and was drawing ahead.   A few seconds more, and her stern was abeam of our mast.

Taken altogether you never saw such a sight in a boat race.   Astern, everything coming down boiling white, with boats of all kinds, some with spars or gaffs smashed, and some little more

than wrecks, scudding for the red-and-white flag
on the line.   Ahead, the town sloping up with the
houses showing among the trees, and down below
the crowds on the wharves.   To starboard—
everywhere—spray blown like steam off the tops
of the waves.   To port, a hundred yards away, the
steamers, whistling, and with a yelling excited
crowd waving their hats and handkerchiefs and
watching the *Osprey* as she drew ahead foot by
foot.   To port, twenty yards away, the *Osprey*
herself, half buried in foam, and with her mast
bending fearfully under the bellying cloud of duck
strained almost to bursting.

Her crew were grouped astern, trying to keep
the bow from burying.   Captain Irland was
doubled up, hanging on to the loose end of the
main-sheet.   Donald was stretched out flat on the
counter with the last three inches of a blackened
clay pipe, upside down, between his lips.   His hat
had been blown off.   He wore a bland smile
which I learned afterwards was reserved for occasions when the majority of men would be excited.   He was gazing critically at the straining
mast and evidently offering the skipper some useful advice.

The skipper——well, no words would describe
the skipper.   She was kneeling on the deck of
the counter beside Donald, struggling with the
tiller, which sometimes, as the boat veered, almost

threw her from her knees. Donald put his hand
out to help her. She shook her head and put it
aside. The brown oilskin with the spray streaming down it and glistening like satin was big
enough for two of her and was blown tight in
against her back, showing the graceful curve of
her lithe figure. Her yellow sou-wester, tied
under her chin, was turned up in front so that
she could see aloft easily, and from under it three
or four wisps of black hair blew across her sun-
browned forehead and cheeks. One moment she
would stand up on her knees and watch the
Glooscap, keenly, like the captain of a revenue
cutter watching a smuggler with a clean pair of
heels. Then she'd crouch, look over the sheets,
glance under the spinnaker at the home flag, look
over her shoulder to windward for an instant, and
then turn her attention anxiously to the *Osprey's*
bending mast and gunter.

Suddenly she made a sharp motion with her
hand and pointed to the masthead. I could see
Irland trying to argue with her, but she waved
him aside, and Donald and he began to haul in
the main-sheet. I wondered what she was trying
now, and felt that if she pulled her main boom six
feet further aft she would jibe, and if she jibed
she'd go over, sure. Wilson never spoke, but
gathered the life-belts under his feet again and

looked puzzled. The sail came further in, and Hans voiced our thoughts.

" She's goin' to yibe! " he said, looking thoughtful.

Just then Donald got on the washboard of the *Osprey*, reached far out and managed to catch the slack of the topping-lift. He cut it, knotted a marlinspike into one end, and brought the other end inboard while the marlinspike ran up to the masthead and jammed. Irland let the mainsail run out again, and Donald carried the topping-lift aft and hauled it taut to a cleat on the counter. It made a beautiful backstay.

" She's saved her mast! " I said.

" Yes! " said Wilson, " and neatly too. Now we'll try to save our race. Haul away, Hans," and Hans hauled on the spinnaker halyards like a Tyne tug on a newly launched battleship. The bamboo mast and boom swung up into place.

" Now, break her out! " roared Wilson.

The Swede ran aft, and the two men threw their weight on the sheet.

" Yoomp! Gaptain, yoomp! " yelled Hans, " Make her fast! "

Wilson sprang and took a turn round a cleat, and the long boom swooped down. With flaps like pistol-shots the big silk sail opened out, and then the wind dragged it forward until the

Glooscap reeled under the strain.   Everything creaked, and the bamboo sticks bent like bows.

" They'll stand it," said Wilson, and smiled again as the whistles of the steamers went off into a chorus of shrieks, and the crowd on their decks danced up and down and howled for sheer joy.   There's nothing a Nova Scotia crowd enjoys half as much as a good boat race.

It didn't take ten seconds to show that we were gaining on the *Osprey*, and gaining fast.   A quarter of a mile more, and we were on even terms, and the bow waves of the two boats splashed together on the tops of the seas.

We were not more than four hundred yards from the finish and were running neck and neck. A white squall came hissing down astern and fairly buried the *Glooscap's* bow.   The *Osprey* staggered, and her improvised backstay broke with a wicked snap and jerked forward from the mast-head like a whip-lash.   Her mast bent like a lateen yard, and then the spinnaker halyard broke.   The big sail shook and went overboard. Miss MacMichael stood up and balanced herself, half crouching, on the slippery deck of the dancing boat.   We could hear her voice clear above the wind.

" Cut it away ; boom and all," she cried.   Donald jumped with the knife, and a few seconds saw the spinnaker drifting astern.

" Thank God! she's safer now," said Wilson,

half to himself; then, turning to me, " Hold the tiller, Ashburn! Here, Hans, give me a hand in taking the spinnaker off."

" But you can carry it to the finish!" I said.

" Yes, but I shall beat her without it now, or not at all."

They had a hard time getting the spinnaker in, and dragged it in the water long enough to more than make up for what Miss MacMichael had lost in the same way. When it was stowed we had time to look at the *Osprey*. We were leading her about a length and gaining a little. The red-and-white flag was getting ominously near, but Miss MacMichael didn't despair. She sent Irland and Donald forward with a spare jib, and at the risk of their lives they spread it with the aid of the signal halyards and a boat-hook. Again the *Osprey* began to catch us. I looked at Wilson.

" Have you got a spare jib? " I said.

" No, and there isn't time to get the spinnaker on again."

Weren't you generous a little too soon? "

He looked at the *Osprey*, then at the red-and-white flag fluttering ahead.

" She'll never catch us," he said, and he smiled at Donald. Donald smiled back, and the *Osprey* gained slowly.

Up she came, and we rushed for the line. Her shining oak stem was abeam of the *Glooscap's* centerboard trunk when the gun roared from the judge's boat. We had won by half a length. The next boat was nearly three hundred yards astern.

We hauled our wind and lay for the boat-house, and the *Osprey* rushed past our stern. Miss Mac-Michael stood up with a megaphone.

" You sailed a jolly fine race! " she cried, balancing herself like a slack-wire walker on the windward washboard of the *Osprey* as she jumped through the short seas. " Won't you come in and talk it over this evening? "

" You sailed a much better one. Yes, I shall be very glad to," was Wilson's reply, and he waved his cap as the boats ran apart.

As we passed the market wharf we had such a list that we could see the cheering crowd over the *Glooscap's* yard. All the boating experts in Caribou who were not afloat, including all the lobster-fishermen, each of whom had gotten rid of a certain amount " o' plain Scootch," were at the boat-house to welcome us. Big Jim MacIntyre, a great crony of Donald's, was the first to get hold of Wilson's hand. Under the influence of perhaps a " thimbelfu' mair " than his share of the Scotch he pounded him on the back in a way that would have smashed the shoulder of a lighter man.

" Mon! Mon! Eet was gran', pairfectly gran'," he thundered.

" Aye! Eet was a' that," came thickly from one of the lobster-fishermen.

" A thocht y' were done for sure afore y' poot an th' beeg speenaker," continued MacIntyre, " but MacMichael'll hae t' go fairther th'n Monthr-real t' get a boat t' beat th' *Glooscap.* Mon, tho', but th't gir-rl c'n sail a boat. Dick Grant here says y'd mek' a gran' pair. Why don't y' marry her? " and the fishermen laughed approvingly.

Wilson laughed too: a laugh which in English would fill a good many paragraphs.

" I'm glad you liked the race," he said, and we left Hans to house the boat and escaped.

That evening we went up to MacMichael's big stone house on the hill, and I had a new experience in life. I saw for the first time a girl on whom attention from men—and the right kind of men, too—didn't seen to have the slightest effect. I thought at first that there was one exception, and that that exception was me. I didn't think this in the cock-sure egotistical way that I might have thought it if I'd been ten or fifteen years younger; but I noted it—or thought I noted it—in much the same spirit as an astronomer notes the bright-ening of a new star,—as a phenomenon, a curious phenomenon.

Captain Irland was there, and was devoted in

a rather naval way, but he was in earnest, though he wouldn't have admitted it even to himself, as he was married.

Billings was there, and explained carefully that the jibe of the *Osprey* had thrown him overboard. Though we all thought differently and perhaps showed it a little.   Miss MacMichael was charitable and eased things for him wonderfully, telling me afterwards that a boy might do a thing once that he would never do again, while I knew that she would never have done it at all.

Henderson came in while we were there, and I saw serious symptoms of his having developed a more than superficial fondness for the heroine of the boat race.   How long he had been in developing it I couldn't tell, though if I could judge at all from results it must have been some time. Then the Honourable Edward Rose, a Nova Scotian, and the Minister of Marine and Fisheries in the Dominion Cabinet, came in from a town a hundred miles away, ostensibly to see Mr. Mac-Michael on business.   He talked business, without going out of the room, about three minutes as nearly as I could time him, and then tried to give the remaining three hours of the evening to Miss MacMichael.   He succeeded only in part, and not more than any of the others, even Billings.   He was older than she, it is true, but not so very old, after all, and surely most girls would have considered him as a desirable,—sufficient of a desirable to investigate at least. But she didn't investigate particularly: she had had many chances before, I learned: and from what I saw then I decided that she cared nothing for social position, as such,—that is, if I knew as much about women as I thought. Later I proved I was right.

As we made a bit of a party, Mrs. MacMichael telephoned for two or three of her daughter's girl friends, and I acquired my first knowledge of the unconventional way in which so many Canadians really enjoy evenings. We in England have more to learn from Canada than most of us would care to admit.

It was an amusing group, though amusing groups of that type must have been common in the MacMichael house. There were a number of men of various ages, and a number of young ladies, all of the latter at least attractive, not in the least an unusual thing in itself: but all the men, with one exception—that exception being myself —seemed to be, not only interested in, but in love with one girl; and that girl in love with but one of the men, her father. Even if Wilson's common sense hadn't told him there was no necessity for it, his natural generosity wouldn't have allowed him to be jealous. So he enjoyed it too, almost as much as did Miss MacMichael and I. Irrespective of preference, all the girls got their

share of attention, for men must talk as well as
women.

Mrs. MacMichael was sweet, though with a bit
of decision in her tone at times that indicated that
she had delivered her ultimatum. This trait evidently went down a little into the next generation.
James MacMichael was keen as any Scotchman
could well be. His eye showed where his daughter's alertness came from, and his straight form
the origin of her litheness. There is but one
English word that describes his smile, the same
old word, " kindly; " and kindly it was, always.

Gertrude MacMichael's two strongest traits
were what in my opinion are the two most attractive traits a woman can have,—Kitty Tyrrel had
them,—frankness and unconventionality. You
mayn't think so; of course it's a matter of opinion.
Then for your own satisfaction and in justification
of your own opinion you may remember that a
good many people say that I'm a crank, at least
in so far as my opinion of women is concerned.
Frankness carries with it generosity, and generosity charity; and unconventionality in a woman
means real true breadth as surely as day is day.
A woman who not only dares to be unconventional, but to whom it comes natural to be unconventional, is sure to be as wide in her views and
loves and as just as it is possible for a woman to be.
But remember, I mean real frankness and real

unconventionality, not the poses. Women of all
ages who pose as frank or unconventional, or both,
are as common as barnacles on the bottom of a
ship when she's been three years out of dock.

Well, as I said, Gertrude MacMichael was frank
and unconventional. She was generous enough
to be nice to everybody, and she was sincere. At
the same time she beat us all at table-tennis,
Wilson included, and gloried in it. I talked to
her father for a while, and it happened that I had
been about everywhere his steamers had been.
She listened and sized me up more nearly than I
have ever been sized up by a woman in the same
time. She seemed to have almost instinctively
scented family, past history, navy, yes, and perhaps adventurer about me, for she inveigled me
into a corner and showed me that she had a great
knowledge of people and things. We seemed to
have a good deal in common in feeling, and it was
then that I deluded myself into the idea that she
was impressed with me. She was, in a way, for we
afterward became great friends, but nothing more.
It was simply that the girl had all her sentiment
left,—thank God!—and wanted to hear of things
I'd done and seen. She knew the spirits of things
as they are in a way that I never saw in a woman,
from the spirit of life in London to the spirit of a
steamer in a storm at sea, and knowing this she

liked Kipling, not because it was fashionable, but for Kipling's sake.

Altogether she gave me an hour's hard thinking, and when I went away I summoned up all the different pictures she had helped to form that day. She was so attractive in all that for the time being Kitty—poor Kitty—melted away almost into nothingness, and I wondered if I too was falling under what seemed to be the universal spell and getting in love with Miss Gertrude Mac-Michael.

Wilson, with all his command over himself, showed in a hundred ways during the evening how thoroughly he was in love with her. To say that a girl with her intuition didn't know it would be like saying that a grebe feeding around the edge of an ice-field didn't see a man with a gun lying behind a hummock a hundred yards further along. The grebe doesn't " raise his head in the air and look long and searchingly in the direction of the intruder." He hasn't time. He goes on fussing around hunting for little fishes, and though there is apparently no particular reason for it he never works down in the direction of the man.

It was not that Miss MacMichael treated Wilson as she did the others. She had an unbounded admiration for any one who could do things better than she could, from talking to sailing a boat.

Wilson had tried to demonstrate to her that she had sailed a much better race than he had.

"No!" she said, "you needn't think I'll admit that the *Glooscap* is a better boat than the *Osprey*. I was beaten, and if we changed boats I'd be beaten again."

She knew the value of his scientific work, and she frankly recognized him as an authority on almost every disputed point, no matter on what type of subject, and often appealed to him and accepted his solutions as readily and as fully as would a child. Yet, when he would do some little thing, perhaps involuntarily, that would show that he could hardly stand the strain without speaking,—something that would escape them all but me,—I'd see a quaint little smile flit over her face, half amused, half weary, and she'd take a sudden and mighty interest in something else. No! she didn't love him; there was no doubt about that: but at the same time I felt equally sure that she didn't love any one.

When we went home it was a clear starlit September night. Up to the northward the first of the Aurora Borealis waved and dimmed the stars, and overhead, unseen, rushed the singing, whistling wings of golden-eyes, dusky ducks, and mergansers.

Wilson hadn't said a word from the time we left the MacMichaels'. I, if anybody, had won the

right to know what he was thinking without asking, so I didn't talk.   At last he spoke:—

"Those ducks sound like autumn: I must be
going north soon!"

"How long have you been in love with Miss
MacMichael?" I asked.

He looked at me quickly and smiled.

"Yes," he laughed, "as I've said before, you're
a deep thinker.   Why—I suppose I shall have to
acknowledge it, though I've never done so before
to any one but myself—I'm afraid I really can't
tell you, for I don't know.   Probably ever since
I came to Caribou,—ever since I first met her."

"Well, I'm not surprised."

"That seems to be a frame of mind shared by
a good many people if I can judge anything by
watching them," he said.

"Now, see here," I said, "last week up on a
wilderness lake you gave me some good advice.
People who may be fools about their own affairs
may have had pretty wide experience, and may be
anything but fools about the affairs of others,
especially in this kind of thing, so you take my
advice and keep at it.   You're bound to win her
in the end, and if she doesn't love you now—and
I don't quite see why—she doesn't love any one
else.   You mustn't mind my talking like this to
you, for I'm ten years older.   You don't, do
you?"

"No, most decidedly not. To be frank, I like it, because I like you, and even a man sometimes welcomes the chance to unburden himself a little. Then," he laughed, "I suppose you rank as an expert. If you say I am to win in the end it must be the case. But concerning the keeping at it, I never intended doing anything else."

"She admires you now," I said.

"Perhaps, though if she does there seems to be a great gulf between admiration and love."

"Yes," I said; "but all things come to him who waits."

"Possibly!" was the reply, "if he waits intelligently enough."

Though I hardly liked to admit it myself, I turned in that night with a little pain at my heart, a pain caused by the second woman in the world who has affected me in the least. Now that the pain has left I have often wondered what it was that made this girl more attractive to me in the time than any other woman had ever been. I believe it was nothing more than her openness and her love for things as they are, coupled perhaps with her absolute independence. Besides all this, there is no man living but would have been in love with the girl's sunburn, her muscle, her willowy litheness, and her grit.

CHAPTER III.

THE next morning Wilson turned me out about seven.

"They are going to have some rowing and canoe races to-day as a finish to the regatta;" he said, "they telegraphed for some Halifax scullers, and they're coming in on the noon train. Oldham, one of their cracks, is coming, and no one here will meet him. They've sent up for me. I'll scull, though I haven't been in a shell for two months, and I expect I shall get beaten. Do you care to come down while I get the boat out?"

"Yes! I shall be glad to. I've sculled a bit, and if you've got another boat I'd like to take a spin with you."

"Good!" he said, "We'll soon find another boat for you."

The storm of the day before had gone down and left a light northerly breeze blowing off the town side of the harbour. A little while after breakfast Wilson and I were chasing each other up and down in front of the wharves. Though I hadn't been in a shell for two or three years I got along decently enough, but Wilson's last wilderness trip had kept him in such training that he could run away from me a length in ten. He rowed a couple of miles on time and then went ashore.

That afternoon I went with the MacMichaels and watched the races. Caribou won the four-oared race and lost the double sculls. We followed them on MacMichael's launch, and fine races they were. These men of Eastern Canada are naturally great oarsmen. Caribou lost the junior single sculls, but the crowd cheered when they won the intermediates, and waited, all excitement, for the senior race.

Oldham had rowed once for the Diamond Sculls at Henley and had missed getting them by less than a length, so he had an international reputation. There were but the two entries, and Wilson had plenty of responsibility as far as Caribou was concerned. The water was choppy, and Oldham's splendid form, the result of steady work, counted for so much that Wilson, even with his gigantic strength, up the whole length of the three-mile course, had all he could do to keep to the tail of the Halifax man's shell. We followed the race with the launch, and from start to finish Gertrude MacMichael's face was a study. She breathed fast and her cheeks glowed crimson. She only spoke once. That was after Oldham, feeling at last the result of Wilson's iron endurance, tried to back-wash him. Then she turned to me for a second and snapped:

"Oh! if I were only a man!!"

A hundred yards from the finish, Oldham by sheer skill and clean rowing was still leading a length, but so hard was he being driven that he was fairly reeling in his boat. The crowd was yelling for Wilson to spurt, but if you have ever sculled a three-mile race with a good man you will know that giant in strength though a man may be he has not much spurt left at the finish.

Then Miss MacMichael seized the big megaphone, and her voice rang as clear over the water as it had rung the day before:

"Only ten lengths more, Dave; now, for my sake!"

Wilson heard her above the cheers of the crowd. Such an effect on a man I never saw before. He sat up, and his chest fairly swelled with the effort. The muscles stood out in brown ridges on his shoulders and arms and legs. His long supple body swung rhythmically, and with the precision of a piston stroke. His sculls bent and boiled through the water, and the bow of his shell lifted at every stroke and hissed past Oldham in a wonderful way. He won, apparently easily, by a canvas-length. Then his head sank on his knees for a few seconds, and a moment or two afterward ne was up again and sculling for the boat-house.

Miss MacMichael turned to me.

"Wasn't that perfectly splendid!" she said, with her eyes shining.

"Yes!" I replied, with more excitement than I'd felt since the fuss at Zanzibar, "it was a great race."

By the time we landed Wilson was dressed and on the wharf waiting for us.

Miss MacMichael ran toward him and held out both hands.

"Here you are, Mr. Wilson, how are you?" she cried, "all right, aren't you?" She remembered how he had sunk down like a tired child at the finish, and looked at him with a face full of girlish tenderness.

"Thank you, Miss MacMichael," he said, laughing, "I feel splendidly, though it was a hard race. I have to thank you for saving it for me. By the way, you just called me Mr. Wilson; I think I have a dim recollection of a familiar voice, through a megaphone, calling me Dave, and asking me to do something for her sake?"

Miss MacMichael laughed. Heavens! what a laugh that girl had.

"Subterfuge, Mr. Wilson, pure subterfuge," she said. "I knew it was a critical time in the race, and really I thought we were sufficiently old friends—that you thought enough of me to do a little thing like that for my sake—for Caribou's sake, I mean."

"Evidently it was subterfuge," he said, "for if, instead of what you did say, you had said, 'Mr. Wilson, for Caribou's sake,' I couldn't have done it." I quite believed him.

Miss MacMichael took a sudden interest in the canoe race that was about finishing while I watched a queer-looking steamer coming up the harbour. She had a ram bow and seemed to be plated like a battleship, while her big funnel told of plenty of power. She had a ponderous way of moving and recalled the ram *Polyphemus* more than anything I had ever seen afloat.

"That's a remarkable-looking machine," I said; "she looks as if she might have gotten adrift out of some unknown branch of the navy."

Wilson was watching her closely. I thought his face twitched once or twice. He smiled as he answered.

"That," he said, "is the *Walrus*."

I looked closely at her stern and saw under her counter—

WALRUS

NORTHUMBERLAND STEAMSHIP CO.

LONDON

"That's one of the boats that helps to pay such dividends, is it? One of the ice-crushers. I'd like to have all my capital in such stock."

"Yes!" said Wilson, "she is something of an ice-crusher, but she could be improved. Sometimes she gets stuck in the board-ice for a fortnight, and that's anything but a paying business."

"If any other line of boats I know of could be sure of doing half as well, its people should be satisfied," interposed MacMichael, who had joined us. "This company has a monopoly. At the same time I don't see that the boats need be as strong as they are. I believe that some of the strongest of our boats—the *Duncrieff* or perhaps the *Dungeness*—could get through the ice, especially where it is more open up about the north of Prince Edward Island. I think some time I shall just arrange to have them make a Gulf port in winter, say somewhere up on the Gaspé Peninsula, or on the New Brunswick shore, Cape Tormentine, for instance, where the ice is kept loose by the tides. I could call at the Island inward and outward bound, and take stuff both to the New Brunswick mainland and to England. Then the Northumberland Steamship Company would have a little healthy business rivalry, and probably their dividends wouldn't be quite so heavy." MacMichael warmed up at the thought of another iron in the fire, and another cent or two on the dollar added to the ever-increasing earnings of MacMichael & Co.

"It couldn't be done, Mr. MacMichael," said Wilson quietly, "the ice up between the Capes would crush in the sides of any ordinary steamer as you would crush an eggshell between your fingers."

"We'll see! we'll see!" mused MacMichael, his Scotch stirred up at the thought of opposition, even from an ice-field in the hands of the Almighty; "some day we'll try it for the sake of the experiment."

Wilson said no more, but watched the *Walrus* as she swept up the harbour toward her berth. Then he turned and walked up the wharf with Miss Mac-Michael.

MacMichael watched the steamer until she glided out of sight behind the Government Pier and only her masts showed above the warehouses, then, as we started up the wharf, he turned to me.

"Have you known David Wilson long?" he asked abruptly.

I told him in part how and when we met.

"When you have known him longer," he continued, "you will find that he is a remarkable fel-fellow. Extraordinarily able. Extraordinarily able."

"I have known him long enough to realize that already," I said.

"Yes! no doubt, no doubt;" he continued, "but you will learn more, much more. He has been 'doing good scientific work, they say. I don't know much about those things, except that they're all useful. He's been tremendously successful in it, I believe: but still, there's no money in it,—at least, not enough. A man of his ability should know that, no matter how much brains you may have, you've got to have some little money to be altogether a success. Not that you've got to be born with it; perhaps it's better not; but you've got to use your brains in such a way that you'll ultimately make a little money. After that you may devote what spare time you have to scientific work or whatever you like. That's the way I look at it."

"It depends something on your definition of success," I ventured.

"Yes! yes! perhaps so; but after all we have only one criterion to go by in this world, and that's the opinion of society. Not that pack of damned fools that call themselves 'Society,' but the people of civilization that the good Lord has blessed with their share of balance. Half the people—half?— nine-tenths of the people in this life will talk about the world, the flesh, and the devil as if they belonged in the same class, while in reality if those same people kept themselves up to the best ideals of the world they'd never need to trouble much about what would happen to them in the future. As far as I'm concerned I've never made much of a success of trying to draw a sharp line between the world and its Creator. That's why I say that a success from the world's point of view, a success with at least a little money in it, will probably be a success from any point of view; that is, supposing you use the money as the Lord intended."

"You think, then, that Wilson ought to have some established employment of some kind!"

"Yes!" was the answer, "I do. Of course it's none of my business, and consequently belongs to the class of things I usually leave alone. But I like him. He's as strong as a horse, and he's always doing kind things. Two winters ago a whole family back on one of the northern harbours was down with diphtheria. They were brought up in ignorance and dirt. That chap went out, helped to clean out their house himself, threw out bodily any male members of the family who objected to his methods, until they came back and begged for mercy, and with the aid of a trained nurse that he hired himself brought them back to health without losing one of them. I wanted him to let me at least pay for the nurse, but he wouldn't hear of it. Why, do you know, I offered him a good position with our firm, but he wouldn't take it! He thanked me, but said the work would keep him here steadily and gave him no chance for his scientific work."

"'If you'll pardon me for saying so,' I said, 'I

think you had better ease a little on your scientific work until you're in a position to keep on making a little money.'

"He thanked me over and over again, and told me that he appreciated the offer very much, but that he didn't feel he could neglect the work he had taken up.

"'Besides,' he said, 'whenever I am in Caribou Henderson always has some work of the Northumberland Steamship Company's for me, and I make something out of that. My knowledge of the Gulf and the ice is of some value to them.' However, the Northumberland Company, like any other steamship company, can't afford to pay a man for work he doesn't do. Wilson is half his time away north up about Labrador or the Gaspé Peninsula, and the work he does while he is here can't be enough to bring him in much of a fortune in the way of an income."

"By the way," continued MacMichael, "while I am speaking about him I may tell you one of the rumors concerning him which one hears once in a while. It serves as a good instance of the ridiculous stories that arise in a small town about a man in whom the people are interested. You'll hear that his father left him large sums of money—his will was never probated—and that David Wilson is rich. You may be sure that if such were the case there would be some evidence of it with a man

as generous as he is.   However, there is one
thing he does do.   He is always ready to beg
Henderson, on behalf of the Northumberland
Company, to give to any charity in the town that
may need it.   The Company is remarkably generous through Henderson, as he has a power of
attorney and does apparently whatever he pleases.
I don't know how the shareholders in London
like it, but I suppose they don't mind, as they
never seem to stop it.   They probably think it's
money well spent in popularizing the firm.   By
the way, I wonder what Wilson's next move is
going to be!"

"He's going north in a short time to do some
work up between the Strait of Belle Isle and
Gaspé.   He wishes to make some tidal investiga-
tions and to look up some fishes and birds.   I'm
going up with him," I replied.

"You are, eh!   Well, you'll have a pretty
rough time.   Are you accustomed to outdoor
life?"

"Yes;" I said, "have been all my life."

MacMichael hummed to himself.   Anybody
who would deliberately start off on an expedition
of the type Wilson usually took, and in the
autumn, too, with no other apparent object than
pleasure, was somewhat of a mystery to him.

We caught up to Wilson at MacMichael's gate.
He and I were invited in to dinner.   We accepted,

and Mrs. MacMichael telephoned for Mrs. Wilson, who joined us a few minutes later.

The uppermost topics were the boat races of the last two days. Miss MacMichael's chief worry in life just then seemed to be that she was not a man, and consequently was not able to scull. One thing I noted. Though Wilson had by the last race evidently made a stride in the young lady's admiration, he was apparently no nearer affecting her emotions than ever. This, however, didn't seem to worry him either then or ever afterward. From that moment on he pursued his course with a bland disregard of its effects. He seemed to have made up his mind that Miss Gertrude Mac-Michael must love him ultimately if it was to be, and he could see no reason why it should not. If the occasion arose he showed her how much attached to her he was as naïvely as would a child. Apparent lack of progress on his part didn't seem to trouble him in the least. He settled down like a strong expedition in a dry country with a convenient base of supplies when it undertakes to starve out a zariba. If one form of attack should in the end be more fatal than any other, this should be the one.

If the girl cared practically nothing for money and the social side of the question—would love a man for the man's sake if she loved him at all— as I felt sure was the case with Gertrude Mac-

Michael, then surely nothing in the world could tell so much in the man's favour as continuous unwavering devotion of this type. If the girl didn't develop an active dislike for the man, and this seemed far from being the condition in the present case, then, if I knew anything of women, the young lady would have to succumb some day, and when she did, Hmm! I'd ask nothing more than to be the man.

Thinking these things over gave me an idea. Wilson had asked me not to speak to any one of the fact that he quietly used a good deal of money for various purposes. Perhaps the rumor was true, and the old Doctor had left him a fortune of his own. In any case he evidently wished it to appear that he had much less money than he actually possessed. Such a thing would seem ridiculous, but now an explanation occurred to me, and one which, knowing the man, didn't seem altogether improbable. He was trying to win the love of this girl, and he wished to do it on his own merits. If she were willing to become his wife at all he wished her to do so as willingly if he were a young scientist and a clerk in the employ of the Northumberland Steamship Company as if he were a man of independent fortune. And yet, why did he give the valuable time he did to the Company. He would hardly do this merely to keep up the effect. Could there be anything

dishonest in the whole thing.   I thought of David
Wilson's face and the man but for a second, and
that thought left me for ever.   Altogether there
was something about it all which remained to me
as an entire mystery.   However, if you leave a
mystery alone it usually clears itself up in time,
and in this case if it didn't it wasn't any affair
of mine.   So alone I left it.

The next ten days Wilson spent a good deal
of the time with Henderson, and after using a
few days in getting some things I needed for my
kit, I had the time free to spend with Miss Mac-
Michael.   She seemed to take to me a bit, and
talked about things in London and Paris until it
made me groan to myself.   She rushed me around
the harbour in her launch, the *Cockawee*, and took
me out into the Gulf, though the days were getting a bit cool for cruising.   She took me out
in the *Osprey*, and I was able to show her two or
three things which would make her harder to
beat the next time she sailed a race.   One day,
just as we were starting out, a block came off her
masthead, and before I got myself pulled together
she had it in her teeth and was shinning up the
spar to put it on: and she did, too.   One day one
of the horses bit at her while she was giving a
lump of sugar to her favourite saddle-horse.   She
dragged him out, put a bridle on him, and, for
punishment, galloped him bareback around a field

behind the stable until he was in a white lather.
She climbed off his back and led him in, docile
and crushed and blowing.

"There! you brute," she said in a burst of
triumph, "now you won't try to bite me any
more, will you!" The last as sweetly as though
she had been leading him to water. Then she
gave him a lump of sugar, which, with his ears
forward, he took daintily between his lips. The
make-up was evidently mutual.

She seemed to know where practical charity
was needed both in town and country, and I used
to drive out with her with a wagon stocked like
the commissariat of a week's inland expedition for
twenty men. Nova Scotia farmers never need to
be given any of the necessities of life, but occasionally, in times of sickness, dainties are welcome
here as elsewhere.

Well, we got to be great friends, and sometimes, to be frank, I was not always as loyal to
Wilson as I might have been: but Providence
took away any chance of my disloyalty being effective, for beyond talking to me about things we
knew and liked in common—and they were many
—she never allowed our friendship to go——.
Why? Because she didn't care any more for me
than she apparently did for Wilson, and didn't
trust my judgment a tenth as much; and this is
how things stood when we left for the north.

The few days before this happened were spent in making preparations. Sleeping-bags were gotten ready, Primus stoves examined and tested, cameras packed, with unlimited plates, dredges and tangles fitted with thousands of fathoms of new rope, little stereoscopic binoculars, deep-sea thermometers, delicate aneroids, dipping-needles, and a hundred more things used on such an expedition added to the outfit, together with such a supply of stores as I never before saw put together for three men for three months. Hans was never given a spare moment for a full week until at last we were ready. We were going up the Intercolonial through New Brunswick to the beautiful Meeting of the Waters at Matapedia in Quebec. Thence we were to go down the north side of the Restigouche River and the Baie des Chaleurs — there is but one such trip — out through the Shick Shock Mountains on to the wild Gaspé Peninsula to the little village of Percé, the terminus of the railway. Here to seaward looms up sheer out of the water the great Percé Rock, while a little to the north, across Gaspé Bay, is the black world-famed, saw-toothed Cape Gaspé itself.

The evening before we left we were at the MacMichaels' with Henderson. MacMichael said good-bye to us both rather solemnly.

"I know Wilson," he said to me, "and when

he goes on these expeditions I never expect him to come back. If he doesn't get squeezed up in the ice some time—well—there's the Percé Rock. The Canadian Government fines or imprisons anyone who tries to climb it,—punishes them as if they were trying to attempt suicide; it's about the same thing: yet he'll attempt it some day, I expect, for the sake of the birds on the top, and then he'll get killed, just like the rest of them." This sounded interesting.

Miss MacMichael was as sweet and charming as usual, but she made no concessions that I could see and probably no admissions. No admissions because she had none to make. She shook hands with us as we left.

"I shall miss you both " (both!) " very much," she said, " but I am sure Mr. Henderson "— looking at that individual, who tried to look quite as conventional as a navigating lieutenant getting orders about a change of course—" I am sure Mr. Henderson, or some of the others," (spoiled it!) " won't mind taking care of me and trying to keep me from getting drowned or shot, or killed in some other violent way, as I expect will be the case some day."

After we had left, Wilson's lips hardened up, and he didn't speak for a few moments. An instant afterward he got back all his courage and poise and was as cheerful as usual.

The next morning, as we left Caribou, the October sunlight was glaring up the harbour, making the Academy and MacMichael's big house on the hilltop stand out, and down below catching the roofs of the houses buried in crimson and gold maples. The air was clear as on a mountain, and as we steamed up over Fitzpatrick we could see far out into the blue Gulf, with Prince Edward Island lying a sharp undulating green and red line along the eastern and northern horizon. There isn't the least use in the world in my trying to describe Eastern Canada in the autumn. You'll have to see it for yourself. It's a funny sensation for an Englishman to be in an atmosphere that he can see through for fifty miles: an atmosphere that makes you feel like running every few minutes to keep from shouting.

I shall not attempt to give you any description of that trip. The scientific results have been published, and, as you probably know, have resulted in Wilson's election to a number of learned societies and still more letters after his name. The story of the trip has been told in print by Wilson himself, but some time I am going to tell it all over again, for he gave no idea in the world of what he did personally. He has told how we got to the top of the Percé Rock and went up and down as we pleased with instruments and birds and eggs, but from his story one would have imagined that Hans and I were responsible for the whole thing. He told how Hans met with an accident, and how " we finally managed to get him down to the boat;" but he didn't tell how he, David Wilson, on a stinging cold day, bandaged up the Swede's head and shoulder on a rock ledge a yard wide, and then, after lashing the insensible man to himself, slid down a three inch manilla rope to the boat two hundred and fifty feet below.

He told of " Captain Ashburn's remarkable presence of mind in saving the steamer *St. Malo* from going ashore on the Labrador Peninsula in a blinding snowstorm." What I did was only the reflex action from long training. Any man with the same knowledge would have done the same thing. He didn't tell how he took his own launch, single-handed, in among the breakers that were thundering at the foot of the cliffs below Cape Whittle, and thus made effective a plan which I had done nothing but propose. I'll never forget the scene when Hans insisted on going with him. He had landed us on one of the St. Mary's Islands, landed us all but Hans, who wouldn't be landed.

" You may get drowned," Wilson suggested pleasantly. The Swede snorted.

" I vill go een, und eef I get drown', vell, I vill haf to die soom vay soom day. Yesus! I'm not scare uv der vater mooch, am I? "

" No! " said Wilson, " I'll admit you're not

scared of the water or anything else that I know of; but this can be done by one man as well as two or twenty. I'll have to be off." He turned to the engine-room, and Hans was thrown off his guard. Wilson reached inside the engine-room door, swung the reversing lever forward, and opened the throttle, and, as the screw churned up the water, he turned quickly toward Hans, picked him up, and heaved him over the rail into the sea. He splashed in not ten feet from where we were standing on a big rock. The crew laughed, and Hans laughed too as he swam ashore, while Wilson, waving a spanner, disappeared in the driving snow. The Swede got some dry clothes out of his kit and put them on, all the time chuckling to himself at the way Wilson had taken to get rid of him. " Dot man vill get drownt vit heemzelf soom day," he said sententiously, " but 't von't be my fault! ' By three o'clock that afternoon we could hear the low growling whistle of the *St. Malo* and the howling shrieking syren of the launch as she guided the twelve-thousand-ton Red Star boat out through the snow clouds into the open Gulf.

The launch turned up about dark, with her skipper very cold and hungry. We had kept the bombs going, and he had found us without difficulty.

"Did Mr. Brun get wet this morning?" was his first question.

"Yaas!" grinned Hans, "Meester Brun got vet, und den he got some dry clodes on, und now he feels fine."

"Ma Crap!" joined in one of the launch's French-Canadian crew, "A don' know, me, but I tink dat's a dam' fine cure for w'at-you-call-it, dose chap dat don' obey orders, a —— mutineer, oui! mutineer."

"Yes!" laughed Wilson, "but if all mutineers were made of the same kind of stuff this would be quite a world in its way."

But I haven't time to tell you of the things that happened to us on that trip. I've spoken of the launch, but I must tell you a little more of her, for if it hadn't been for the launch and the ideas she helped to give us this story would never have been told. When we arrived at Percé I found that Wilson had there a regular little headquarters of his own in the shape of a four-roomed log cottage by the shore, a cottage with big stone fireplaces that threw their warm light out into rooms full of dredges, stuffed birds, bottles containing sponges and molluscs and echinoderms from the bottom of the Gulf, and a thousand other interesting and wonderful things.

Below the cottage was anchored the steamer which Wilson usually spoke of as "the launch."

She was a good lump of a boat, about a hundred feet over all, with a low house, and was named the *Scoter*. I went down and looked her over carefully. She was built of heavy steel plates, evidently to stand work among the ice, and had a squat, wide funnel. Her bow was rounded like that of a canoe, a peculiar shape for the bow of a steamer, and she was fitted with an extra steam windlass and a derrick for handling the dredging apparatus. Her crew were French-Canadians, men who knew the Gulf and the Grand Banks almost as thoroughly as did Wilson himself.

The *Scoter* took us all over the Gulf from Belle Isle to Cape North, and from Cape Ray to west of Anticosti. Even when the bay ice began to form and the big clumpets began to run down in bunches from the north, she carried us through. One day we were trying to get through some thin field-ice. We would back up and run at it, break it for two or three lengths, and then we'd stick, and have to back up and go at it again.

" Now, that is precisely what the *Aurora* and the *Walrus* do," said Wilson meditatively. " When they are working among loose floating clumpets they are practically perfect. The clumpets hit them now on one bow, now on the other, and are pounded aside. But when the clumpets freeze together, or the boats get into board-ice, their bows wedge in, and there they stick until they back up and have another try at it. Now, if we could only devise some plan by which the boats could get through field-ice as readily as through loose pack, it would be a great help to the Company."

We thought it over, and finally decided that designing the boats to run up on the ice would probably solve the problem. So one day we cleared the *Scoter* of everything movable forward, got the crew to put in tons of coal and scrap-iron aft, so as to raise her bow out of water, and, with a full head of steam, started off for the ice-field with six feet of her keel forward out of water. We rushed at the edge of the field, slid up on it, and with the ice grinding and crushing down under the *Scoter's* weight went through for half a mile and came out in open water on the other side. The experiment was a success.

"With your help," said Wilson, "I'll design a boat for that kind of work, and we'll offer it to the Northumberland Steamship Company. If they accept it—and I think it is extremely probable that they will—they'll no longer be troubled with steamers getting caught in the ice occasionally and not getting in for a week. Consequently their dividends will increase, which, other things going satisfactorily, should enable the firm to survive the vicissitudes of business rivalry," and he smiled.

"Yes!" I said; " considering that the Company

has no competitors, and has paid a dividend so far which the De Beers concern in its best days would have to struggle to equal."

So, during a few spare evenings while we were at the cottage, we turned out a rough design for a steamer such as had never been before. She was armoured almost like a cruiser; had trimming-tanks aft that would sink her stern and hoist her curved pram bow five feet out of the water and trimming-tanks forward that would sink her bow and throw her screw into the air high enough to have new blades lagged on at sea. Then Wilson forwarded the design to Henderson. Six weeks or so later he told me that the Northumberland Steamship Company had adopted the plan, and had placed an order with a big Tyne firm for the steamer, which was to be two thousand tons gross and to be delivered the following December.

" Henderson," he added, " has asked me to select a name, and I think I shall let you have the honour of christening the first ice-crusher in the world, especially as you did most of the designing."

" I ! " I said. " Let me see." I thought for a few moments. For some reason my thoughts ran back to Kitty Tyrrell; and the picture of the little village, with the Shannon winding through it, where she was born and where I first saw her, came strongly before me.

" How would the *Shannon* do? " I asked.

" Splendidly," said Wilson; " there's nothing like having something to recall old Ireland. The *Shannon* it is."

So it happened that on the fifth of the following December a round-bilged, pram-bowed, low-set almighty-looking steel steamer, unlike anything in the heavens or in the earth or in the waters under the earth, with flags flying, ploughed her way ponderously into Caribou harbour, and under her counter were the words—

SHANNON

NORTHUMBERLAND STEAMSHIP CO.

LONDON

All the winter before I had been with Wilson. When the ice came down from the north the *Scoter* was docked for the season, and we took to the pack itself, sometimes with ice-boats and sometimes without. Then I learned things that no book and no man can teach. So it would be perfectly useless for me to tell you and expect you to know. I learned of an entirely new experience in life. I learned of the feeling, of the new grasp of all things, that comes to the man who has been out for days and weeks on the shifting ice-pack, when the grey seals come up in the lanes beside the murres and the burgomasters; when, at night, with glinting light above, and glinting light from crystal down below, and nothing else, there is a great shining silence like the silence between the worlds; when the Northern Light reels and flashes green and red and sends a faint silky rustle that makes the silence deeper all around; and then, more wonderful than all, when, without even a movement of air, the great silence breaks. In from the east sounds the weird harmonic cry of the cockawee, and down from the north come deep booms and low muffled roars as the pack stirs, as though the hand of God had beckoned and the Great White Silence had moved to do its appointed work.

These are the things which touch a man more deeply than anything else in nature. You may or may not agree with me; but the man who has seen and heard these things knows that what I say is true, and he who has not can never understand. If you take the trouble to learn, you will find that every Arctic explorer, no matter what manner of man he may have been before he went to the North, under the influence of the infinite vastness of things will have recovered all his sentiment and will have preserved it in all its simplicity, like that of a little child.

During this time I learned other things, and among these things I got a knowledge of the ice

and its movements and little idiosyncrasies which
served me well later.

In the spring of that year I fished.   In the summer I went with Wilson up to the Grand Falls of
the Hamilton River in Labrador, and later spent
the greater part of August boat-racing in Caribou
harbour.   In the autumn I hunted and shot.
When the time for the *Shannon* to turn up drew
near, I began to tire of lack of employment.   It
bred thoughts of Miss Kathleen Tyrrell and times
that were; and these were things that I had been
devoting a year to forgetting.   I was struck with
a new idea, and one day I broached it to Wilson.

" See here! " I said, " I know a good deal about
navigation——"

" You should! " he interrupted.

" And since I've been roaming around the Gulf
with you I've learned a good deal about ice.
Now, I wonder if the Northumberland Steamship
Company would take me on as the captain of the
Shannon for a year at least."

" What under Heaven do you want to be the
captain of the *Shannon* for? " said Wilson.
" You've got money enough to buy the *Shannon*."

" Perhaps so, but I'd like the experience, and
more especially the employment.   It's hardly
necessary to explain to you."

" Then you had better see Henderson.   He has
entire charge of that, and I feel sure that if you

really wish to try the *Shannon* he will be glad to give you the chance."

I went with Wilson, told Henderson in confidence all that was necessary concerning my previous experience, and he agreed to give mĕ command of the *Shannon* on her arrival.

When she steamed in, all Caribou turned out to see the new ice-crusher, and sea-going and shipping Caribou freely gave its opinion, or rather its various opinions, on such an anomaly on the face of the deep. The opinions were not all favourable, and six weeks later, after a hard frost, the enthusiasts and a good many others drove down on the ice to the mouth of the harbour to see her attempt to come in. The *Aurora* had tried it two days before, the *Walrus* the day before, and neither had been able to pound her way a foot further in than the lighthouse beach. There they had had to lie and be unloaded into sleds on the ice.

When the crowd arrived at the mouth of the harbour the *Shannon* was pulverizing clumpets a mile outside and working in at a good clip. However, the *Aurora* and the *Walrus* could both do that: not so fast, perhaps, but they could do it. But when, after reaching the lighthouse, the *Shannon* stuck her big nose up in the air and crashed up the harbour through thirty inches of solid green ice, and that so fast that the sleighs beside her could hardly keep up, criticism collapsed, and some of the critics were almost willing to bet that she could steam through a sea of mercury with a boiler-plate surface. - Donald Mc-Donald stopped me as I stepped ashore.

"Thut's a gre't boat y' got there;" he said warmly, though slowly, as usual. "Eef a were you a'd coom oop thro' th' light-hoose beach th' nex' time y' coom; 't w'd mak' the channel straighter 'n' more convenient."

That day The Honourable Frederic Ashburn, late Captain in Her Majesty's Navy, and the captain of the *Shannon*—captain and part designer—was exceedingly pleased with himself.

The *Shannon* was such a success that I was not surprised when Henderson told me one day that the Company had decided to put on another similar boat, somewhat larger and more strongly constructed. I recommended some changes which would make the new boat half as strong again as the *Shannon* and a more efficient ice-crusher. The suggestions were adopted, and one moonlight night in the following December a boat of twenty-five hundred tons gross steamed up Caribou harbour and berthed at the Northumberland Company's wharf. She had a straight stem above, but with her bow cut away below so that it only reached her keel level away aft under the step of the foremast. Her stern was sharp and curved

so that she could run backward almost as well as
forward, and under her counter were the words—

LIFFEY

NORTHUMBERLAND STEAMSHIP CO.

LONDON

The precedent of naming the first steamer after
an Irish river had been followed.

The *Liffey* differed in one important particular
from the *Shannon*.   She flared everywhere above
the water-line, so that if she were nipped between
two moving ice-fields she would be lifted clear out
of the water, while the *Shannon*, with her straight
freeboard, would run a chance of being crushed by
the resistless pressure.

During the first winter that I was on the
Shannon, and during the following summer, I saw
a great deal of Miss MacMichael, and as nearly as
I could judge she hadn't made much progress in
the direction of getting in love with anybody, even
Wilson.

During the early spring the MacMichaels went
off to Europe and didn't get back until June.
About the same time Wilson went to England
with some scientific papers and saw something of
them in London.   It was during this trip that he
was elected a Fellow of the Royal Society.   While
he was in England he inspected the *Liffey* and

gave me an enthusiastic account of her when he came out.

After he arrived in Caribou he took a little time to himself, and devoted most of it to cultivating Miss MacMichael. Apparently they were but friends as usual. When I think of that summer it keeps me laughing, and still wondering to myself. Caribou had a big tennis tournament. Dave Wilson and Gertrude MacMichael went up and practised together two hours a day, six days in the week, for a month or more beforehand. When the tournament was on they each beat all their opponents, who included the best players of the three Provinces.

The girl was like Kipling's Fuzzy-Wuzzy, like " a injia-rubber idiot on the spree." If she fell in the court, as she did once or twice, she would light on her hand, and be up and at it again like a prize-fighter. She'd wipe her hand off on her skirt as an international champion does on his trousers, grip her racket after feeling it two or three times, crouch, and be all over the court at once. She whipped every woman mercilessly, and toted each and all of them around the harbour in her launch afterward. She talked like a whirlwind when the spirit moved her, and kept the assembled youth and beauty on the rush in the attempt to keep up with her vagaries. She threw the whole MacMichael establishment open to the tourna-

ment, and was the leading spirit in the dances that
were given every evening. She sang songs from
all the new operas she had heard, sweetly and
effectively. All the men, independent of age or
peculiarity, adored her, and she laughed at the
adoration of them all, which of course only made
it the more vigorous. The girl was steel—and
violets.

Wilson was as brown as an Indian and in splendid shape. He beat his men with the precision of
an engine, and enjoyed the whole thing like a small
boy. And as Miss Gertrude MacMichael had the
men of the party in tow, so did he have the women.
Perhaps his new honours had something to do with
it. Undoubtedly, insensibly, they had——a little,
but very little——. He told them stories; he went
down to the harbour and practised canoe-upsets for
them; he danced with them, irrespective of age; he
swam with them; and he took them for drives in
the mornings before the games started, and showed
them the beauties of Caribou in the glory of a Nova
Scotia summer. Then he took them to the tennis-
field and delivered them up to be beaten by Miss
Gertrude MacMichael. The majority of them
would have done anything in the world for him,
including marrying him, if he had wanted them
to,—but he didn't. This is a most peculiar
world,—in spots.

I saw it all and took part in it all, and finally it

began to hurt, for I found that it brought up Kitty Tyrrell again in her connection with scenes not dissimilar twenty-five hundred miles away. I was beginning to find that the memory of Miss Kathleen Tyrrell was one of the things that wouldn't die of itself and objected to being killed.

CHAPTER IV.

S O much for all that.

Winter came on, and the *Liffey* turned up, as I have told you. From the time when, on the second day of the regatta two years before, Mac-Michael had spoken about sending one of his own steamers to a Gulf port in winter, and calling at Prince Edward Island inward and outward bound, the idea had evidently never left his mind. It wouldn't have been MacMichael's mind if it had. I would come in off the *Shannon* after having made an easy trip across in four or five hours, and he would ask me just how easily I got through; whether I found much open water, and so forth. I would have to admit that there was a great deal of open water.

" Yes," he would say, " and up above there would be more, up where the ice runs more freely, to the north of the Island. I believe I could get the *Dun-crieff* in without any trouble in the world."

He asked Wilson his opinion again.

" Mr. MacMichael," was the answer, " I should strongly advise you never to attempt to drive an ordinary type of steamer into any part of the Gulf

of St. Lawrence between the months of January
and April. If you do, you may expect to lose her.
If the wind was southwest and the ice light, you
might get in almost anywhere, but even then you
might get caught. But a southwest wind is indeed
a rarity in this Gulf in winter, and in any case would
hardly last more than a day or two. Suppose you
were in, and a northeast storm came down and
brought fields and lolly and clumpets and bergs from
Belle Isle itself, and piled them up against the shores
of the Maratime Provinces. Where would your
steamer be unless she were built for ice-work?
Crushed into junk, dropped into the bottom of the
Gulf, and, if you were in shoal water, pounded into
that bottom by ice."

MacMichael hummed to himself and talked about
the weather.

" When MacMichael "—Donald McDonald used
to say—" goes humpin' aroun' hummin' t' heem-
self like a leaky pop-valve, y' may as well gie o'er
tryin' conveence him o' onything. Y' cood as well
go oot een a sou'west gale an' by gently expostulat-
in' wi' the sheet-iron rooster on th' kir-rk steeple
expect heem t' tur-rn his tail t' th' win'." So Mac-
Michael, of necessity, was left to his own opinions.
But the *Shannon* and the *Liffey* did all that was expected of them, and it was evident that the Northumberland Steamship Company would soon get rich
if it went on as it had been going. I could see that

this inclined MacMichael more and more toward making some move in the direction of working into the Gulf trade in winter.

January came around. The *Liffey,* with Malcolm Fraser in her—Malcolm who used to have the old *Aurora* when she first came out—was making a great record for herself, running with the regularity of one of the Holyhead boats, though often you could look out over the harbour and see her coming up without a streak of open water in sight. Yes, and the *Shannon* was holding her own. We were carrying plenty of passengers and full freights, and, do you know, I got to take as great an interest in the line—real wholesome interest—as I ever did in my naval work.

By the way, about the first of January MacMichael had gone to England on business, but this time he'd gone alone. The same week Wilson took Hans with him and went off up to Gaspé.

" I shall be down about the first of April," he said, as he left.

One day—it was the twenty-first day of January—I was bound in to Caribou. We had had a tough fortnight of it. Hard frosts for four or five days had filled all the bays with field-ice. A westerly gale lasting for a day had driven the fields off shore, then an easterly gale had smashed them up and the pans had blown together and frozen into big clumpets. Then the wind shifted to the north-

northeast, and drove those clumpets, together with a lot more from the north, hard down into the southern bight of the Gulf, until Northumberland Strait was packed with ice from end to end. Even the *Liffey* had her work cut out, but still the *Shannon* had been ramming her way through it beautifully.

When I first sighted Caribou Light it was about two in the afternoon and the sun was shining clear over the glistening clumpets between me and the harbour. The *Shannon's* bow would ride up, far up, on a stiff piece of ice, and then, with a grinding crash, break its way down to water again. We were making good headway when the first officer, who had been standing outside the wheel-house on the bridge, looked in.

" Caribou Light seems to be flying some signal, sir," he said.

" Signal! " I answered. " This time of year! Who could it be for? "

" I don't know, sir, unless for some boat of this line. Perhaps it's for us."

" I can hardly think they would need to signal us for anything. Hand me down that binocular. There! Now go and see if you can make it out."

A minute afterward he came back.

" It's our own house flag and pennant, sir," he said, " they want us."

" They do, eh! Here, let me see the glass.

Yes," I said, " you're right, Mr. Ferguson; run up your answering pennant."

He did so, and the signals on the light station were gradually changed until they spelled out the message:

Shannon will proceed in with all possible despatch. Critical. Do not spare boat. If Liffey in sight, signal same.

I signalled back:

O. K., Liffey not in sight.

" Well, I'll be hanged! " I said.

" Evidently something serious, sir," said Ferguson.

" Very evidently.   Don't spare boat, eh!   Hmm! Go to the chief, Mr. Ferguson; tell him about this message and tell him to do his best, to get out every ounce there is in her."

Twenty minutes afterward the *Shannon* was trembling from stem to stern, trembling so that the glasses wouldn't stand on the shelf outside the rack. Her funnel was sending out a cloud of black smoke, with an occasional live coal, under the pressure of the forced draught which had been turned on.   The throttle was wide open, and up from the engine-room came the throb, throb, throb, of her big engine. From outside came the crash of breaking ice and the swish and swirl of churning water. We ran straight at what seemed to be the thinnest parts of the barriers, and we generally went through.

In the meantime I was forming theories as to the cause of the signal. What could be the trouble? Each theory was formed only to be rejected, and when finally I got inside Caribou Light and started up through the board-ice I was as badly puzzled a man as you ever saw.

When I steamed up to the wharf I was surprised to see Wilson talking to Henderson outside one of the warehouse doors. Near the next door stood a great crowd of coal-passers, with baskets already filled with coal on the wharf beside them. They were talking among themselves, and were evidently a bit excited.

Before we could get a line ashore Henderson ran out to the edge of the wharf.

" Captain Ashburn," he shouted, " will you make arrangements to coal at once. Fill every bunker and all the spare space you have. You might put your own men on in addition to these." He spoke hurriedly and excitedly.

I passed the instructions on to the chief, wondering still more what it could mean. Coaling like that must be for an ocean trip.

As soon as the gangway touched the deck the coal-passers streamed across and began work. When I got ashore Henderson had already called the steward and was giving him instructions about provisioning for three months. Just then Wilson came up and we shook hands.

" What does all this mean? " I asked, " I thought you weren't coming back till April! "

" I hadn't any intention of coming back until April," he replied; " but come along up with me and I'll tell you all there is to tell."

We walked up the hill and seated ourselves on the carriages of the old guns on the battery. On the way up he gave me a description of the trip up to within a few days before.

" Last Saturday afternoon," he said, " I was in the cottage at Percé, writing up some tidal work. The Gulf was jammed with ice as far as I could see. Hans had been edifying the Frenchmen by coasting around on the hills on a pair of ski, when he burst into the cottage and said that he could see smoke out in the Gulf.

" ' Smoke out in the Gulf? ' I said. ' Why, what do you mean; there can't be any smoke in the Gulf this time of year; you must have seen a puff of mist or something of the sort.'

" ' Meest,' he said, ' Meest! Yesus! deed you efer see meest dot vas black? Breeng your glas' und see for yourself! '

" I took the glasses, climbed up to the top of one of the hills, and went out to the edge of the cliff. There were a lot of excited Frenchmen there waving their arms in argument and pointing seaward. I asked Louis Bourgeois, one of the *Scoter's* crew, who was among them, what they were pointing at.

" ' I donno', me,' he said. ' Bot she look lak de smoke of one steamer. *Mais* she can't be dat, for dey don' fin' it de kin' of steamer yet dat can come op here in winter.'

" ' There are one or two that might get here all right,' I said, ' but this couldn't be either of them.'

" I looked to seaward. Nothing but ice, ice everywhere, with here and there a narrow lane of open water. Away off on the southeastern horizon was the black smudge Hans had spoken of. It was smoke. There could be no doubt about that. I looked through the glass and could make out a single-funnel steamer. She was in open water, but locked in by ice on every side, and big ice too. Of course I was surprised. How any steamer could have gotten into the Gulf in winter I couldn't imagine. I looked closely at her again. She was evidently a good-sized freight boat, perhaps six thousand tons gross, with two masts. Beyond that I could make out but little, not even the colour of her funnel. If she was flying signals she was too far away for me to make them out. I watched her running at the thinnest places in her ice prison and trying to break her way through. Each time she would be turned back and have to try another spot. I thought at the time that she might as well attempt to break through the Isthmus of Panama. When it came down dark she was drifting away north with the ice.   It was a fearful position for a steamer to be in.

"That night I thought of a scheme to signal her. It was luckily perfectly clear, and Hans and I took the big oxy-hydrogen light—the one I had for making enlargements from microscopic slides—put it on a toboggan with the gas cylinders, and with snow-shoes on dragged it to the top of the hill. We looked out in the direction we had last seen the steamer.   We could see nothing but stars and the Northern Light.   We set the big jet up in the snow, put a condenser in front of it, and started to send flashes of light out across the Gulf.   We kept sending a few flashes at intervals of ten minutes, from eight o'clock until about two in the morning without being able to make out anything in return.   At first it wasn't so bad, but later a breeze came up—northwesterly—and blew the fine snow over the crest of the hill, crystalline and sharp as knives. There wasn't very much in quantity, for it didn't hinder our seeing in the least, but the quality was superb.   We could hear it hiss against the barrel of the lantern.   Some of the Frenchmen came up at first, but it soon got too cold for them, and they left.   Finally I thought we should freeze to death. However, Hans stuck to it like a man——"

"And you?" I said.

"I," continued Wilson, "Oh! I couldn't let the steamer and her crew get crushed in the ice if I could do anything to help them—though just then it wasn't very evident what I could do," he continued musingly. "Well, we kept at it, and about three o'clock just as I was going to turn the light on again, a faint red light showed up away to the eastward. It was a rocket. It was followed by a blue light, then a red, then another blue, then a white, and finally another red. Red, blue, red, blue, white, red.

"Hans had been so cold that but for the mechanical movements he made in helping me with the light you might have supposed that he was in a state of coma. But when he saw the signal lights flash out he jumped up and watched them until the last one faded away.

"'Red, blue, red, blue, vite, red,' he ejaculated; then his expression suddenly changed, and he slapped his hand on his thigh—you know how he does it—

"'Yesus!' he yelled, 'it's a MacMichael boat!'

"Yes, it was a MacMichael boat. Red, blue, red, blue, white, red, is MacMichael's night signal. Then the whole thing suddenly became clear. MacMichael had often threatened to send a steamer into the Gulf in winter, though I never supposed he was quite in earnest—that is, unless he got one built something after the pattern of the *Shannon* or the *Liffey;* but now he had done it, and the inevitable had happened. Now that she had seen our light I wondered if it would be possible for her to send us a message. I decided to try her with the Morse code. I sent a couple of preparatory signals. Then, with long and short flashes, I slowly spelled out the message:

"'*What boat. What condition are you in.*'

"I turned a pair of night-glasses on her and watched for perhaps a quarter of an hour. Then the flashes came, red—they were using red Bengal fire—and this was the answer:

"'*Duncrieff. Leaking. Cannot get ashore. Need assistance. Owner aboard.*'"

"What! I said, feeling the fearfulness of the situation strike me as perhaps I've never felt anything of the kind before, "Mr. MacMichael aboard! Where is he now?"

Wilson looked down, and his voice got unsteady for a second as he started to speak. Then he controlled himself quickly.

"God knows!" he said.

"What reply did you give them?" I asked.

"This," he answered:

"'*Save ship as much as possible. Shall try to reach you with Shannon or Liffey. David Wilson.*'

"After that they tried to send another message, but a slight snow squall came between us, and though I could see the flashes for a minute or two I could only make out two words. They were

' *Owner wishes*——,'   Owner wishes what, I wonder."

" Heaven knows," I said, and we were both silent, probably because each was weighing in his mind the chances for ever knowing what the red flashes said to the floes and the clumpets and the seals.

" I wonder why he came out in the *Duncrieff* when he was trying an experiment of that sort with her ? " I said.

" Just because it was an experiment," said Wilson.   " If you knew MacMichael as well as I do, you'd know that if there was an experiment to be carried out by the MacMichael boats he would be present in person if such a thing were possible. That is the reason the MacMichael boats are known wherever the sun shines."

" You said that the *Shannon* or *Liffey* would attempt to go to the assistance of the *Duncrieff*. What does the Northumberland Steamship Company say ? "

" Henderson has agreed to send either or both of the boats," said Wilson.

" It's rather generous of the Company to offer to send its two finest steamers to endeavour to save the boat of a line that is trying to become a rival." Wilson said nothing.

" Do you think the *Shannon* can do it ? " I continued.

"You should have a pretty accurate idea. But I think she will." Then a shade passed over his face. "If there is anything to do by the time she reaches there," he added.

"When did you see the *Duncrieff's* signals?" I asked.

"Last Saturday night, or rather Sunday morning. There was no train from Percé until late on Monday, and as they had no engine there I couldn't get a special made up. So I started from Percé, alone for the sake of lightness, at four o'clock on Sunday morning, and drove nearly two hundred miles to Campbellton in New Brunswick, in time to catch the Maratime Express on Monday. I used up five horses on the way, poor beasts, but I got them each in a comfortable place before I left them.

"By-the-way, if I didn't know you as well as I do, Ashburn," he continued, "I should ask you whether you cared to go on this trip. I shall be able to do the navigating, as I know that part of the Gulf pretty well. Of course you know that I feel there is very considerable danger that the *Shannon* may never come back, and that her crew may never come back either; though if the worst came to the worst we would make a hard fight to get ashore in the ice-boats. I simply want you to feel that you are not bound to the ship in any way on this trip, though I suppose anything I may say is useless."

"Perfectly useless, Dave," I said; "if anything

did happen I don't know that I am so useful but that this world could get along satisfactorily without me. But, do you know, I have a feeling that if this must be done we can do it."

"Well, then," said Wilson, "it must be done, and we shall do our best to accomplish it."

"Does Mrs. MacMichael know yet?" I asked.

"No."

"Nor Miss MacMichael?"

"No, not yet. I must go and tell them now."

"I shall go back to the *Shannon*," I said.

"No," said Wilson, "come with me. You are a great friend of Miss MacMichael's and I should prefer it, if you don't mind."

"Whatever you wish," I said, and we started up the hill.

Night was closing in, and when we approached the MacMichaels' gate we could look back down the hill toward the Northumberland Company's wharf and see dimly the masts and funnel and big pram bow of the *Shannon*—God bless her—and down below we could see the flaring lights and hear the ceaseless rattle of coal down the iron chutes.

We found Miss MacMichael alone and were glad that it was so, as we felt we knew better how to tell her than her mother. She was sitting in front of a blazing wood fire that gave the only light in the room. She had evidently been gazing into the flames, as we all love to do at times, and she looked up as we went in.

"How do you do, Captain Ashburn," she said, as she got up and turned on the electric light. "Why, Mr. Wilson! I thought you were away up on the borders of the Arctic Circle somewhere. You've got a pleasant little habit of surprising people in a nice way. You may feel deeply honoured to know that in spite of Captain Ashburn, who has been really extraordinarily nice, and Mr. Henderson, who has been actually devoted, I have been lonely since you left."

"I've felt honoured at lesser things," said Wilson, smiling slightly, "but Miss MacMichael——"

In an instant she saw that something was wrong. She looked from Wilson's face to mine for a few seconds with a half-curious, half-frightened expression. Then she thought for a moment, evidently summing up the happenings that could come to her as bad news. Her mother——was in the house: her father——away—in England. Her keen, unerring intuition flashed up a picture of something amiss with him.

"My father——" she said, hardly above her breath. She sank on a sofa and looked to Wilson for an answer.

He had himself under the control so characteristic of him in times of danger or trouble. His deep voice carried hope in its every tone and was as soft and as sympathetic as a girl's.

"Your father is in no immediate danger, I hope," he said, "but it is of him we have come to tell you. You are a very brave girl, and I shall simply tell you how things stand. Your father was in England, and evidently decided to send the *Duncrieff* out to a Gulf port in January. He must have decided to come out on her himself. Last Saturday I sighted the *Duncrieff* off the Percé Rock, caught in the ice, and she signalled that your father was aboard."

"The *Duncrieff!*" she said faintly. "When he went away he told us he was going to have her strengthened to try a trip through the ice, but we never thought that he——O, Dad, dear old Dad! Why did——" and MacMichael's daughter buried her face in her arms and quivered with sobs.

Wilson's lips became a thin line, and I swallowed a lump in my throat.

Only a few seconds passed, while the room was still. Up from the wharf below, sounding far in the distance, we could catch the continuous rattle of coal falling on the iron chutes.

Miss MacMichael stood up quickly, and with eyes brimming with tears—the only time I had seen them so since the little chap of Ranald MacKenzie's died in the Cottage Hospital—she came over and put her hands in ours.

" You'll think I am very weak, but——now, tell me, what is to be done? " She was the girl of the boat race and the ski again.

" The fact that the *Duncrieff* was to be strengthened for work in the ice puts an entirely new light on the whole thing," said Wilson. " It gives her a hundred per cent better chance. I managed to telegraph a message to her on Sunday morning, in which I said that we should try to get to her with the *Shannon* or the *Liffey;* and—listen!—do you hear that coaling down at the Northumberland Company's wharf? That's getting the *Shannon* ready for the trip. I'm going up with her, and now— God helping us!—I feel that we are bound to win." He spoke with the same enthusiasm and confidence that had carried away the big hypercritical audiences at Burlington House.

Miss MacMichael took both his hands in hers.

" David Wilson," she said, " you're one of the dearest chaps alive, and I shall never know how to thank you. But the Northumberland Company,— are they willing to send the boat? "

" Yes," said Wilson, " Mr. Henderson is quite willing to send either of them."

" Then the Company shan't suffer! "

" Probably not," was the meditative answer.

" When will you start? "

" The instant the *Shannon* has finished coaling and provisioning. I shall telephone down to Henderson and see." He went out into the telephone room.

Mrs. MacMichael came in, and her daughter told her the whole story. She bore it with the strength which was one of her characteristics.

" Are you going with the *Shannon,* Captain Ashburn?" she asked.

" Yes," I said.

Wilson came in and spoke to Mrs. MacMichael for a few minutes. Then he turned to us.

" Luckily," he said, " they had all the stores in stock and are getting them aboard, so that the boat will be ready as soon as the coaling is finished, which Henderson says will not be later than three to-morrow morning. We shall go then."

Miss MacMichael's lip trembled for a moment, while she seemed lost in thought. Then she clenched her hands and steadied herself with an effort.

" I shall go with you!" she said.

" You! Miss MacMichael!" said Wilson, with a look more of satisfaction than of surprise.

" Yes! that is—if Captain Ashburn will take me," she continued, looking appealingly at me. This girl had given me more surprises in life than any other woman ever had, but this crowned them all.

" I wonder if you realise that there is a good deal of danger in such a trip," I said,—" yes, and perhaps a good deal of discomfort and a possibility of hardship. But as far as I am concerned I shall be glad, as you very well know, to do anything I can to make you comfortable if you really wish to come. What does Mr. Wilson say?"

She turned to him.

"I can only say that you yourself are the best judge," he said; "but unless one of the stewardesses will volunteer to go—and I very much doubt it—you must remember that you would be the only woman. You could hardly go under those circumstances."

"From a conventional point of view, perhaps not," said the girl; "but Betsie would go with me, mother, wouldn't she!"

"Yes, dear," said Mrs. MacMichael; "if your heart is set on going, and you think it best, Betsie will go with you I am sure, though I cannot see, Gertrude dearest, that you can be of any use."

"When Dad is found I may be of use where no one else would," she said simply, and for a moment the tears came to the eyes of both women.

Betsie was an old Highland Scotch general servant who had been in the MacMichael family for the past fifteen years. She was one of the two women I have known in whom fear, as a constituent of their make-up, seemed to have been entirely left out. Some time I shall tell you about the other. Once in Betsie's younger days, or, at any rate, in the days of the dim distant past—tradition says she didn't seem younger then than now—she cooked for a lumber camp.   One day, when the men were all away at work, one of the horses broke through the ice into the lake.   Betsie got a noose around his neck, strangled him into insensibility, and, after tying the rope to a tree, bent on a sampson purchase and snaked him ashore.   She brought him around with brandy, and when the men got back to supper the only proofs of the story were the hole in the ice, and a happy horse, with a bare ring around his neck where hair had formerly been, and a breath that smelled of cognac.

During the same period of Betsie's career two Indians, both very drunk, came to the cook-house when the men were away, and threatened to shoot the cook if they weren't furnished with dinner. They would undoubtedly have gotten the dinner under other circumstances, but Betsie's wrath rose. With a deft movement of a hot poker she got their feet inextricably tangled so that they fell; then she annexed the two guns, and, seizing an axe, chased the owners across into the woods on the far side of the clearing.

After she got older and went into MacMichael's employ she indulged in feats of a milder type; until, in the last few years, one of her famous exploits recurred as regularly as any of the numerous female cats that lived in the outbuildings of the MacMichael establishment brought a litter of kittens into the world. Betsie had a butter-tub—disused as such—with a cover which fitted accurately. This tub she used to secrete in a place known only to herself, and when it appeared before the eyes of mortals it was a sign to all that passed that way that Toodlums or Kippy or Maudie had been fruitful and had multiplied. About the time that Maudie was particularly solicitous after food, Betsie would disappear for a period, and emerge from the barn a little later with her hair filled with hayseed, but with the butter-tub in her hand, and in it a litter of kittens. She would fill the tub to the brim with water, and put on the cover, on which she would sit and smoke a short black T. D. pipe until long after the last gurgling *maeows* had ceased to come from beneath her skirt. From this it must not be inferred that Betsie was hard-hearted. Far from it. She merely knew that these kittens could not be allowed to grow up, and so she arranged that they should depart at an early age.

Betsie was the one woman in all the world that sympathized with all the vagaries of Gertrude Mac-Michael. That young lady herself told me that when, at the age of twelve, she had carefully dragged a toboggan made of barrel staves up a ladder to the peak of the stable roof, and, using the roof as a slide, had brought up in a snowbank thirty feet below, and when, as a consequence, the parental wrath had descended, it was Betsie who took her into the pantry and stuffed her with fresh ginger-bread and milk, telling her that she would have done the same thing at her age.

So it merely remained for Betsie to be consulted. She was found and brought in. Wilson explained the situation to her, and told her of the possible dangers of the trip, knowing away down in his heart that the more he brought the dangers into prominence the more would Betsie wish to go. She had a reputation to sustain, and she knew it.

"If Mr. MacMichael's in trouble, and it's not too dangerous for Miss Gertrude to go with you, it's not too dangerous for me," she said, and that ended the discussion.

"We shall call for you at half-past two," said Wilson, as we left.

He went to his home, and I went down to see how things were going with the *Shannon*.

CHAPTER V.

THE news had already sifted out, and a crowd of people were on the wharf, watching the gangs of men at work. Henderson was rushing about, giving orders for half a dozen operations at once. Engines were puffing back and forward, taking away empty coal-hoppers and bringing up full ones. Two long lines of men, all black and unrecognizable under a coat of coal-dust, were passing the full coal-baskets aboard in a steady stream along one gangway and the empty ones ashore along another. Engineers were rushing about, now stopping under a deck lamp to examine and measure a new piece of packing, then disappearing down a ladder through a hatch from which came a stream of yellow light. One of the winches was rattling away, hoisting aboard cases of provisions, while another, with a big gang of men in charge, was groaning under the job of getting aboard extra blades for the propellor and stowing them in the hold. Down in the stoke-hold the stokers were knocking clinkers off glowing grate-bars and sending them up the rattling ash-hoist, from which they hissed into the icy water. The big centrifugal pumps that could empty every tank in the boat in thirty minutes were being tested for the last time before starting, and great streams of white, frothy, salt water were pouring from the ice-crusher's sides. Down below, the dynamos hummed, and every port in the *Shannon* showed a gleam of light.

It was a clear, cold night, but the crowd on the wharf increased every minute,—men, women, and children.

When Henderson saw me he ran over to where I was standing.

" As this is special service," he said, " we want the crew to volunteer to go. Hadn't you better call them into the saloon and tell them."

" Yes," I said, " I shall. Mr. Ferguson, get every member of the crew into the saloon." When everyone was there, from first officer to firemen, I said :

" Men, the majority of you, perhaps all of you, know where the *Shannon* is bound to-night. The *Duncrieff*, with James MacMichael on board, has been caught in the ice up near Cape Gaspé. The *Shannon* is going up to try and save the *Duncrieff*, or at least to save Mr. MacMichael and the *Duncrieff's* crew. As this may be considered special service, and as the danger will be much greater than in regular work, the Company wishes each man to feel that he is under no obligation to go, and that anyone who may be married, or who for other reasons may consider it unadvisable to go, will say so at once, so that his place may be filled by a volunteer."

There was silence for a minute or two, then a whispered conversation between some members of the crew. Then the chief engineer, old Sandy MacKinnon, noted for his lifelong attention to saving his salary, stepped forward.

"A'm prood t' be able t' say for the crew, sir, that not a mon among 'em wishes to leave."

Henderson thrust a note into my hand, and I read it.

"And I am very proud," I answered, "to have a crew that will stick to the ship under such circumstances. I have just had a note handed to me which states that every man of the *Shannon*'s crew will, on his return to Caribou, receive from the Company the sum of twenty-five dollars, and the officers fifty dollars, above their ordinary pay. You may go, and remember that every moment gained gives us a better chance of saving the *Duncrieff*."

The men had been very quiet. There wasn't one among them who hadn't felt the direct benefit of the MacMichael boats, no, nor one of them who hadn't been greeted with a pleasant word and that ever-kindly smile by James MacMichael himself. Now, as they turned to go, they cheered,—cheered so that the crowd on the wharf surged forward to see what

was happening, and when they went back to work
they gave no mercy to the winch engines or themselves.

Everything was going well, and I went ashore
to go up to Wilson's home. The wharf was now
almost covered with people, old and young, each
trying to get some further particulars of the *Duncrieff's* position, or some corroboration of the ru-
mour that MacMichael was aboard.

Jim McIntyre stopped me.

"Ees it true, sir," he asked, "thut th' *Duncrieff* ees jammed een th' ice oop off Cape Gaspé,
'n' thut Meester MacMichael's aboord?"   Twenty
men in the crowd listened for the answer.

"Perfectly true, I'm sorry to say," I said.

"'N' air ye goin' t' her asseestance wi' th' *Shannon?*"

"Yes," I said, "if we can get to her.   We shall
leave about three o'clock."

"Aye!" he said meditatively, "a mus' tell Tonal.
He might wan' t' go," and he departed in the direction of the fire station, where, since leaving the
Dungeness, Donald McDonald presided as chief engineer of the Caribou Fire Department.

I felt that I shouldn't mind having another chief
of Donald's ability aboard. He used to be the
chief in the *Dungeness,* the biggest of the MacMichael boats, and had a splendid record in her. Besides, in moments of danger and excitement Donald

had a reputation for coolness and fearlessness that was absolutely unique. It was generally believed that he drove the *Dungeness* at the speed he did by carrying half as much steam again as he was allowed. It was Donald that had fought the new fire-engine at the time of the Academy fire and had saved the Academy, and, as a result, had been given a gold watch by the town council. In the back of the case of the watch was the statement that it had been given for a certain service which Donald had performed " at the risk of his own life, and incidentally of the lives of several of his fellow men." Yet throughout the performance of that service Donald had smoked the three-inch black pipe, answered inane questions suavely, and talked pleasantly about trivial and irrelevant things.

I found Wilson in his library straightening out papers unlimited. Some he was filing away, and some he was putting into envelopes addressed to various learned societies.

" You never can tell! what may happen on a trip of this sort," he said in explanation, " so it is better to be prepared."

I spent the greater part of the evening with his mother and himself. Mrs. Wilson seemed to have made up her mind that Mr. MacMichael was safe, and that whether the *Duncrieff* ever came back or not, the *Duncrieff's* owner and crew were as certain to return safely to Caribou as if they had never been caught by the floes up by Cape Gaspé. It's a curious thing in some women, this seeming to have an intuitive knowledge of when things are going for the best. One more superficial, or having a lesser knowledge of women than I, might think that the lack of fear of results in such a case could only arise from ignorance. But Mrs. Wilson was surely as far removed from being ignorant as was any woman this earth has seen. Even if she had been but ordinarily intelligent, with such a husband and such a son she could hardly have lacked knowledge of things in general; but she had a faculty for generalization and for the best application of the things that tended to ultimate truth such as has been given to few women. It could not be ignorance either of fact or principle that gave Mrs. Wilson the belief she had in the safety of James MacMichael. I don't know what it was, but I've seen it so often in women, and so often have I seen it work out right, that it gave me confidence as nothing else had. His mother's attitude must have done much toward cheering Wilson, though I must say he didn't seem to need it at that moment.

"There!" he laughed, as he folded up the last paper and put it in a drawer, "I have just finished my last will and testament for the eleventh time since my birth. Whenever I go away north I make a will, probably chiefly because a man who prepares to be accidentally killed never is."

It was one o'clock when Wilson kissed his mother good-bye, and with an extra sleeping-bag and a sack full of clothes we started down over the crisp snow toward the sounds of activity still coming from the Northumberland Company's wharf.

Just as I was stepping aboard the *Shannon* old Donald McDonald came up.

"Captain Ashburn," he said, "Jim McIntyre tells me y're goin' oot wi' th' *Shannon* t' try to get Jeemes MacMichael 'n' th' crew o' the *Duncrieff*. Froom my way o' thinkin' eet w'd ha' been better eef y'd taken th' *Leefey*. Noo, when y' get two ice-fiel's coomin' t'gether eet's better t' have a boat thut climbs oot on top o' them th'n one that stays there and waits t' get squeezed. Howefer, a dare say th' *Shannon* can do th' wor-rk. A wanted t' ask y' eef y'd min' my goin' along wi' y'. A wiz wi' Mac-Michael for a long while, 'n' a thocht a might be o' soom use."

"Yes, Donald," I said, "I shall be glad to have you with me. Be aboard before three. The only reason we didn't take the *Liffey* was because she was not here, and we didn't wish to lose any time: I hope, as you say, that the *Shannon* can do the work without her."

"A'll joost go an' get my kit, 'n' get Perry t' look after th' engines. Eef th' toon cooncil doosn' like eet—weel—a'm sorry," and he disappeared in the darkness.

We went aboard and learned from Henderson that he would be ready by sharp three. As we left the boat and started up the wharf to call for Miss MacMichael, the crowd, which had thinned out, had begun to gather again to see the *Shannon* off. We found Mrs. Wilson at the MacMichaels', and she had succeeded in a wonderful way in making Mrs. MacMichael as cheerful as herself.

The girl was ready when we arrived. She was dressed in a grey blanket snow-shoe suit faced with crimson, and her sweet, clear-cut features and sun-browned brilliant colouring made her as lovely a picture as a man may see in this life. I have often sat in the old St. James, and in later years in the Carlton and the Savoy, and looked around at the crowd, especially at the women. Heavens! what an exhibition it is for a man that loves sincerity and simplicity. If you had stripped the majority of those women—some who have been known as beauties for many seasons—of their dress, their jewels, and their powder and paint, ripped their nets off, loosened their hair up a bit, dressed them as this girl was dressed, and compared them with her, how many would have stood the comparison. It makes me laugh now to think of the row of beauties as they'd show up in those blanket suits. And this girl was not only more beautiful than they, but she could talk better, perhaps sing better, and certainly do everything else in the wide world much better.

She could beat the majority of them—perhaps all—at tennis, and some other things; if she had them in a boat race with her she'd frighten them into hysterics—most of them; her greatest pleasure was giving, theirs receiving; they were always blasé, she never; and, though I had never seen her at it, I had a deep-rooted idea that when she loved she would love better than they. Withal she was but mortal. I don't believe in paragons. She wasn't one. She was impetuous—too impetuous—and she had a bit of a temper which was not always under perfect control. Remember, too, that I am far from underrating the others, those of the Savoy and the Carlton—though some of them you couldn't underrate—for I have spent many pleasant times with them, but this girl leads, leads them all. Why? Not because of anything more than the fact that with the natural brilliancy of the best of women she combined a moral sanity that led her to love things for their own sakes—not because they were loved by others—and, well, she never posed.

Betsie turned up dressed, as far as I could make out, in a brown shawl as big as a staysail. All I could see of her was her sharp face with its bright, shifting black eyes, a wisp or two of grizzled hair, and an angular arm that carried a bundle—her "kit"—done up in a patchwork quilt.

As we walked down between the smooth spruce hedges, half buried in snow, that bordered the driveway to the MacMichaels' gate, we looked back and could see the figures of Mrs. MacMichael and Mrs. Wilson in the open door as we had left them. The girl couldn't trust herself to speak, and walked on in silence beside Wilson, who had captured Betsie's bundle, which he was swinging while he whistled softly to himself.

It was a typical Canadian winter night, clear, cold, and without a breath of wind. The snow glittered and crunched under our feet. The sky was a blaze of stars, with Sirius and Orion glittering away to the southwest. The harbour, frozen solid, showed as a dim white sheet stretching away to the dark line of woods on the opposite shore. Ordinarily, except for the street lamps, Caribou would have been dark by eleven o'clock, but now there was hardly a house that didn't show a light. The *Shannon* was going to try to rescue James MacMichael and the crew of the *Duncrieff*, and Caribou must see the *Shannon* start.

I must confess, however, that I was surprised when I reached the pier. Out on the end of the wharf the last ounce of coal had been stowed, and everything was quiet. The *Shannon* loomed up, and from her funnel the smoke poured black. Sandy was firing up. From the boat to the head of the wharf stretched a solid black mass of people, men, women, and children.

As Wilson and Miss MacMichael went through,

Betsie and I, as we followed, could hear what they said :—

"It's MacMichael's daughter!" said one, "I saw her face as plainly as I do yours."

"Well, if that girl ain't got the grit of the devil!" said another, to which Betsie nodded violent assent. I could hear them carrying the news to the women :

"It's Miss MacMichael. She's going too, and Betsie is with her," and soon they all knew it.

Donald joined us as we went up the gangway.

"Are you coming too, Donald?" said the girl, speaking for the first time since she had left the house, "I'm so glad!" She evidently thought that the presence of Donald, the imperturbable, the fearless, added another chance of success to the expedition.

As soon as we were aboard she asked me to help her find Henderson. This was soon done.

"Mr. Henderson," she said, "my father and I owe the Northumberland Steamship Company a very great debt for offering this boat to go to the assistance of the *Duncrieff,* and you may be sure that it will be repaid as fully as we can do it, though I am afraid that nothing we could do could tell you how grateful we are."

"Miss MacMichael," he answered, apparently with some embarrassment, "if it were not a great pleasure to the Company it would still remain a duty, and I feel sure that if you can appreciate the services of the *Shannon* half as much as the Company appreciates the chance to give them to your father and you we shall be well satisfied."

Just then the first officer came in.

"Ready to cast off, sir," he said.

We went on deck and found Wilson standing by the gangway.

"Good-bye!" said Henderson, "I hope three weeks will see the *Shannon* back with Mr. MacMichael and all of you." He turned to go ashore. Miss MacMichael held out her hand.

"Good-bye! Mr. Henderson," she said—I examined the knob on the engine-room door, and Wilson, apparently taken with a sudden desire to know the direction of the wind, gazed fixedly up at the main truck—"Good-bye! for the present. Perhaps I shall know better how to thank you when I get back." Henderson murmured something, fled down the gangway, and disappeared in the crowd. A minute afterward the last shore hand went over the side.

"Miss MacMichael," I said, "come up on the bridge with Mr. Wilson and me. Mr. Ferguson, you may cast off." Two hawsers were stowed, and the last wire spring fell on the ice and was dragged aboard. They had been useless for hours, for the ice had been making fast and the *Shannon* was frozen in.

From the bridge we could look out over the heads

of the almost silent crowd to where the lights of the
town and the white streets sloped up to the black
line of trees and houses against the stars.   Out to
the east, away down the grey-white stretch of harbour, blinked the Caribou Light, and a faint white
line showed the silent Gulf outside.   Above all, to
the north, the Northern Light shook, green and
pink.   A winter night in this, the most glorious
climate in the world, is something to be remembered for all time.   It's cold, to be sure, but a cold
that braces every nerve, and the air comes into your
nostrils keen and pure.   The *Shannon's* funnel was
pouring out a cloud of black smoke that blotted out
the stars as it drifted off to the southeast.

"All clear, sir," said Ferguson.   I opened the
pilot-house door, turned on the electric binnacle
light, and called the quartermaster to take the wheel.

"Now, Miss MacMichael," I said, "ten hours
after arriving we're ready to leave.   Ring to stand
by."   She reached for the handle of the engine-
room telegraph and swung it over and back, and in
an instant the clanging response came up, indicat-
ing that Sandy was ready.

"I'll leave you to do the next thing," I said.
She looked at me and smiled.   She swung the brass
handle back, and then forward to the very last
notch—"Full Speed Ahead."   I smiled to myself
as the response came back with a vicious clang that
indicated Sandy's surprise at such a sudden start.

Then up from the engine-room came the deep booming throb of the *Shannon's* mighty triple-expansion
engines; I say mighty, for these ice-crushers are en-
gined as are no other ships in all the world.   The
ice smashed astern, and the water spurted through
as it cracked and ground on every side.   Then the
silent crowd broke into a deep roaring cheer that
rang in waves for a full half-minute and then echoed
bellowing back from the woods across the harbour.
It was a Canadian cheer with a good deal of Scotch
in it, but it was more than that.   It was a cheer
that told as nothing else could tell just how much
James MacMichael—yes, and James MacMichael's
daughter—were loved by the people of Caribou.

Gertrude MacMichael smiled; then, touched as
only a woman of her type can be by the feeling
shown in that roar of voices, the tears came, and,
as the *Shannon* raised her nose in the air and started
to gather way, she walked out on the bridge and
stood silent until the lights were twinkling far away
over the path of broken ice and black water astern.
She pulled her hood up and came to where Wilson
and I were sheltering ourselves behind the wind-
shields.   She talked of the glory of the stars, of the
keen air, and of the aurora.   She felt as we did the
overwhelming majesty of a northern night.   I have
seen many things done by God and man.   Of all
the things that humanity has tried to make impressive I have seen but one that touched me deeply.

It was the sight when, with the eight destroyers ahead, the Great Queen passed for the last time down the line between the ships, ships that stretched so far ahead that I could see the flashes and never hear the thunder of their guns.   As this was to all other human spectacles, so is a northern winter night to the rest of things as they are.

We watched; watched as the *Shannon* settled down by the stern and roared out past the Caribou Light and past the red range lights, rounded the end of MacDonald's Reef, and, with her steel stem cutting the fields and pounding aside the clumpets, went thundering up the Strait of Northumberland toward the Northern Light and the saw-toothed cape where the ice-floes held the *Duncrieff*.

Wilson had been almost without sleep ever since he had left Percé, and took the chance of turning in while it offered.   I knew this part of the Gulf as well as did he or any other man, but up above it was different.   Miss MacMichael stayed on the bridge with me until the Gull Rock Light was abeam and the light on Wood Islands showed up away off the starboard bow.   Then we went down and found Betsie, who had her own room and the girl's fixed up as if she had been aboard a week.   I left her, and went to the wheel-house till daylight, which found the *Shannon* hunting around for thin places and lanes of open water off Point Prim.

That day I turned out late to find everything

brilliant sunshine, shimmering water and glittering snowy ice, and as night came down—another night of stars and Aurora—we had Cape Tormentine Light flashing away to port, and the light at Sea-Cow Head on our starboard bow. Then for a day or two we got into heavy ice and a few snow-squalls, but the *Shannon* did nobly, and won the approval of Donald, who divided his attention between the bridge and the engine-room. If there was any heavy ice to be encountered he was to be found either in one place or the other at all times of the day and night. Sometimes as we would run at a particularly heavy pan, he would lean far over the rail of the bridge and watch the ice as it broke and went boiling down into the green water under the two thousand tons of steel. Then he'd suck at the little black pipe for a second and turn to me:

" Eet's marvellous, pairfectly marvellous! " he'd say. Donald was one of those men who was an engineer by birth. He loved an engine for its own sake. He would search around for half a day with a spanner for some little knock that nobody else could hear, until his engines ran as though they were the spirits of engines that had lived in some previous cycle, and had died—like us all—to obtain perfect rest and quietness in doing the work they loved. The *Shannon* was a great machine, and, as such, she took his fancy. If a piece of machinery took Donald's fancy he got in love with it, just as

a man may get in love with a woman. He used to
be in love with the old *Dungeness,* and for a solid
month after leaving her he looked incredibly solemn. He got in love with the old Ronald fire-engine, and used to treat her like a child until it came
to a fire, and then he had been known to——well,
it was with her he fought the new engine and won.
This last was the key-note of one of Donald's peculiarities. No man treated an engine so well, and
no one got so much out of it when a crisis turned
up. So Donald fell in love with the *Shannon;* and
I've looked down into the engine-room and seen
him sitting on the bottom of a bucket, smoking the
black pipe, and watching, for an hour at a time, the
three big polished cranks and crank-rods as they
whirled glinting around in the dim light. He got
Sandy to let him take a sort of supernumerary position, and, armed with the inevitable spanner and
a hammer, he wandered around adjusting glands
and stuffing-boxes, and aiming vicious blows at flying cross-heads and crank-pins, until the *Shannon's*
8,000-horse-power was turned out almost as noiselessly as the 6-mouse-power in a small boy's engine.

Miss MacMichael and Wilson spent a good deal
of the time on the bridge—together. The girl
knew as well as I did just how much Wilson had
done toward getting the *Shannon* off in a hurry to
the assistance of the *Duncrieff.* She knew that if

things went as we hoped they would that Wilson—and Wilson alone—would be responsible for it all. She knew that he had driven two hundred miles in the stinging cold over the Gaspé Peninsula—he didn't tell her, but I did—to save twenty-four hours' delay. She also knew that he had gone to Henderson, and that for some mysterious reason—it was really an extraordinary thing for him to do—Henderson had offered not only one but both of the Company's best boats to go on an expedition from which neither might return, a contingency which would probably ruin the Company itself; and all without any guarantee of any sort that the loss would be made good. She was grateful, deeply grateful; that was evident; but, as far as I could see, that was all,—all, at least, for a time.

One day we were working along off the low snow-covered beach at Tracadie. The lagoon inside was frozen, and the board-ice extended well out into the Gulf. The wind was northwest and stinging cold, and the clouds hung low and grey. Outside it was clumpets,—clumpets everywhere, coming down from the north,—and big clumpets too. Among them were murres and guillemots, auks and puffins, glaucous gulls and grey harbour seals. Wilson was smothered in furs, working away with glasses and a note-book. Miss MacMichael decided that she wanted to see too, but it came down so cold that even in her blanket-suit she shivered.

In spite of her expostulations Wilson whipped off his fur coat and made her put it on. He armed her with a binocular, then put on a leather jacket and went on with his work. She watched the birds and seals and clumpets, and the spray that dashed over the stem and made a great mound of ice on the *Shannon's* fore deck; and —— I watched Miss Mac-Michael. Finally she leaned back in the deck-chair, snuggled down into the warm fur collar, and looked at Wilson. She watched his every movement as he worked,—noted, probably, as I did, his sun-tanned cheeks and clean-cut lips. Then an entirely new expression came over her face, and she smiled,—but not as I had ever seen Miss Gertrude MacMichael smile before. Her smile was always sincere, but this time it had something new in it. It was sentimental, actually sentimental. Suddenly she looked at me, and her cheeks flooded with crimson. I was looking at the New Brunswick coast at the time through a glass; but the eye-pieces of those glasses do not fit very closely, and I saw it all. I made a page or two of mental notes, and then my thoughts ran back to Miss Kathleen Tyrrell, and I made a few more.

"Mr. David Wilson," I said to myself, " I'm beginning to think you've won, and if you have I don't see why I——Well! we'll have to let the matter rest for the present."

The next day the *Shannon* had her hands full.

The wind came in from the northeast and it snowed, and for a while I couldn't see the length of the ship. We were getting up near Shippegan and Miscou, and the ice was getting heavier every minute and jamming in until the *Shannon* would often be enclosed in a pond and have to back up and hammer her way out.   Wilson knew this part of the Gulf better than the Admiralty charts.   He lived on the bridge and in the wheel-house, and for the next day or two he went by soundings.   He had nothing else to go by.   At last, on the second night, it cleared up just in time for us to see Miscou Light disappearing astern.

The *Shannon* fought her way across the mouth of the Baie des Chaleurs—just then there wasn't much to indicate why Jacques Cartier had named it so— and in the clear morning sunlight sighted to the northwest the dark cliffs of the Gaspé coast.

We were in waters where we might sight the *Duncrieff* at any time, and I kept a double watch and offered ten dollars to the first man who should see her.   We had a little open water and worked up toward Percé, but without seeing a smudge of smoke or a light.   Above, the ice was heavier again, and when at last the Percé Rock loomed up, the *Shannon* had a struggle to get near enough to the village to send one of the ice-boats ashore.   Wilson went in, and came back with the news that the *Duncrieff,* with her bow deep in the ice in which she was apparently frozen solid, had drifted south the day after he had seen her, and then away to the north again. Since then she had not been seen. The news was bad enough in a way, but it had one hopeful side; the *Duncrieff* was frozen in so probably would not sink.

"I'll remember for a long time Miss MacMichael's pitiful expression when Wilson, looking unconsciously a bit grave, climbed up the *Shannon's* side after he'd come back with the ice-boat.

"I hope——" she faltered.

"The *Duncrieff* was seen after I saw her, and she was safe then, so we'll hope she is yet," he said. "Trust the *Shannon,* Miss MacMichael; she'll find her,"—and the *Shannon* went to work at the task. She pounded off north, and then turned northeast toward the coast of Anticosti. Wilson stuck to the bridge almost night and day for four days.

It was about two in the morning of the fifth day out from Percé. It was clouding up heavily to the north and west. There was ice enough everywhere, but up to the north the blink hung glinting over a big field of apparently very heavy pack. The Aurora, rolling to the zenith in green streamers, was being blotted out by the rising clouds. Donald had been up having a smoke and talking to me, and Wilson had just come up. I was going to turn in. Donald, with his eyes fixed on the blink over the ice ahead, was telling us of a peculiar accident that had occurred on the *Dungeness,* and had just gotten to the crisis of his story when he stopped suddenly, looked ahead more intently, and said:

"A've na doot thut thet rocket wiz fired by th' *Duncrieff.*"

"What rocket?" I said, and jumped forward to see.

"Joost t' poort o' th' starboard riggin'." Wilson and I looked and could see the trail of a rocket fading away.

"It's the *Duncrieff,*" said Wilson, "nothing else could be in the Gulf." He spoke quietly, but his eyes sparkled.

"Weel, a'm fery glad she's safe!" said Donald with a sigh, and he lighted the black pipe and finished his story. Wilson and I looked at each other and laughed, partly at Donald and partly for joy, and Donald smiled and allowed a match to burn up close enough to his fingers to be crushed out conveniently without using his other hand.

I got out a Northumberland Company's light signal and burned it. Then we waited. At last across the ice and water came the flares:—red, blue, red, blue, white, red.

Wilson bowed his head. "Thank God!" he said. My hand shook as I put away the rest of the signals.

I went down and told Miss MacMichael. The girl had needed all her pluck for the last four days, but she had the pluck to call on, and she had stood the strain marvellously. Now nothing would do but that she must go on deck. I told her that there was nothing to be seen, but she got into the blanket suit and went up in the wheel-house with Wilson. I was staggering tired, so I turned in.

Miss MacMichael stuck to the bridge, and when I turned out at grey dawn and went up to the wheel-house again Wilson was standing with his hand on the engine-room telegraph, and the girl, who was outside, braving the cold and hardly moving, was gazing over the wind-shields into the grey white ahead.

Wilson had been taking the boat through all the open water he could find—the clumpets were too big to be hit for the sake of hitting them—and always working toward the pack over which the *Duncrieff's* lights had flared.

Donald had been on the bridge most of the time after the MacMichael signal had been seen, and now went down with Wilson and Miss MacMichael to get a cup of cocoa.

We at last came out into open water with only an occasional clumpet in sight, and away up to the east and north the jagged white edge of the big pack showed up with the clouds hanging low above it.

" East-northeast! " I said to the quartermaster at the wheel.

" East-northeast! " he repeated. I went out on the bridge. It was beginning to blow hard, and we were running right in the teeth of the wind. The *Shannon's* bows and forepeak and rigging were coated with ice. A lot of seals were about, and flock after flock of golden-eyes went whistling overhead down to the southeast. The light began to brighten up, and each minute I could see further. It blew still harder, and a flock of white-winged scoters came struggling up the wind, working toward the ice pack ahead. The light was now bright, and I watched them as they whistled to windward low over the water and ice until they showed as a black speck against the pack. The speck half faded away, then became stronger again and seemed to become stationary and to increase in size. I put up my glass. The speck was a steamer's funnel, and I could make out the masts and the sheer of the stern. It was the *Duncrieff* at last, but she was a good ten miles away, and we were at least five from the edge of the pack. I howled and danced up and down, and ran into the wheel-house and slammed the door.

" The *Duncrieff's* in sight," I said to the quartermaster; " steady as you are."

" Steady it is, sir. Where away? " he asked, looking at me a bit amused.

" Dead ahead," I answered, and ran down to tell Wilson, who with Miss MacMichael and Donald came up to the bridge again. We could now see the big boat plainly enough—what there was to see. She was lying in the centre of a great field of heavy ice which extended, broken and ragged, far out of sight, away to the northern horizon. To the east there might be open water beyond—we couldn't tell. Around the *Duncrieff* was piled some of the heaviest ice I had ever seen inside the Gulf. The whole body of the pack was made up of clumpets which had been driven together by the gales of the last few weeks and had been frozen into place until they formed one great field without a lane of open water in sight. The surface was so rough that it would have needed almost superhuman efforts to drag even a light broad-runnered ice-boat over it, and to have taken across such boats as the *Duncrieff* had was beyond the power of men.

Wilson and I, with our glasses, went over every yard of the edge of the great pack looking for a thin place. There wasn't a place that looked even promising. Donald inveigled Miss MacMichael over to the other end of the bridge and fitted her out with a pair of glasses so that she could study the *Duncrieff*.

"Dave," I said, "that's one of the hardest looking pieces of ice I ever saw. If the *Shannon* can go through that she is indeed a wonder."

"She will have to do it if it can be done," he said. "We shall have to make her do her best, I am afraid."

At last the sun came up and made a great brilliant copper-red band along the eastern horizon. I have seen many sunrises and sunsets in many lands, but for variety and gorgeousness there is none like the winter sunrise over the ice in the Gulf of St. Lawrence. That morning we four watched it as it changed every floating clumpet and the great pack, with its pinnacles and pans, into glinting red fire, turned the grey clouds above into copper-red and rose-gold, and lit up the big white waves that roared out from under the *Shannon's* bow.

"It's a bad-looking sunrise," said the quartermaster.

"Yes," I said; "it looks as if we were in for a breeze of wind."

"It's blowing half a gale now," said Wilson, "and increasing every minute."

Twenty minutes later we were at the edge of the pack. I rang the engines slow, and we ran along looking for a thin spot. The swells washed against the field, and below we could see the ice extending out far under water, showing that much of the field was too thick to be broken by any human agency, even with a weapon like the *Shannon*. We looked at the *Duncrieff,* and now it seemed that there was open water a short distance beyond her. If this were the case it might be better to try to find a way around the field. It would take at least a day, but seemed safer. But even as we were discussing it the wind howled stronger through the *Shannon's* rigging and we saw that it had shifted to the south-east.

"How's the glass, quartermaster?" I asked.

"Falling."

"And the thermometer?"

"Rising."

Wilson stood in silence and watched the edge of the great pack.

"Look," he said, "it's running hard to the west." The water was swirling as it swirls under the lee of a ship full aback.

A storm when you're in the ice isn't much like a storm in the open sea. To be sure, there is the wind, screeching through the rigging and shaking the chain and wire funnel-guys as if they were so much cod-line. But there's no hanging on to rails to keep from sliding overboard; no winding your arms and legs round a ventilator until ten tons of green water has washed over you and left you coughing and gasping and trying to get your wind; no breaking of four-inch lines and splintering of wood as your boats go overboard; no poor chaps going sprawling across the deck hoping to bring up in the lee scuppers, and going off on the top of a white-crested wave instead. No. In a storm in the ice the wind may blow as it will, but there runs no sea at first, and never unless there is open water, and lots of it, away to windward. But there is some-

thing which is worse, far worse. The ice moves.
The great resistless, pitiless ice moves. Slowly, deliberately, but with a force nothing can resist.

I've seen two fields meet,—heavy fields through
which neither the *Shannon* nor the *Ermak* nor any
boat that man could build, could go. Some were
driven by ocean currents proper, some by wind, some
by tides. I have seen them approach each other
noiselessly and slowly, and as their edges met I have
heard the fields crack for miles and seen the edges
broken and crushed, and, with a continuous noise
like the thunder of heavy guns, great cakes weighing tons on tons piled higher than a topsail-yard, or
carried up on the crashing ridge to slide down on
either field, as a piece of toffee slides down the side
of a plate. The wind—you never hear the wind;
there are too many other things to think about.

A swell running in from the open sea may break
up a field, especially a field of clumpets such as the
Duncrieff was caught in, and if this field broke up
and the clumpets crunched together, where would
the *Duncrieff* be, even supposing that she had been
sufficiently strengthened to be sound as yet!

Wilson called Donald.

"What condition do you think the *Duncrieff* is
in?" he asked.

"Her bootom?" inquired the engineer.

"Yes!"

Donald looked over the ice toward the spot where
the big MacMichael boat's stern and funnel showed.

" She's poonched like an ir-ron bucket th're usin'
t' bur-rn charcoal een," he said.

" I think as much myself," said I.

" Then," said Wilson, " there is but one thing
to be done: the *Shannon* will have to try to go
through. The wind is getting heavier every minute. If this pack should break up, it might help us
to get through, but the *Duncrieff*——"

" There w'd be no *Duncrieff*," said Donald, 'n'
th' cod-feesh 'd hev a gran' loomp o' scrap ir-ron t'
eenvestigate."

Miss MacMichael came up to the group.

" There is some new danger; " she said, " tell me
all about it, Captain Ashburn; I should prefer knowing."

I told her all there was to tell.

" I shall trust the *Shannon* and you all," she said.
" I thought I knew both men and boats before this
trip, but I have found I knew neither. If the *Shannon* cannot get through, then it is almost better to
die with the knowledge than to have lived without
it. If the *Shannon* does get through I shall know
how to thank you as I never knew before." The
girl spoke with a peculiar gayness, yet she was serious enough. The iron in her came out, and though
she realized the odds as well as any of us she had
but one thought. The *Shannon* must go through.
She had no personal fear and possessed unlimited
confidence.

CHAPTER VI.

THE *Shannon* still ran up and down in front of the field. There was a crack, and a clumpet that had been frozen to the edge of the pack broke off and turned over with a crash, sending a wave rolling across the short seas. Wilson watched the edge of the ice as a few loose pieces slowly rose and fell. He looked at me meaningly, and stepping into the wheel-house, took the wheel and rang " Full speed ahead." The ice-crusher rushed around in a quadrant and went boiling down on a low place in the field, doing her eighteen knots and with her nose high in the air. It was a great sight the way she ploughed into that pack and hurled aside the clumpets. Her stem would go up as though she were going to climb out on top of the ice, and then with a great hissing of water she would break her way down through. There she'd stick, and Wilson would back her up and go at it again. After an hour or so of this work, two small pans closed in suddenly while she was backing, and she shook from stem to stern.

" Propeller broken, sir," came through the engine-room speaking-tube, and we had to empty all the after tanks, and open the sea cocks into all the forward ones, until the boat's bow sank and her stern came up far enough to throw the big wheel out of water and allow us to lag on a new blade in place of one of which only a stump was left. The men worked hard, but it was after noon before we were ready to go on. In the meantime snow-clouds began to fly over the ice, and before the *Shannon's* nose was again up in the air we could no longer see the *Duncrieff*. Wilson had noted that the direction had changed but little. Evidently the pack was not turning.

All afternoon the *Shannon* banged at the heavy ice, making a few yards at a time, then backing off and charging again like a bull at Madrid. The snow blew thicker and thicker, and the wind yelled overhead as it does in a tropical hurricane. All the afternoon Wilson stood at the wheel and the girl stood beside him, working the engine-room telegraph.

I offered over and over again to relieve her.

"Do let me stay!" she said finally; "I know I am not doing any good, but I feel as if I were."

"I'm not so sure that you're not doing any good," I said. "You know we sailors are a superstitious lot, even the supposedly intelligent and case-hardened ones like myself. I've seen the *Shannon* in such places this afternoon as she's never been in before, and she's gone through them,—places that I would have sworn no boat could have gone through. The least you seem to be doing is inspiring Mr. Wilson with a knowledge of thin places in the field that it would seem to need some superhuman agency to discover."

Wilson smiled.

" I only hope Miss MacMichael can give me some inspiration as to how to get through that ring of clumpets ahead," he said, pointing to a curved line of small bergs showing through the flying snow just over the port bow. " It looks impossible, but it is hard to believe that anything is impossible to the *Shannon* now. We can only try it." He backed the boat down the broken track she had left for two hundred yards and drove her at a point between the two smallest clumpets. Just beside the clumpet to starboard was a piece of thick board-ice that had been forced up on edge by the fearful pressure when the ice had come together, and now towered sixty feet above the water, almost overhanging the path through which the *Shannon* was trying to force her way. The boat went at the space between, sending a wall of water roaring off from her bow. She ran up until it seemed as if she would never come down, but the ice was solid. Wilson backed her up and tried it again. This time the ice cracked, and part of it broke away. The third time the barrier heaved and went down, and the *Shannon* wedged into the crevice. The clumpet on the right, with the great weight of ice over it, pressed against the boat's bow and sank grinding down. With the crash of breaking ice there was a sound of creaking steel, and then the great tower of solid green-white board-ice to starboard, with its base dragged from under it, leaned over slowly and majestically and came thundering down on the *Shannon's* fore deck. The boat shook and shivered from truck to kelson.

I rushed out to the end of the bridge. The deck plates were crumpled like tin, and the starboard bow was stove in from rail almost to water-line. I ran back to the wheel-house.

" I suppose it is the number two tank," said Wilson quietly. " Is it far down? "

" Not to the load water-line."

" Is that all. I'm glad it is no worse, but I am afraid there are some rivets sheared off down below ; it sounded like it before that Cleopatra's Needle came down. Mr. Ferguson, send the carpenter into number two tank to report." He backed the *Shannon* out and sent her boiling up at the débris.

" There, you brute! " he laughed, as she rode over the shaft of the fallen ice-tower and ground it into lolly, " That will teach you not to break in steamers' decks." All the time the girl's eyes sparkled with excitement, and Mr. David Wilson, unwittingly, or at any rate unintentionally, made another great step in her estimation.

A few minutes later Ferguson came back, somewhat excited.

"Carpenter reports twenty-two inches of water in number two tank," he said: "eight frames sprung in number two, and seven plates opened; seven frames sprung in number three, and five plates opened; eleven inches of water in number three."

"H'm!" said Wilson; "have them pumped out, and tell the carpenter to wedge the plates."

"Very good, sir!"—and as Ferguson walked away I could hear him talking to himself, something about: "You'd think he was having new signal halyards rove, or giving orders to have the ventilators painted." Turning to me as he passed, he said confidentially,—

"I don't believe either he or old Donald would get excited if the *Shannon* went to the bottom of the Gulf and left them sitting on a clumpet. Donald would get out a pencil and paper and begin to calculate the amount of suction as the boat went down, and *he'd* get out a little glass and hunt for some new kind of beasts on a string of kelp."

"Yes!" I said; "and then they'd make a fire with the kelp, and if their luck held as usual they'd drift ashore the next day."

Well, Wilson drove the *Shannon* ahead as if nothing had happened, and just as night came down she smashed two blades of her propellor, and again we had to stop and put her down by the head. This

time it didn't take so long to get the forward tanks
filled.   You could listen down the hatch and hear
the water coming in like a cascade by ways it had
never come before.   But in spite of the wedging it
took longer to pump it out.

We hadn't seen the *Duncrieff* since eleven o'clock ;
but as dark came on she began to fire bombs to guide
us, and rolling down the wind every thirty minutes
would come a boom that told us that she was
still above water.   It was not cold, but the snow
was as thick as before.   The men worked as though
their own lives depended on getting the blades on
that boss, and by eleven o'clock we were up and at
it again.   In the meantime the movement in the
pack had increased and the clumpets were breaking
all about us.   It made things easier for the *Shannon,* but we all knew, though no one said so, that
the *Duncrieff's* chances were lessening every moment.

Miss MacMichael kept up her wonderful pluck.
The *Shannon's* search-light was turned on, and she
saw it blaze through the glinting snow and show
up the ever-widening lanes of black water.   The
girl knew what it meant as well as we did, but she
never gave up, nor did Wilson or Donald, though
at last I'll admit I thought we should never see the
Duncrieff again.   But each half hour the boom came
growling down the wind, and the girl's eyes would
light up in triumph.   The steward brought up hot

cocoa and chops and toast, and she would eat peering out into the snow and with her hand on the telegraph.

All the time the *Shannon* pounded ahead, now winding her way through a lane, now hurling herself on a barrier, as a rorqual bears down on a whale-boat. Still the booms came down the wind, sounding nearer and nearer, and the snow whirled in clouds, blotting out everything.

About four o'clock we came out into a streak of open water,—an opening in the centre of the field running across our course. The snow came less thickly, and we could see a wall of heavy ice beyond the water, perhaps two hundred yards away.

" It is twenty-two minutes since the last bomb from the *Duncrieff*," I said. " It sounded very close. Don't you think we had better wait until the next one is fired? The boat may be somewhere on the edge of this crack, and we would get to her more quickly than if we went into the ice on the other side."

Wilson agreed with me, and we stopped for three or four minutes in the edge of the ice. Wilson was peering out into the darkness.

" Perhaps," he said, " she would be near enough to hear our whistle. We can try it." He pulled down the lever, and the *Shannon's* syren howled through the snow. We listened, and the report of a bomb rang out almost directly across the crack.

I turned the search-light in the direction of the sound. If you've ever been in the ice you'll know what we felt when, instead of seeing two hundred yards of open water, we saw the heavy ice up to within seventy yards of us and rapidly closing in. The two parts of the field were closing up, and the *Shannon* was between without even room to turn. Wilson took in the situation in a second. His lips hardened, and as he looked at Miss MacMichael an expression of sharp pain crossed his face. It lasted but for an instant, but she saw it and breathed more quickly.

"Full speed ahead," he said,—"*hard!*" She slammed the handle over, then back and over again. Sandy understood, and the telegraph-bell fairly howled in reply. The *Shannon* went straight for the oncoming ice and buried herself in it. She was carried back, and a minute afterward the two fields met. There was a long, indescribable crash of clumpets grinding clumpets to lolly, a rush of iron ice mounting on ice and crashing on steel, until pieces weighing tons came raining down on the *Shannon's* deck and upper works. The pressure was fearful, and the boat's starboard side at the number three compartment was being literally crushed in, while she was forced over to port until we could hardly hold our footing on the floor of the wheel-house. Just forward of the wheel-house to windward a big flat piece of board-ice stood up on edge for a mo-

ment, and then toppled over and smashed one of
the boats into firewood. All the time the grinding
of ice on ice and of ice on steel was past the power
of human words to tell, while loud above everything else we could hear the booming cracks of
breaking clumpets.

This lasted for a good quarter of an hour, and
then the pressure slackened, and the *Shannon,* battered and shaken, righted up again. She was wall-
ed about with great irregular hummocks, and
though a little open water was in sight she was no
more capable of moving than if she had been a mile
inland.

Everyone had been silent, awed by the wonderful scene and the noise. Donald, who had been
hanging on to the binnacle to save himself from
falling through one of the wheel-house windows,
was the first to speak:

" Eet's a great peety that solid steel won't float,"
he said slowly; " eef 't wud, a'm thinkin' a cood
beeld a boat thut 'd stan' thees kin' o' theeng f'r a
hoondred years 'n' never cut a reevit: 't th' same
time a don't know onytheeng else thut wud."

Miss MacMichael started forward.

" Look! " she cried, pointing to starboard, in the
direction from which the pack had come. We could
see a shower of sparks and the glaring coloured
balls of a signal-light shooting up through the snow.
Red, blue, red, blue, white, red. Below we could

catch the gleam of two or three yellowish lights.
I turned the search-light in that direction, and there,
towering far above the pack, and almost as white
as the ice itself, was the big stern of the *Duncrieff*,
so high that we could see her screw, and not more
than two hundred yards away. Though not one
of us were at all sure that we, at that moment, did
not ourselves need rescuing as much as the crew of
the *Duncrieff* ever had, we cheered,—yelled with all
our might—including Donald,—and the cheer was
echoed by a roar from down below.

There was comparative silence for a few minutes, then down from windward again came the
sound of breaking ice, and we could see the *Duncrieff's* stern drop slowly. There was a minute of
fearful suspense. Even Donald's face was drawn
and set, for it seemed for the time as if the *Shannon's* great fight through hundreds of miles of ice
was to be for nothing, and that the *Duncrieff* was
to sink before our eyes. Miss MacMichael buried
her face in her hands and swayed. Wilson put his
hand on her arm and steadied her.

" Poor child! " said Donald.

For a minute she did not speak, but then faintly
came, " Dave, O Dave! can't we do something! "

" See," he said; " the *Duncrieff's* stern is no lower. We shall try." Again the ice began to break
and force itself against the *Shannon's* battered sides.
There was another movement of the pack, and this

time we were glad it was so, for its pressure might hold up the big MacMichael boat, or what was left of her, until we could make one more effort to get to her assistance.

This time the *Shannon's* bow was forced up, but the quarters, just abeam of the after hatch, got a fearful squeeze. I asked Ferguson to go down and bring up a report of the damage, and he came back with a white face and the news that six plates were buckled in the number six compartment back of the engine-room, and many of the frames were badly strained. Wilson noted the weakness, and spoke with an imperative sternness I had never seen him use before. His eyes snapped and shone.

" Have them wedged," he said; " and keep them pumped dry!—dry, do you understand. Donald," he continued,—his tone changing to its usual calm as Ferguson left,—" would you mind keeping an eye on the job? "

" Aye, sir," was the answer, " a'll do thut; " and Donald went after the disappearing first officer. We knew that number six was in good hands; and five minutes later, above the noise of the ice, we could hear, coming up from the after hold, a clanging of hammers and a ringing of sledges that sounded for all the world like a boiler-shop in full blast. Donald had the faculty of getting work—and hard work too—out of every man and boy in sight, and if we could judge anything by sounds he was using that faculty to advantage.

In a little while the ice ceased heaving, the grinding eased, and the *Shannon* settled down again. The movement had stopped and the pressure was over, at least for the time.

Now, I am no coward! I know that by comparing myself with other men,—men I have watched in action and in all sorts of nasty corners. Then I've been told it by men who have watched me; men whose judgment in the matter should be above appeal and who wouldn't lie. But, do you know, during the time when the *Shannon* was being squeezed between those grinding, crashing fields I was anxious—perhaps even more than anxious at times. When there is a force that can be resisted by some force, perhaps equally strong, under your own control, then if a man has any pluck he proceeds to resist; as he would, for instance, with a cruiser against a cruiser, or even with a cruiser against a battleship. Even if there is a force that is resistless, like an oncoming ice-field, a man with pluck will try the only way of dealing with a resistless force, getting away from it. But if there is a resistless force and you can't get away from it, if there is nothing to do but throw yourself on its mercy, and it seems to have none, then a man is justified in doing a great many things that he wouldn't do otherwise, perhaps even in getting frightened.

Yet, during all the time that the *Shannon* was being pummelled by the ice, Gertrude MacMichael, as far as I could see, actually wasn't frightened. Her one fear seemed to be for her father's safety. This is one of the things that made me say what I said at first,—that she was a wonder—a living wonder.

I am afraid that at times, when I think of some of the situations that girl and I have been in together, I let myself dwell too long. I must stop it.

Well, the pack had hardly quieted down when Wilson turned the search-light on the ice between the *Shannon* and the big freighter and looked over it carefully for a few seconds.

" H'm! Now I'm going to the *Duncricff*," he said. The *Shannon*, wedged in as she was, and knocked full of holes, could as easily have gone to Mars.

" How do you intend getting there? " I asked.

" Ice-boat," he said.

" Can you take an ice-boat through that? " I pointed at the piles of ice and patches of open water in the path of the search-light.

" Not alone, but with Hans and four others I can try," he answered.

" May I go too? " said the girl.

" Through that! " I gasped.

" Miss MacMichael! " said Wilson, laughing; " if you will pardon my saying precisely what you said to me before we left home, I think ' you're one

of the dearest girls alive,' and almost too brave to
be real; but you cannot go with us through that
pack in an ice-boat. Beside the danger, you would
take the place that would otherwise be taken by one
of the *Duncrieff's* crew on the return trip. I promise you that we shall bring your father back to the
Shannon in the first boat-load, whether he is willing to come or not."

"I was wrong to ask," the girl replied, looking
down at the cocoa matting on the wheel-house floor,
"there was no bravery in it. It was only that I
wanted to see Dad. Dear old Dad!" and her eyes
lighted up as she glanced over to where the yellow lights shone.

Wilson called Hans, and with four of the strongest of the crew—and the *Shannon* had some mighty
men in her ship's company, for they were nearly
all Nova Scotia Scotch—they lowered the lightest
of the ice-boats and climbed down beside her. If
ever a boat was manned by giants it was then. They
slipped the gunwale-straps over their shoulders, and
with Wilson on the starboard bow they started.
The snow had by this time practically stopped and
the wind was rapidly going down. We gave them
the full benefit of the search-light.

Miss MacMichael and I watched from the bridge.
I could see that though Wilson was going quietly
about it he was moving quickly. Evidently he did
not trust to the ice holding the *Duncrieff* above wa-

ter long, and he swung all his enormous strength
onto the strap.   The clumpets were piled into barriers over which it seemed impossible to drag the
boat, but she went up places like the side of a house.

Once, while the men were grouped at the stern
trying to force her over a steep ridge, she stuck and
could not be moved.   Leaving the others to keep
her from sliding back, Wilson crawled forward, put
his shoulder under the bow, and literally heaved
her over a hummock, so that she went sliding down
the other side, dragging her crew with her.   Every
man worked with tireless energy, now chopping the
tops off hummocks, now dragging at the straps, and
again rowing over a lane of open water.   The ice-
boat would disappear for a minute or two, and then
reappear on the crest of a ridge in the full blaze
of the search-light.   At last, as she came up on the
top of a splintered clumpet, a cheer came down the
wind from the *Duncrieff's* crew.   They had seen
her.   It was not a faint cheer, but a hearty ringing
shout, and the girl at my side fairly danced as she
heard it.

It aroused an entirely new feeling in me, and I
felt more distinctly proud of myself than I ever had
felt before.   Even with James MacMichael aboard,
the *Duncrieff* had been to me a sort of vague objec-
tive point toward which we had been struggling,
anxious and almost sleepless, ever since we had left
Caribou.   But when I heard that shout from hu-

man voices come down the wind, voices of men of
blood and bone like myself, I felt that I would
willingly have undergone ten times the hardship for
the same result, and, though I had not done much
myself, I thanked God I had had the chance to do
even the little.

At last we could only get an occasional glimpse
of the ice-boat.   Finally she disappeared altogether,
and for a few minutes there was silence,—the deep,
wonderful silence of the ice, that came in curious
contrast to all the noises of the last few hours.
Then from the *Duncrieff* came cheer on cheer.   Wilson had reached her at last.

The crew of the *Shannon* began to pour from
every door and hatch, deck-hands, stokers, engineers, and officers.   Donald emerged from the after hold carrying a sledge and a couple of hardwood blocks.   His sleeves were rolled up, his hands
and arms black with oil, and his clothes soaked with
salt water.   He came up to the bridge.

" Y'd be surprised t' see th' rips een the skin o'
thees boat ! " he said, meditatively, lighting the black
pipe, " y'd theenk she'd been roon into by th' Aurora."

" Is it very bad ? " I asked.

" Bad !   We've got two o' th' beeg centreefugal
poomps on, 'n' can joost keep th' water doon.   Eet's
comin' een like th' str-ream from a circulatin' poomp.
A can feex her oop so she'll float a' right, but a doot

eef she can efer go thro' ice again befoore she goes t' dock."

"If she can't go through ice, how are we to get out of this," I said, pointing at the hummocks shining under the search-light.

"Wait teel they melt," he said sententiously, "oor"—after a pause—"send foor th' *Leefey.*"

"The *Liffey!*" I said, laughing, as I usually had to do when Donald spoke, no matter how serious the purport of what he said. "How do you propose sending for the *Liffey?*"

"Y' might joost write Malcolm a note 'n' send eet ashore een an ice-boat."

A shout came up from below. Wilson, with a much increased crew, was on his way back from the *Duncrieff,* and the ice-boat was being fairly lifted over the ridges. The *Shannon's* crew gathered on the forward deck, and, as the boat came nearer, cheered themselves hoarse. As the men came close enough for the search-light to show their faces, a voice from the deck yelled:

"Is that you, Aleck? How are ye?"

"Hello! Simmy, we're comin' aboard to breakfast," came the reply. The relief had evidently put the crew of the *Duncrieff* in good spirits.

Then from the deck arose again another voice:

"Where are y' bound?"

And from the boat came the time-honoured reply in the Gulf:

"Potatoes, oats, and servant-girls."

"What have y' got aboard?"

"The North Pole."

Another voice from the deck:

"Y' must have been huntin' for it, to get up here."

A minute or two more and the boat was on the solid ice that surrounded the *Shannon,* and the ten men from the *Duncrieff,* who had come as the ice-boat's passengers—though they had worked their passages—climbed over the last clumpet and scrambled over the broken ice toward us, while Wilson and his crew, without stopping a second, rushed the ice-boat back again over the rough path toward the wreck of the big freighter.

Miss MacMichael watched the ten men as they clambered toward the *Shannon's* side. They were so close now that they were out of the path of the search-light, which was glaring toward the *Duncrieff.* I swung it down for a moment.

"There's Dad with Captain Cameron," she said eagerly; "see, there they are ahead!" James Mac-Michael, wearing a heavy reefing-jacket and a fur cap, was picking his way over the last few yards of ice with the captain of the *Duncrieff.*

"I shall go down on the fore deck and meet your father," I said. "Will you come?"

"No!" said the girl, trying to look as if she wasn't trembling with excitement. "I told Mr.

Wilson not to tell him I was here. I shall stay on
the bridge where I can see everything and not be
seen. Bring him up to the wheel-house and let me
surprise him."

I ran down the ladder and joined the shadowy
crowd below, leaving Donald with Miss MacMichael. The crew made way for me, and I went out
into the circle of light by the gangway just as Mac-
Michael came up the ladder. As his foot touched
the deck the *Shannon's* crew cheered,—danced and
cheered as I don't think I ever heard men cheer before. MacMichael ran forward and gripped my
hand, and his face was a study.

" Ashburn——" he said; then he choked up and
stopped. He looked around him at the men,—the
blue-jerseyed deck-hands; the black-faced, hairy-
chested, bare-armed stokers; the greasy, water-soak-
ed, dog-tired engineers and the blue-reefered officers, all cheering for sheer joy; he looked at the ice-
covered rigging; the splintered boats, the bent and
twisted rail, the broken, battered deck, and the
crushed side of the poor old *Shannon*. The tears
came into his eyes and poured down his cheeks.
He controlled himself with a great effort.

" Thank you—, thank you, men," he managed to
jerk out huskily.

" Come to my room," I said. " Mr. Ferguson,
tell the steward to send up some supper. Captain
Cameron, come along too." We went in through

the saloon and up to my room, which was just abaft of and under the wheel-house. I called Donald in, and MacMichael shook his hand warmly.

"This is a great surprise," he said. "What brought you out on an expedition of this sort? Caribou may burn down while you are away."

"Eef eet tr-ried a've no doot eet cud bur-rn doon as well wi' me there as away," he said, slowly. "But let me tell y' fir-rst a'm fery glad t' see y', for t' tell y' th' trooth a was not too shure thut a wud. As to what tempted me t' coom, a thocht a might be o' soom use, and a fin' they can gie me a job o' tinkerin' occasionally. Joost 't present a'm—oor rather a ought to be—wor-rkin' on soom holes een the noomber seex compairtment thut y' can steeck y'r ar-rm thro'; holes communicatin' wi' th' Goolf o' St. Lawrence. As t' your bein' sur-prised at seein' me on sooch an expedition, a may say thut a'm joost a leettle surprised t' see you on sooch an expedition yersel'. A hope th' good Lord has made Hees argument suffeeciently str-rong against y'r tryin' to navigate thees pairt o' th' Goolf in weenter een anytheeng but an air-sheep." Donald was merciless, but MacMichael knew him of old and laughed.

"I shall give up Gulf-navigation with steamers of the *Duncricff's* type," he said, and the old engineer, wearing his most bland smile, went down to have another spell at the number six.

Of course the first thing MacMichael asked about was his own family.

"I hope Mrs. MacMichael and Gertrude didn't get too much of a fright when they heard that the *Duncrieff* was caught," he said, with a troubled look.

"We left your wife very well," I said. "Mrs. Wilson was with her, and they seemed to have every faith in the *Shannon* getting to your assistance. Your daughter is away from home at present."

"Gertrude away!" said MacMichael, with a look of surprise. "Where is she?"

"Somewhere north, I think," I answered. "Oh! excuse me a moment—I want to speak to Ferguson."

I went up on the bridge and told Miss MacMichael what I had said. She followed me down; and when the girl in the grey and crimson blanket suit ran down those stairs—or rather jumped, as she did, from top to bottom—you should have seen MacMichael's face. It had been a study when he came aboard——but now he fairly gasped.

"Gertrude, my dear girl!" he said; "have you too come up here through four hundred miles of ice?"—and a second later MacMichael and his daughter were wound up in each other's arms.

Captain Cameron and I left them and went on the bridge. Cameron's face was white and worn-looking.

"Captain Ashburn," he said, "in the last three weeks I've had the hardest time of my life, and I'm a good deal older man for it. Mr. Wilson and you and the *Shannon* have done a piece of work such as has never been equalled. When we drifted to the north after getting Wilson's message off Percé I hadn't any hope in the world of ever being heard from again. Yet I had to keep a brave front and keep everybody cheered up,—everybody but the boss, and he didn't seem to need it. I suppose that is why I'm a captain and he is the owner of the MacMichael boats. It got worse and worse, and the *Duncrieff* got jammed up until the part you can see was the only part that even looked like a steamer. The rest is just one big junk-heap. We kept fires under the boilers to work the pumps as long as it was worth pumping; but when it was a case of pumping out the whole Gulf we drew the fires for the last time and saved the coal for heating,—heating, as I thought, until the ice should break up and let us drop in a few hundred fathoms of water. I fired rockets every few hours, more as a matter of duty than anything else, and when your signal showed up the night before last it was the happiest minute of my life.

"I knew that the pack was strong enough to hold up the wreck of the *Duncrieff*," he continued, "and I couldn't believe that any steamer could get through. We could see your search-light, long before you could see us, and I expected every minute to see it disappear. When the first big crush came I think even the boss had about given you up; but when the crush was over, and the light still came through the snow, every man on the *Duncrieff* believed that no ice that moves could hurt the *Shannon*. Plenty of them had given up hope a week ago, thinking it was only a matter of a little time more before the old boat would go under. It's bad enough to see one man that's condemned to death; but when you live for days with half a crew that has given up entirely, it's a pretty solemn business, especially when you yourself are a good deal of their way of thinking.

" When the snow eased up a little while ago, and we saw that ice-boat coming, the men went wild with excitement. Half of them just hugged each other and blubbered; and, to tell you the truth, I felt sort of funny myself.

" I never saw such a man as that Wilson. He did half the work of his crew, and he has a great crew, too. He stuck to the bow strap, and three or four times he was in the water almost up to his arms, and it's pretty cold. He sent four of his men ahead to help us with our dunnage, and he and the Swede yanked that big boat along for forty yards over some of the roughest ice you ever saw. Look at him coming back!"

I looked. The ice-boat was on her way with another load.   The night had become perfectly clear, and now the stars were paling before the coming daylight.   Mr. MacMichael and his daughter came out on the bridge.

"The ice-boat is coming back again," I said.

The two came over to where Cameron and I were standing and looked out toward the *Duncrieff*. The ice-boat was being rushed along at a great rate. Every man seemed to be doing his utmost, and, as they came nearer, we could see Wilson still on the bow strap, now pulling the boat toward him and hanging on to the gunwale as she rushed down a sharp slope, and now putting his broad back under the bow and jamming it over into some new path. They came to a widening crack we had not noticed before.   He plunged into it waist deep on the shelving ice, and we could hear him shouting to the men to get in the boat.   A moment afterward he climbed in, streaming with icy water, only to leap out on the pan on the other side of the crack a moment later. The men jumped out, ran the boat over the pan to the next crack, and splashed in again.

"The man will kill himself!" said MacMichael, "why under Heaven is he working himself and his crew like that?"   I hadn't time to answer before I heard a shout from the boat.   It was Wilson's voice:

"Send four fresh men out for this boat."

"Mr. Ferguson," I called, "send four of your

strongest men to the edge of the first lane." I turned to Mr. MacMichael.

" The reason he is working like that," I said, " is that the field is opening up, and after being broken as it has been by this crush he is afraid the *Duncrieff* will go down before he gets all the men off. Look! those lanes are widening every minute. How many men did you have aboard altogether? "

" Sixty-two," said MacMichael gravely, and a bit nervously.

" He's bringing fourteen this time. That leaves thirty-eight yet aboard."

Wilson struggled up the ridge of the last hummock and stopped long enough to roar:

" Lower away another boat, Ashburn, and put a crew in her. Hans will take charge of her. Send an extra man for this boat. The *Duncrieff* can't hold up much longer; I've ordered all the men out on the ice." Then the ice-boat slid down and into the last lane. As she ran on the solid ice the fourteen men from the *Duncrieff* left her and came up, carrying their baggage, and the four big Scotchmen who had been serving as Wilson's crew for the last hour dragged themselves wearily behind, one limping and supported by two of the others. Behind them came Hans, apparently as strong as ever. There was more cheering as they came aboard, and the crew of the ice-boat grinned faintly collectively, and bowed a mock acknowledgment of the part that was meant for them—and it was no small part, either. Ten minutes later I passed them sitting in a row, dog-tired and wet, but determined to stay on deck until they saw the last *Duncrieff* man aboard. They were talking of Wilson and Hans to the men around:

"So help me God," Tom Grant, a big red-whiskered chap was saying, "she was wedged so as the four of us couldn't move her, 'n' him 'n' the Swede jumped 'n' took hold of her alone. They hefted her once, 'n' then she came up 'n' slid, 'n' if she hadn't hit Jack's leg there she'd 'a' been goin' yet."

By the time I'd gotten the second ice-boat down, Wilson had his new crew and was off for the *Duncrieff* once more. Captain Cameron had left when he did to bring aboard some valuable private papers of MacMichael's. When I had finished, and Hans was selecting his crew, I went back to the bridge. Cameron turned to me:

"I think I'd better go back to the *Duncrieff* with Hans," he said. "It's better to have a look over things to see that nothing is left, and besides, I'd like to have one more look at the old boat. She and I together have made a good deal of money for the firm."

"Just as you please, Captain," I said, and called to the Swede, who was passing forward with his men, ready to start: " Hans, Captain Cameron will go with you."

" Too late, Cameron, too late, look!" said Mac-Michael, pointing over the ice, " the boat is going, and one of the finest freighters that ever took a cargo she was." All of the *Shannon's* crew, with the exception of those away with the ice-boat and those with Donald in the number six compartment, were on deck, and with a shout of excitement they climbed in the rigging and on the house to get a better view.

It was now almost broad daylight. Every eye was turned on the *Duncrieff*. It's very seldom that it's given to a man to see a steamer sink, and yet more seldom that he sees one sink under such conditions: grey morning, white ice and silence, and the possibility that all the men might not be off. Cameron gazed across the ice like a man in a trance. MacMichael stood with his arm around his daughter. The girl drew him closer, and I could see her trembling. The woman's heart conquered the iron nerve when she thought how close he had been to death. Every man in the crew became silent as he watched.

The breath of air that was left drifted down from the big steamer and carried with it the occasional low grinding of ice. There were one or two sharp cracks, then silence again, and the *Duncrieff's* great ice-covered stern began to rise slowly into the air, carrying with it a plate of board ice that broke off at last and crashed down onto the pack thirty feet below.   The blades of the big manganese bronze propellor were twisted and useless, and the quarter showed the plates ripped and torn away and the frames bent and broken for forty feet.   The stern came further up, and the foremast cracked and splintered off against the edge of the pack.   Finally the deck was almost vertical fore and aft, and the rudder, with its head broken off, fell over to port with a bang.   Then, with her crumpled bow pointing straight at the bottom of the Gulf, the boat that knew all the waters from Scatari to the Great Barrier Reef, the boat that had been the finest of the MacMichael line, with the possible exception of the *Dungeness,* slid downward and sank, and a few little clumpets and some lolly swirled in to cover the place where she disappeared.

"She died game!" I said; "she held you up until the *Shannon* came."

"It did seem as if she tried to hold out till we were safe!" said Cameron feelingly.   "Day in and day out, when the pack moved, I couldn't see why she didn't do just what she's done now, and leave us all on the ice like those fellows," pointing to the rest of the crew, who we could now see plainly, standing on a flat clumpet waiting for the ice-boat. "I wonder," he continued, "how much chance the *Shannon* would have had of finding us then."

"It was a wonderful escape," said MacMichael. "A man has a tendency in business, especially if he gets along pretty well and doesn't think about much besides shop, to get a mighty belief in his own infallibility. But if he gets left out here in the ice for a few weeks, and then gets rescued just in time to get his breath and see his steamer sink, he begins to remember that Providence takes a little hand in things as heretofore. It's a good sermon, a good practical sermon, and I shall never forget it."

"We're not home yet," I said, "and the *Shannon* has some holes in her."

"I don't care if she is riddled," was the reply, "The good Lord doesn't save people from a fate like that," pointing toward the spot where the *Duncrieff* had disappeared, "to drown them later in the same trip: at least, that's my belief,"—and MacMichael hummed, which, according to Donald, was the signal that argument had ceased.

I looked at the ice-boats. Hans was hurrying toward the men on the clumpet, and Wilson was working along slowly and carefully toward the *Shannon*. As the boat came closer we could see that a number of men were lying under the thwarts. The boat was brought up the sloping ice as near the steamer as possible. Wilson looked up at the bridge.

"You will have to build a new *Duncrieff*, Mr.

MacMichael," he said, " the old one has finished her work."

MacMichael smiled: " After I get home I shall have one under way as soon as the cable can carry the message," he said.   " What's the trouble? "

" Four of your men were hurt by falling ice, none of them seriously, I hope.   They are cut a little about the head and are stunned."   He stooped, and picking up one of the men carried him up the ice slope and up the ladder onto the *Shannon's* deck as though he were a child.   He left him in a berth in an empty stateroom while Miss MacMichael and Betsie bandaged him up.   One by one he brought up the others and went back with the ice-boat again. Back, yes, and he never gave up until the last man and the last piece of baggage was aboard.   Then, after the boats were up, with Hans barely able to crawl behind him, he staggered, wet and tired, into his room, got into dry clothes, and came out into the saloon looking fit to do it over again.

CHAPTER VII.

TEN minutes later came the call to breakfast. It would have been hard to find a better illustration of how men's feelings are affected by comparative rather than absolute conditions. A little while ago every man of the *Duncrieff's* crew had been silent in the fear—or, at any rate, in the thought—of death. Now the *Duncrieff* was at the bottom of the Gulf, and from down forward on the *Shannon*, where the same men were eating with the *Shannon's* crew, came roars of laughter as they talked over the happenings of the last few eventful weeks and days. Outside, the sky was cloudless blue, the light wind had hauled around to the northwest, and, looking out through the ports, we could see fantastically shaped glittering white clumpets, with lanes of dark-blue water between, and nothing else. The sun was shining with a warm glare over everything, making as innocent-looking and pretty a picture as a man may see. In the saloon Mr. Mac-Michael and his daughter and Wilson and I sat down. All the fearful strain of the last few days was gone—though the traces could be seen on each face—and we were as light-hearted as children, and showed it. If you had looked in you would have thought we were on a yacht cruise.

Where were we? In the north of the Gulf of St. Lawrence, somewhere between the coast of Anticosti and Cape Gaspé, in the early part of February. Around us was a great ice-pack which looked just then sweet and harmless and innocent enough, to be sure, but we knew what it could do. We were in an ice-crusher that had been crushed, and crushed badly, and over the sounds of the laughter of the men forward there came from the number six compartment the continuous clang of sledges, where Donald, the indefatigable, was working to keep the *Shannon* afloat. As to getting ashore, there was not much more direct prospect of it apparent than there had been in the *Duncrieff*, though, at least, one had a better chance of remaining above water.

The inconsistencies of the people of this world are marvellous, and it's wonderful what a little sunlight will do in the way of encouragement. It's well so.

MacMichael and his daughter and I were already at the table when Wilson came in and sat down.

"Mr. MacMichael," he said, "at last I have a chance to ask you about the *Duncrieff's* last message that night you drifted north from Percé.

It began: ' Owner wishes——' and then a snow squall came up and I could make out nothing further."

" You didn't get that message!" was the surprised reply; " then I have much more to thank the Northumberland Company for than I thought. I knew before that I owed you all more than I could ever give, for you risked your lives; but now I find I owe still more in gratitude, for the Company has sent this wonderful boat without any guarantee that her damage or loss would be made good. The message was: ' Owner wishes Northumberland Company to understand that he will assume all responsibility if *Shannon* is damaged or lost.' "

Wilson laughed. " Was that all?" he said. " I think you will find when you ask Henderson that the Company would have sent out the boat just as readily without that message as with it.

" Just at present," he continued, " the problem is how to get ashore. I have seen Donald, and he says the *Shannon* simply cannot go through pack ice before she goes to dock. She could work along in open water if the sea was not too high, but there is practically no open water in sight."

" I asked him how we were to get out," I said, " and he suggested that we wait until the ice melts, or, as an alternative, that we send for the *Liffey.*"

"And then he smiled and lit that pipe," said MacMichael, with a laugh. "How did he intend to get the *Liffey?*"

"He suggested that we write a note to Malcolm and send it ashore in an ice-boat."

"Good idea!" said Wilson, quickly; "this north-east gale must have carried us pretty well toward the Gaspé Peninsula. We shall get an observation in a little while now and learn where we are. We are probably between fifty and a hundred miles from Percé. If this proves to be the case, Hans and I can take a crew and work our way in. It may take a few days——."

Miss MacMichael leaned forward and put her hand on his arm.

"Out day and night in an ice-boat in ice like this in the open Gulf!" she said, with the colour coming and going in her cheeks. "Mr. Wilson, you have done enough for us already, without offering to go to almost certain death." She impulsively took his hand in one of hers and laid the other on her father's arm. "Dad," she continued, "he has been like this from the moment he brought us the news that the *Duncrieff* was caught. He didn't spare himself; he spared no one but us. He crushed the *Shannon* into what she is now, he stayed on the bridge night and day, and laughed when Captain Ashburn and I knew he was so tired that he couldn't speak. When everyone else was under cover he stayed out in the cold and watched, never trusting either the men or the officers of the watch while he could keep awake; and he may say what he likes about humanity, but I believe he did it all for you ——and me," and the girl laughed as she turned to me for confirmation.

"It is all perfectly true," I said, "and there are other things which Miss MacMichael didn't see, and which I daren't tell you while Mr. Wilson is here."

"And now," continued the girl, "he wants to go out into the ice in a twenty-five-foot boat for our sakes again." She turned to Wilson and closed her brown hands over his right hand and wrist. "Promise me," she said, "that you will not run this awful risk; better to stay here until the *Shannon* can go through herself, or if she cannot be strengthened, if Donald cannot——oh! surely there is some other way!" She spoke earnestly enough now. There was more than ordinary concern in her voice, and Wilson saw it and glanced at her with a curious smile that made her withdraw her hands.

"I am sorry," he said slowly, "but there is no other way. However much I should like to promise anything you ask"—I gazed at the

N. S. C. on my serviette—"I am afraid it is impossible to promise this. As far as the danger is concerned, Hans and I have been on worse expeditions,—or as bad, at any rate,—and with a much worse crew than we shall have this time. With regard to my past conduct," he laughed, " I regret to say that neither Captain Ashburn's nor Miss Gertrude MacMichael's descriptions can be classed as scientifically accurate. I hope I would have done the same for any steamer in the same position as the *Duncrieff*. I don't say that my motives would have been the same. You can't always govern your motives, you know." The last with a half-veiled smile.

"True, O Sage," said the girl, with mock gravity; " I have noticed that myself;" and she dropped her eyes before Wilson's quick interrogatory glance. MacMichael drifted back to the days when the *Duncrieff's* bottom hadn't lost its first brilliant red, and began to tell me of a charter in which she gave him nine thousand dollars clear profit, when Cameron won a sudden promotion by hiring all the hydraulic cranes in Havre and loading over the tops of moving trains. I listened, but the other conversation came sifting through. " You might argue," the girl went on, " and no doubt you could demonstrate to the satisfaction of the rest of the world, that your sole reason for leaving the *Shannon* and going ashore in the middle of winter in an open ice-boat was a selfish one,—yes, and you might convince me,—as much as logic ever convinces me of anything,—but still I shouldn't believe you. So if I were you I shouldn't argue; for at the end I shall still believe that, if you persist in going, you are doing it for the sake of us all; and," she added, "even knowing the great danger, I shall have to admit that I am weak enough, and have enough vanity and conceit, to feel that you are going partly for my sake and to be pleased accordingly." Wilson's face lighted up under the influence of the words, and the smile that accompanied them. I knew his feelings, and knew that he would undertake a trip to either or both of the Poles in an open boat, or without a boat, for that matter, for the girl that spoke.

"Do you remember," he said, "that once, in much less of a crisis than this—in that race with Oldham two years ago—you asked me to do something for your sake, even called me by my Christian name through a megaphone, and told me afterward that it was subterfuge?"

"Yes," was the reply, "and so it was, but for your own sake,—yes, and partly for my sake, too, for I wanted to see you win."

"And now," said Wilson, "you don't ask me to do anything for your sake. You say that you know I am doing a number of things at least partly for you already, and that, as a result, you are pleased.   Now, what is this subterfuge for?"

"It isn't subterfuge."

"Remarkable!" he laughed, "what is it?"

"Truth."

"How am I to know that?"

"By my saying so."

"Why do you say so?" he asked, with the air of an inquisitor.

"Probably because I've changed.   Perhaps because I know you better.   I hadn't spent ten days with you in the *Shannon*, fighting ice, and running races with death, and seen you—see here! Mr. David Wilson, you ask too many questions, and I answer too many too frankly,"—and the girl attacked a chop that had been getting cold. Wilson laughed.

"I am getting away from the subject," he said, turning to Mr. MacMichael, "and I usually pride myself on not getting away from subjects until I am through with them.   My plan, then, is to work my way to Percé with an ice-boat, telegraph to Henderson to provision and coal the *Liffey*, go to Caribou by rail, and bring the *Liffey* up here.   She has a knot or so more speed than the *Shannon*, and she is much heavier and stronger; and more important still, as you know, her bilges are shaped so that she is lifted by an ice crush instead of being caught and squeezed.   I am sorry

we didn't have her from the first. I actually
thought of waiting until she got in, and finally
decided to bring the *Shannon*. It is well I did.
If we had arrived a day later—we might have
found you on the ice, but I am afraid the chances
would have been smaller, much smaller."

"If the *Liffey* can do more than the *Shannon*
has done," said MacMichael, "she must indeed
be a wonderful boat. When you were coming
through the pack Cameron stood on the bridge
with a glass as long as he could see you, and
afterwards he watched your search-light. He
swore that every quarter of an hour would be
your last, and when finally he heard your whistle
I thought the man would go crazy with joy."

"Wait till I get to Caribou," laughed Wilson,
"and I shall try to demonstrate what the *Liffey*
can do. Some day, in say ten days or two weeks,
while you are drifting around in the centre of an
ice-pack as the guest of the Northumberland Company's steamer *Shannon*—may her shadow never
grow less—you will hear a roar on the southern
horizon. You will see a large black object vomit-
ing black smoke and live coals. You will see
clumpets the size of a house describing parabolas
on each side of the object, and lighting in the
sea a hundred yards or so distant. You will see
small clumpets clinging to the whiskers of seals
and begging to be towed out of danger. As it

comes nearer you will see that the black object is the *Liffey*. She will thunder up alongside the *Shannon*, take off her passengers and part of the crew, and start for Caribou, Nova Scotia, with the *Shannon* following in her track. I forgot to say that on the *Liffey's* bridge will be a long individual resembling an Indian and with a ferociously determined expression.

MacMichael laughed.

" A very attractive and exceedingly gorgeous picture," said the girl.

" Yes, and better still," said Wilson, " with a few slight modifications, a true one. Wait and see ! "

After breakfast Miss MacMichael went down to her patients. She had had no sleep for thirty-six hours, but, tired though she was, she had to be captured by Betsie and forced to turn in.

Wilson hunted up Hans, told him of the proposed trip, and set to work selecting a crew and the kits for them. He examined every sleeping-bag, overhauled every piece of cordage, tested every Primus stove, and looked to every detail himself. He had had but an hour or two of sleep in three days, and in the last five hours had tired out two crews of as tough men as you would find in many a long day's travel. Yet when I came on him in the steward's pantry, working away with a can-opener, opening and testing specimens of the tinned stuff he was going to take with him, he was by turns whistling like a small boy, thundering the "Armourer's Song" from "Robin Hood" and making jocular remarks to the steward's cat, who was also testing specimens.

The chief steward didn't attempt to hide his amazement, but then the chief steward didn't know all the facts. He didn't know that it was only the memory of the pressure of a pair of brown hands on his, and the memory of a few words spoken and a few things done, quite involuntarily, —and there lay the charm,—that was the cause of this outburst. If the chief steward had known he wouldn't have been much the wiser, for he probably hadn't been educated to the differences between thoroughbreds and other girls. Not only did the chief steward not know, but probably Wilson himself was not quite sure why the sky was a little more blue and the ice a little more white than usual. Even I, with all my experience in such things, was only entitled to my own opinion, though it was probably correct.

"When do you want to start with the ice-boat?" I asked, breaking in on a sentence in which he was explaining to the cat the number and variety of things it would suffer from if it persisted in taking condensed milk after tinned lobster.

"To-morrow at daybreak, if the weather looks satisfactory," he said.

"Then, my dear boy, you'll have to turn in at once.   You haven't had three hours' sleep in three days."

"I've had as much as you have," he replied; "turn in yourself.   Have a good sleep until three o'clock, and I'll keep an eye on the ship,"—and, do you know, though he was going out in the ice at dawn the next morning, I had to promise to turn in too before he would go.   I left the *Shannon* in charge of Ferguson, and slept, after what had been the most remarkable experience of my life.   With the exception of the watch, and Donald and his gang in the number six compartment, every soul aboard turned in and slept, slept until the sun swung over to the westward and sent the *Shannon's* black shadow lengthening out and spoiling the glitter on the pinnacles of the clumpets that stretched away toward Newfoundland.

I was wakened a little after three, and sat up to find that the sounds of hammering down aft had ceased.   When I went on deck Donald and his men were struggling over the side with some pieces of timber.   The old man had taken an iceboat, gone over to where the *Duncrieff* had sunk, sawn up the foremast, which had been left on the pack, and was bringing the pieces aboard as braces for the number six compartment.   He climbed on deck and leaned on the rail to direct his men.

"Noo, lads! Soop 'er oop. Hi! Alex, don't be standin' there like a goat. Y'll have eendigestion eef y' don't tak' more exercise 'n' thut. Stirr-r y'r stoomps, mon. Noo, why are y' all heavin' like thut; we can't get thut ventilator and we wouldn't want 't eef we cud." He turned to me. His face was streaked with red iron rust, white lead, and grease, and but for the grey eyes and the three-inch pipe I would hardly have recognized him. His overalls and jacket were soaked with bilge water and stunk with the great indescribable stink peculiar to that liquid.

"A'm a sight!" he remarked.

"You are!" I said.

"An' quite coomfortable 'n' happy!" he added with his bland smile.

"No doubt," I replied.

"An' a'm makin' a gran' good job o' the noomber seex; thut ees, 's good 's y' can make wi' wood, 'n' a leetle hand reevetin': good enough not t' leak more th'n three thoosan' gallon' a day, in smooth water, wi' no ice. A hear thut Meester Wilson's goin' t' Caribou for the *Leeffey!*"

"Yes," I replied.

"A'm sorry thut a can't go. A'd not be mooch use een an ice-boat. But a theenk a cood breeng th' *Leeffey* oop smairt. She's got a gran' good nest o' booylers, has thut boat." Yes, I thought, and they would be worked as they were never worked before if you had charge for the trip.

I went on the bridge. The day held fair and cloudless, with a light northwesterly breeze. It was only a little below freezing, and the sun was still strong enough to make a coat unnecessary. Everywhere in the lanes were numberless seals and sea birds, working for a living, looking extraordinarily pretty in the light of the setting sun, and keeping a respectful distance from where the *Shannon* sat black and solitary in the midst of the clear white silence.

Ferguson came up.

" I got an observation at noon, sir," he said,— 48 degrees, 85 minutes north; 63 degrees, 17 minutes west. That puts us about fifty miles from Cape Gaspé and almost directly east of the Cape."

" Good! " I said, " much better than I thought. If the weather holds as it is Mr. Wilson will be able to get away in the morning:" and the weather did hold.

At dinner the girl tried to be cheerful, but didn't make a tremendous success of it. I thought at the time of how I had seen the piece played through. I thought of the girl with the iron nerve that raced the *Glooscap* to a finish. I thought of the evening after, when she treated

a salon of admirers with consideration—and con-
tempt—; of a good many such evenings still later;
and of the tennis tournament and her impartial
distribution of favours. I remembered the way
Wilson had smilingly settled down to win, and how
he had apparently made no more progress for two
years than if he hadn't existed. I had watched as
the girl began to see that something was wrong
with her lines of defence, and had struggled not
to believe it. She might have struggled on for
weeks, or perhaps months longer, but to cap the
happenings of the last little while, happenings
that would break down any barrier if given time,
came this ice-boat business. He treated it as
lightly as he did other things with danger in
them. But the girl was too practical to be de-
ceived. She knew there were dangers even down
in the Strait between the Capes, but up here in
the open Gulf she knew they were a hundred times
greater; and she was afraid, not for herself, but
for him; and this did its work, as ever.

That evening came the climax—one climax.
What an evening it was! The wind dropped dead.
An hour after sunset the thin, cold crescent of
the new moon slid down behind the clumpets and
left the night to the stars and the Northern Light.
Captain Cameron, worn down with the strain of
the last few weeks, had turned in with the rest of
us in the morning, and had never turned out even

for dinner. I had sent the steward in with some
soup and roast beef and plum pudding, and told
him to sleep ahead. Donald, tired out at last, had
turned in too. MacMichael came to my room
after dinner and talked over some future plans
for his boats. He was going to be up before daylight to see Wilson off, so, in a little while, he too
started for his stateroom. Miss MacMichael and
Wilson had gone on deck bundled in furs, for the
evening was getting rapidly colder. I was left
alone. I picked up an old copy of Brassey and
looked over it, but I soon got tired of ships and
guns and barbettes; so I put on my reefer and
went up to the wheel-house. Everything was
dark. I sat on the locker by the open door and
watched the weird waving streamers of the Aurora
to the northward, watched Orion and the Big Dog
glittering away to the southward, and heard the
bark of the dog-seal coming in faint over the pack
from the east, and the occasional sharp crack of a
clumpet. Lord! what a sense of solitude and of
the grandeur of the Universe. I have already
told you of the feeling, and I can say no more:
you must see for yourself. The things I had seen
and done in all my life came up in review. I had
begun to drift back to the days with Kitty Tyrrell,
to feel the same glow, which time refused to kill,
when suddenly I heard the voice of a girl, soft
and clear. It is almost treason to tell it,—yes,

and, for that matter, almost useless, so long as I tell you the result. However, what she actually said was characteristic enough of her:

"Dave, dear heart, I love you as I don't believe a woman ever loved a man."

By Heavens! I almost believed her, for I believe it is given to but few women to love as that girl could. You see, she was twenty-five and had never been even scratched as the arrow went past. I wonder where you would go to find such another!

Well, I kicked the locker two or three times and kicked over a tin chart-case beside, but even then I evidently didn't make noise enough, for when I went out on the bridge two figures over by one of the wind-shields were wrapped in each other's arms. I fled quietly to my room and started from the bottom of the stairs whistling Mendelssohn's *"Wedding March."* This time, when I got as far as the wheel-house door and stepped out, the two figures were standing close together—they were both too diplomatic to stand far apart—and studying, or apparently studying, the ice. I kept on whistling as I sauntered up.

"Isn't this a night worth living a life to see!" I said.

"Yes," said the girl, with her voice as steady as an organ tone, "and you seem to be at peace

with yourself and all the world.   Does that tune
call up tender memories?"

" Not exactly tender memories, but many pleasant ones.   I'm very fond of the tune itself.   Its
contrasts are so ingenious.   I suppose you find the
same thing to be true," I continued, " but I always
get some tune indissolubly connected with each
little period in my life.   For instance, whenever I
hear that ' Frangesa ' march I think of two seasons ago when I was in London, and the orchestra
used to play it at the Savoy.   In the same way
when you or Mr. Wilson next hear Mendelssohn's
' Wedding March,' wherever it may be, you will
remember a night on the old *Shannon* with the ice
all around, and the stars and the Northern Light;
and you'll hear the cockawee, and the whistle of
unseen wings overhead, and the bark of the dog
seal.

" Now, we've got to be up early, so I'm going to
turn in.   Good-night."

" Good-night! Ashburn," said Wilson, laughing,
" you're all right in your way, but a little mis-
guided as to your own interests."

" Good-night! " said the girl, " the next time I
hear the ' Wedding March ' I shall try to remember the *Shannon*."

" You won't have to try," I said, and I went
below.

Ferguson turned me out at half-past three.   The

Aurora was still bright, and the night was cold, with the lightest breath of wind from the north. In a little while the steward had a smoking breakfast on the table. With the exception of Wilson everyone was a bit quiet. He told us of experiences he and Hans had had in ice-boats in all parts of the Gulf, and some of them were bad enough too. He told us how once, down between the Capes, when the men got drunk and wouldn't leave with the Government ice-boat, and there were important despatches to go, one of the Allen boys took the despatches, and with nothing but a pike pole, to help him in jumping from clumpet to clumpet, crossed in safety the nine miles of loose ice from Cape Traverse to Cape Tormentine.

But though he treated the crossing of the fifty or sixty miles between the *Shannon* and the Gaspé Peninsula as though it were already accomplished, the girl was downcast, the only time I had seen her so in all the while I had known her. The little fat god must have pulled to the ear. There are times when, judging from effects, I think he must lay aside the little bow and use a six-inch gun. This was one of the times. Miss Gertrude Mac-Michael, the impregnable, was conquered. In most conquests it is a case of conquest first and then assimilation, but in this, conquest and assimilation seemed to have come together. A new light was in the girl's eyes. I had seen it before in

many other eyes, among the palms in St. Lucia,
in a hot ball-room at Melbourne, on a balcony looking over the moonlit Mediterranean at Monaco,—
yes, and in other places, many other places,—
though I wasn't responsible, that I could see,—
and I knew what it meant. I chuckled to myself
every time I thought of the change. However, it
was a case of valour rewarded.

By the way, one thing I never told you about.
This was the way the girl held her admirers for
all time. Every man she knew admired her, some
more, some less: the majority more. She never
gave any of them the least encouragement, but
they stuck to her, apparently for ever. Perhaps
that's only man nature after all. I wondered how
they would stand the shock when they saw the
change,—that is, if they ever did. In the excitement of the rescue of the *Duncrieff's* crew, and the
feeling of the danger of the ice-boat trip, we had
almost forgotten that another such crush as that
of the day before would in all probability send
us to the bottom of the Gulf, to keep the *Duncrieff*
company, long before the *Liffey* or anything else
could get to our assistance.

After breakfast the last preparations were made,
and a little later, before the stars in the east had
even begun to dim, Wilson changed a leather
jacket for a light cardigan in preparation for hard
work, and we went on deck to make a final

inspection.   He had chosen the same long, light, fine-lined ice-boat he had used the day before.   The crew included the *Shannon's* boatswain, and was made up of the strongest men she had.   Of two of them, " Long Henry " and " Little Willie," the former stood over six feet four, while " Little Willie " stood a shade over six feet six in his socks. As a strong man, the fame of another, Malcolm Macpherson, went far beyond the district of Caribou.   They tell many stories of him.   It was he who surprised Jennings, the boss, and the rest of the section gang.   Jennings had worked with his men for a good solid day to get out a big black birch knee which he was going to use in some repairs to the turntable.   It weighed about six hundredweight, and they had brought it all the way from Irish Hill on a trolley.   They were about to unload it in the station yard when Jennings saw Malcolm coming along the track, on his way home from the *Shannon*.

" Boys," he said, " we'll have some fun with Malcolm."   Macpherson was getting past when Jennings called him.

" Malcolm," he said, " here's a piece of black birch we don't know what to do with.   Would you have any use for it? "   Malcolm stopped and eyed the big knee critically.

" Are y' shoore y' don't want ut, Meester-r Jennings," he said, and the men looked at each other and grinned.

" No!" said Jennings, " it's no use in the world to me."

" Och! weel! then eef y'r shoore y' don't want ut a don't doot ut'l mek firewood." He went to the trolley, almost derailed it in jerking the knee over to the edge, bent down, slid his shoulder under the six hundredweight of birch, and with half a dozen grunts straightened up again. Then, swinging slowly around with his head sideways, he looked out from under the stick at Jennings.

" A'm shoore a'm fery thankful t' y'," he said. "Coot-tay," and he swung ponderously around again and walked away, leaving Jennings able to say one thing only,—" Well! I'm damned." The section gang spread the story, and the next day eighteen men called at the section shanty during the morning, each of whom wanted to know if Mr. Jennings had any hardwood suitable for grate fires to give away. When it got dangerous for men to go they sent a small boy who said that if " Mithter Jenningth would pleath leave Mithter Carterth hardwood in the thtathion yard he'd call 'round with a truck for it Thaturday morning," or something to that effect.

Needless to say Malcolm was a good man for the ice-boat crew. Then there was the boatswain, a New Brunswicker named McEachern. He wasn't over five feet eight, but he had a forty-eight inch chest and a fine pair of shoulders. He was a lobster fisherman before he came to the Northumberland Company, and had the record of having fished four hundred traps and pulled them every day in the last season except three. In those times he used to go into Caribou and get drunk occasionally, and then his favourite amusement was to go into old Johnson Hendrie's store, buy a dozen thick glass goblets, and amuse the crowd by chewing them into splinters, a good deal to the detriment of his mouth. Once Wilson hired him to go on a winter trip with Hans and him. It was a hard trip, and McEachern found that both the Swede and the Nova Scotian, neither of whom drank, would come in fresh at the end of the day, with him dog-tired.

"I'll not be beaten by any man of me age!" he said. "It's the whiskey," and he stopped it. A little later he went to the *Shannon* as boatswain.

So, altogether, the ice-boat had a good crew. These four men with Hans and Wilson should get ashore if there were any such thing as getting ashore, and the men on the *Shannon* felt sure they would succeed.

The crew had the boat swung out and were standing by the falls when we reached the after deck.

"Is everything in, Hans?" asked Wilson.

" Yaas! " was the reply, " Everydings."

" Lower away then! " Wilson gave me a few final instructions about the signals I was to keep going after ten days or so, to help the *Liffey* in finding us, then, after shaking my hand, he turned and said good-bye hurriedly to Miss MacMichael and her father. The girl may have spoken, but I didn't hear her, and when MacMichael and I looked again Wilson was climbing down the ladder and she was leaning on the rail, alone.

Her father took her arm.

" Come, Gertrude dear," he said, with an attempt at matter-of-factness, " come up on the bridge with Captain Ashburn."

By this time it was grey dawn, and the sky was getting pink in the east. I switched on the searchlight and turned it down on the ice-boat and the men standing beside her. "Long Henry " and "Little Willie " were letting out the midship straps to suit their height. The boatswain and Malcolm had theirs on their shoulders and were " hefting " the boat by lifting her stern clear of the ice and dropping her as though they were running a rock-crusher. Wilson and Hans retained their places on the bow straps, this time with the Swede to starboard.

Every man in both the crew of the *Duncrieff* and that of the *Shannon* was on deck, and when the six of them slipped the straps on, and, after waving their hands and giving us a shout, started the boat bumping over the pack toward the west, the crews cheered as they did when MacMichael had come aboard, only that, with sixty new voices, the cheer was a mightier one.

The light brightened rapidly, and MacMichael's daughter, hardly moving for half an hour, leaned over the rail of the bridge and watched the boat as she would come up on the crest of a ridge and then go down out of sight again. Then she turned away cheerily and began to hum an air from " San Toy," and afterward, day in and day out, the only way I could tell that she was thinking of the captain of the ice-boat was by an occasional wistful expression and a certain little absent-mindedness.

I kept a glass on the boat for over two hours, and the places she went through were marvellous. Out about three miles from the *Shannon* was a pressure ridge, where two parts of the pack had been forced together and the ice jammed forty feet in the air. I saw the six men sit on the boat's gunwale and rest at the foot of it. Then they got into their straps again and buckled to, and the way that ice-boat, with her load of provisions, went up that wall of ice was a sight. She swung over the crest, her stern went up in the air, and the last I saw was the boatswain and Malcolm being jerked off their feet as she slid down the slope on the other side.

CHAPTER VIII.

THE next day Donald finished with the number six compartment and commenced patching up the number two and the number three, until at the end of a week he had done his best. He rested, and he needed the rest.

Every day of the first week was fine, though for two days it blew a westerly gale that carried the pack off shore. Then came four beautiful cloudless days, two of them as warm as April. The field was solid all about the *Shannon,* and the two crews turned out on the ice and stretched their legs. They ran races, had boxing matches—using bunches of waste as gloves—, and with three empty beef barrels, a couple of coils of hawser, and some old boatcovers as properties, had a combined obstacle and hurdle race that was rendered doubly popular— with the spectators—by the fact that every man after struggling through a tunnel of canvas, which, for the time being, looked like a big worm in severe pain, came out as black as a Hottentot. They had been cleaning the tubes that morning, and it was rumoured that Donald had been seen going toward the old boat-covers with three buckets of soot. Donald himself remarked " eet was a gran' race," but he didn't see " why th' laddies shood get so dir-rty een goin' thro' those boat-covers."

One day I took my gun and went for a walk around the edges of the lanes nearest the *Shannon*. I managed to get ten or eleven ducks and a seal. The next day Miss MacMichael decided that she wished to come also, and of course she came. She climbed to the top of any clumpet that looked in the least dangerous, and dared me to follow her, and it wasn't always as easy as it might have been. Like a small boy she slid down anything that offered a slide, and I, of course, had to do that too; though I took good care that I was on the side of the clumpet away from the ship if I could manage it. She explored every crack, and just saved herself from falling into one by jumping six or seven feet across it.

" Pretty nearly got wet that time! " she laughed. Finally she persisted in going out to the extreme point of the solid ice in that part of the field. It was low—typical board-ice—and we investigated the wide lane that ran on two sides of it. Then, as the sun was getting low we .turned back. We went perhaps two hundred yards and came to an open lane a good thirty yards wide. The end of the point had broken off, and we were on an ice island, and the *Shannon* a good mile away.

" Do you know that we're adrift! " I said.

"I do, O King," was the reply, "so have we been even for six days."

"Yes," I said, "but we have been in the *Shannon* and now we can't get back to her."

"I also recognize that fact," she said, looking somewhat dismayed, but without a shade of fear. Then she laughed, sat down on a hummock, rested her elbows on her knees and her chin on her hands, and looked at the ice across the lane, which was slowly receding.

"Well," she said, still smiling, "this is a pretty predicament.

> "A polar bear on an iceberg sat
> All up in the Arctic Sea :
> But the iceberg went to Newfoundland
> And left that bear on a foreign strand;
> And he's waited there for fourteen years
> For a berg bound north, and his wife's in tears,
> As she probably long will be."

"Yes," I laughed, "and unless we can make a big enough fuss it will probably be the case with us."

"Captain Ashburn!" she said with assumed dignity, "I always thought you incapable of anything of that sort. But, to be serious, what are we to do. See this pan is almost touching on the other side. Can't we work back that way?"

"We would probably have to cross twenty impassable lanes," I said, "but we can get on that part of the field and climb on a clumpet from which we can see the *Shannon*." Even from the clumpets we could only see the boat's masts and funnel, and I fired away nearly all my shells in the effort to attract attention. Finally they signalled they were coming, and though it was after dark when the iceboat with Donald in charge reached us, and though MacMichael, who came with them, was a good deal worked up and frightened, the girl was cool, perfectly cool, and seemed to take the whole thing as a matter of course, as a pleasant little incident to break the monotony of waiting, and on the way back talked more about the prospect of supper than anything else. Yes! she had splendid nerve.

We had taken observations regularly and found that we were drifting northeast. Two days afterward, in the early morning, we sighted the coast of Anticosti, the big island that the French chocolate king, Menier, bought from the Quebec government. I decided, if we got near enough to the coast to make it at all possible, to land Mr. MacMichael and his daughter and the *Duncrieff's* crew, as they would be much safer than in the *Shannon* in her present state. But I was spared the trouble of even a trial. The wind came in from the northeast, and for two days we had just such another snowstorm as when we were fighting our way to the *Duncrieff*.

At last our pack and the ice that came down with it must have run into a field near the Gaspé shore,

for another crush began, as bad as either of the
first. There was the same grinding crash of ice,
and the old *Shannon* shivered and shook and strained and groaned; and besides, there was the noise of
bursting rivets and the sounds of rending timber,
when Donald's repairs in the number six compartment began to give way under the fearful pressure.
It was a hard experience, but it was short, much
shorter than the others, and the men stood it splendidly. When it was over and the ice was piled to
starboard in windrows as high as the top of the
Shannon's funnel, the centrifugal pumps went to
work, and Donald, undismayed, went down with a
gang of men and worked in the seething icy water
until he was numb.

But even Donald couldn't keep the water out this
time. Hour after hour he worked. Hour after
hour the sound of hammering came up from below,
until nothing more could be done, and, tired to
breaking, he turned in and slept for a whole day,
to the ceaseless accompaniment of the pumps.

Then, in day after day of bright sunlight and
northerly winds, we drifted slowly south, south of
Cape Gaspé and off the mouth of the Baie des
Chaleurs. We never once sighted land. Every
day was blue sky, glittering blue water and glinting
ice: every night flashing stars, waving shooting Aurora, clear cold, and silence, with later a growing
moon; and always drifting off to leeward the black

cloud of smoke from the funnel, and down below the ceaseless beat and whirr of the pumps. But the pumps took coal, and the coal could not last for ever. It was dwindling away, but I said nothing and waited, waited with stores ready for the ice-boats, and the ice-boats ready for work. Two weeks had gone since the ice-boat and her crew of six had left the *Shannon* for the Gaspé coast, and not a smudge of smoke on the horizon anywhere. We didn't even know that the ice-boat had reached the land, though the weather had been all we could have wished.

I could see by little things that the girl was feeling the strain, though she carried a surface like a Krupp armour-plate. Once when she thought no one was about I saw her sink down on the locker in the wheel-house and bury her face in her hands. A minute afterward she was up and walking around the bridge whistling.

Four more days passed. It was getting along toward the beginning of March, when the ice from the north comes down into the southern part of the Gulf, and the *Shannon* was going south with it. Surely if the *Liffey* were coming she should be up by this time. Wilson knew the currents and the effects of the wind so well that he should have found us by then. So probably thought the men, for they began to show their uneasiness.

One day it was snowing briskly, with a light

breeze from the north. We kept the usual signals going and fired a gun every half hour. The men were particularly gloomy. The girl saw it, and—bless her heart—she came and asked if she might have a concert in the saloon.

" Miss MacMichael! " I said, " you're a jewel, and you're grit all through."

" I wish I had half as much grit as I should like," she said, " but Dad feels a little solemn, I think, and a song or two might cheer him up, and might cheer up the men, too." We went about among the officers of both crews, and, as usual, managed to find a trio of banjos, two or three mandolins, and flutes, flageolets, fiddles, and piccolos enough for an orchestra. That evening at eight the men came up, crowding in from the snowy deck to the saloon, which was as comfortable as that of a liner. Every man not on duty was there, and wonderful was the variety of neckties, the badge of full dress at sea. Donald stayed outside and smoked, and looked in through a port which was open for ventilation. The saloon was so full that there was hardly room for the performers around the little piano. For an hour there were songs, and solos of various sorts, and each got its applause. Then Miss MacMichael, playing her own accompaniment, sang, " We'd Better Bide a Wee." Her voice was gloriously sympathetic, and I watched the faces of the men as they sat in perfect silence. The mighty contrast be-

tween feelings brought up by the ice, the uncertainty, the excitement and the strain of the last few
weeks, and the feelings awakened by the girl's rich
voice and the old song they all knew so well, was
too much, and many a man who was remarkable
for nothing so much as the string of oaths he could
put together when he thought occasion demanded
wiped his eyes on his hand or coat-sleeve and looked
at the floor.   When she finished they clapped and
yelled so that the girl looked at me in a bewildered
way.

"What shall I sing?" she said,—and, do you
know, she was trembling.

"Whatever you like best yourself.   They will
appreciate it."   She sat down again and sang
"The Fairies."   The beautiful ripple caught their
fancy and they smiled to a man.   She drifted off
into "Nancy Lee," and the men swung into the last
chorus.   Her mood changed, and she sang simply
and sweetly a stanza of the great hymn, "Eternal
Father, Strong to Save."   There was silence as she
finished; then Donald, removing the black pipe from
his lips, stuck his grizzled head in through the port.
He was wearing his most benign smile.

"Captain Ashburn," he said, with his voice most
impressively quiet, "A don' wan' t' eenterroopt th'
cooncert, but th' night's cleear noo, an' y' may be
eenterested t' know thut th' *Leefcy* ees breakin' oop
ice an' makin' a moost ungodly foos aboot three mile'

oop t' wind'ard." There was a dead silence for a second or two after Donald had finished speaking, then the men rushed at the saloon door and out on deck. The concert was never finished.

The girl got up from the piano laughing with joy. She seized her father's hand and darted for the door at such a rate that MacMichael had to do some careful navigation to steer clear of chairs and the end of the sideboard on the way. They went up on the bridge and I followed.

After the last big crush the broken ice had drifted away from the south of the *Shannon* and left her on the edge of a field with heavy ice piled up on one side and open water on the other. Then had come four or five nights when the spirit went far below zero, and over the open water had formed a great stretch of board-ice which had gone on increasing in thickness. This field, to the east and south, reached away to the horizon. Over it, through the haze left by the last of the snow-storm, shone the full moon, its reflections glinting up from a broken band of the field near the *Shannon*. Away off to the southward, with lights gleaming and with a great cloud of black smoke pouring from her funnel, was the *Liffey*. She was a full three miles away, but down on the light wind was borne the sound of breaking ice. It was no case for stopping and backing. She came up in the shadow as steadily as through open water, with her steel-clad stem now high in the air, now crashing its way down to water again.   The night is deceptive and she seemed to be doing twenty knots.   Donald had come up with Captain Cameron and stood puffing the little black pipe and looking on with approval.   Mac-Michael rubbed his mittened hands together, Miss MacMichael sat on the rail beside him with her arm around his neck, and the *Liffey,* with every port ablaze; with her big black funnel, her lofty wheel-house and flying bridge, and her round-bottomed ice-boats standing out against the sky; with splintered ice and spray thrown in a glittering cloud from under her curved merciless stem; and with her stern low down and her big screw grinding the ice into lolly, came roaring out into the path of the moon.   *Bup bup bupety-bup boom bupety-bup boom boom bupety-bup boom bup crash.*   Have you ever heard the song of the ice breaking under an ice-crusher's stem?   If not you should go up to Caribou and cross to Prince Edward Island on the *Liffey.*   We on the *Shannon* hadn't heard it for three weeks, and it came as welcome as a monsoon after the doldrums.   The girl gazed motionless as the *Liffey* thundered along in the moonlight.

"Isn't it a splendid sight?" she said, with all the enthusiasm of a child.

"Splendid enough," said Cameron, "but you should have been aboard the poor old *Duncrieff* and seen the men cry and hug each other when the

Shannon whistled after fighting her way through the pack that night. This field no more compares with that pack for strength than a spun-yarn does with a nine-inch hawser. But that boat has had many the hard fight before she got here. She's got the same hand on the wheel, and he'd drive her."

"Aye," said Donald, "an' an ir-ron han' at thut! Aye! he'd drive her!" To know how much this meant coming from Donald you would have to know Donald. MacMichael's daughter knew, and her eyes sparkled in the entrancing way they had when she was pleased.

The *Liffey* never eased. She swung astern in a big semicircle, and the throb of her engine didn't stop until she pulled up alongside us not a hundred feet away. To the cheer from the deck of the *Shannon* came back a shout from across the ice which, a few minutes later, was black with men. Miss Mac-Michael and I went down the ladder and met Wilson wading through the light snow toward the *Shannon*.

"What do you think of the *Liffey* now?" he laughed as he took the girl's arm and we started back. The *Liffey* got her full share of praise. He turned to me.

"You've got some of the big pumps going!" he said. I told him of the last crush and its effects.

"She's a wonderful boat is the *Shannon,*" he mused, "Bless her old heart, it's a marvel that she's not at the bottom of the Gulf crushed as flat as a flounder. Whenever anything happens to her—but I hope that will not be for many a long year—I shall put up a block of granite to her memory."

There was a great handshaking all round, and then the work of transferring the *Duncrieff's* men to the *Liffey* was begun. Everything had been packed and ready to move for days, and the ice-boats, piled high over the gunwales with sailors' kits, plowed their way back and forward through the moonlit snow between the ships, with thirty men each to drag them.

" When are you going to start? " I asked Wilson.

" The moment I get all the men on the *Liffey*," he replied, " By-the-way, both Malcolm " (Malcolm Fraser, the captain of the *Liffey*) " and MacIntosh, the first officer, got hurt two days ago by falling ice. They are both laid up and I have had no sleep worth speaking of for a week. Will you come aboard and take the *Liffey* and leave Ferguson with the *Shannon?* "

" Certainly! " I said, and passed the order for the fires to be brightened up in preparation for a start.

At last every man belonging to the *Duncrieff,* from captain to cook, had seen his last piece of dunnage safely stowed on the *Liffey,* and had followed it himself with a greater sense of security than he had had for many weeks.

I never liked anything less than I liked leaving the old *Shannon.* She had saved the lives of over a hundred men. We had trusted her when the most hopeless-looking fields came down, and she had never failed us. She had been crushed until she had groaned with the strain of thousands of tons of ice, but she still floated. For Wilson she had done more than for me, for she had conquered a heart that had seemed unconquerable; a heart that it had needed an ice-crusher to conquer.

" I feel that I should like to stick by her all the way down the Gulf!" he said, patting her rail affectionately. Our own things had all been transferred, and finally Betsie turned up with the bundle done up in the patchwork quilt, and we were ready to leave. By the gangway stood Donald, smoking the black pipe and studying the *Liffey* meditatively.

" Hello! Donald," I said, " did you get your bag over?"

" Oover wheyr-re?" he said, with the pipe still clenched in his teeth.

" To the *Liffey,* of course!" I replied.

" The *Leefey!* A'm noot goin' t' th' *Leefey!* A may be o' soom use t' th' *Shannon* yet. When she tr-ries t' go thro' after that boat my leetle repairs 'll proobably need soom lookin' to. Eet'll be a har-rd strain, 'n' oonless a wiz heear a wud no' guarantee she'll go far." Donald, as I have already told you, had gotten in love with the *Shannon* as a man gets in love with a woman, and now, in the hour of her weakness, he was not going to desert her. He also knew his own worth and capabilities and was frank about it, perhaps more so than about any other one thing.

" Is it that bad? " asked Wilson, with a voice as full of genuine concern as if he were asking about a sick friend.

" Aye! " he said, " eet's bad enough, but a've na doot she'll go thro' eef th' men are not afraid o' her."

And there we left him, while MacMichael and his daughter and Betsie and Wilson and I climbed down the ladder and went to the *Liffey*. Twenty minutes later I rang the engines ahead, and the *Liffey* raised her nose and went careering at the heavy ice around the *Shannon*. It took half an hour to cut her out, and then, as we drove past her bow, we heard the jingle of her engine-room telegraph and the throb of the big engines that had been so long still.

We turned south; the *Shannon,* battered, and with the pumps throwing heavy frothing streams from her sides, swung into our track; and the procession started for Caribou. Three hours before, the men had been gloomy enough, and Miss Mac-Michael—little wonder that the man on the pier at Caribou had said she had " the grit of the devil "—

had been trying to cheer them up with a concert.
Now they were homeward bound : so everyone was
light-hearted.   Down below the men roared somewhat modified bits of the songs the girl had sung
for them.   It was funny to hear the carpenter of
the *Duncrieff*, with a chanty voice, and to an air that
was evidently original, thundering :

> " Soom nicht, when th' soon een dairkness deeps,
>   W'll seek thet dreamland oolden ;
>   An' y' sh'll tooch wi' y'r feenger-teeps
>   Th' ivory gates 'n' goolden."

Up in the wheel-house the reaction was felt as
strongly as down below, and the feeling came out in
noise as ever.   MacMichael went off into a plethora
of expletives referring to the magnitude of the
thick-crowded events of the last few weeks.   Wilson wore a smile that wouldn't be repressed, and
told of the ice-boat trip and of the little idionsyn-
crasies of her remarkable crew.   The girl was
boiling over—I hadn't seen her in the same humour since the tennis tournament—and she whistled and sang and talked like the patter of rain in a
tropical thunder-storm.

At last everyone turned in and left me alone with
the quartermaster at the wheel.   The *Liffey* listed
now to starboard, now to port, ran up, crashed
down, and hammered her way along ; and astern,
through the fine snow that was blown over the surface of the ice, shone the lights where the *Shannon*

was wallowing in our wake, looming black in the moonlight.

For three hours she kept on, and then came a howl from her syren. She had stopped. We had been going through some heavy clumpets. I stopped the *Liffey,* and the *Shannon* came slowly up to within hailing-distance.

" What's the trouble? " I shouted.

" Boat's making considerable water," came the answer from Ferguson; " we'll have to stop and repair." So stop we did. I turned in and left orders to be called as soon as the *Shannon* was ready to proceed. A little later the second officer came in and told me that Ferguson, and Donald and Sandy MacKinnon, the *Shannon's* chief engineer, were coming aboard to see me. By the time I got out the three were on deck. Sandy and Ferguson looked troubled, and Donald's lips were set into a thin line.

Ferguson was the first to speak.

" The men want to come aboard the *Liffey,*" he said, hesitatingly.

" Soom o' th' men! " rasped Donald, with biting emphasis on the " soom; " " but they're na great shakes,"—and his jaw closed with a snap. I was surprised. Never before had I seen Donald give the slightest indication of losing control of his temper,—not that Donald hadn't a temper, but he seemed to take a peculiar pride in keeping it from exploding by surrounding it with bland, sarcastic, or jocular verbal safeguards as deliberately as he would pack a box of dynamite in excelsior.

"Want to desert the *Shannon!*" I said,   I had the search-light turned in her direction.   Her appearance was a bit startling.   The pumps were still going full blast, but her bow was deep down and she had a heavy list to starboard.

"Aye!" snorted the old chief of the *Dungeness*, "Desairt s th' worrud.   But eet's only a few booys that're scared.   They've never seen a boat a leetle doon een th' water, an' soom o' Sandy's lads 're afraid she might go steel fairther doon wi' them een th' englne-room.   Barrin th' boat, eet'd be na great loss eef she deed : but th' *Shannon's* a gran' good boat yet, an' sooch an engine a've never seen. Eet'd be a great peety t' loose her when a few days een a doock wud mek her as good's new."

Sandy's temper rose, for Donald's smile was now even and aggravating, and seemed to reflect in some way on his—Sandy MacKinnon's—conduct.

"Desairt be damned," he yelled, dancing about the deck.   "Three-quarters o' all th' men aboord want t' leave, an' th' rest o' them, like Meester Mac-Doonald heere, wouldna ken whayther a sheep wiz sinkin' or no.   She's got eight feet o' water een th' noomber seex compairtment an' twelve een th' noomber two, een spite o' th' fact that Meester MacDoonald repaired-red them."

Donald grinned and lit the black pipe.

"Saundy," he said softly, between puffs, "Y're foonny when y're mad. Eef y' c'd do 't t' oorder my advice'd be for y' t' leave th' engineerin' beeznees 'n' go een a show uz a wild man. Y'd mek more money, 'n' thut's what y'r leevin' for. Noo, y' know fery well thut eef y'd done thet repair-r joob een place uv me, th' *Shannon* 'd ha' been t' th' bootom o' th' Goolf long ago. But what a wiz goin' t' say wiz thut when y're mad, tho' we don' min' you pairsonally—y' can keeck holes een onything y' like, but a shood advise y' t' try a theen spoot een th' ice, as when y' geet th' hole made eet'll help t' cool y' off. As a wiz sayin', tho' we don' min' you pairsonally, we oobject t' y'r tendency t' exaggerate. A theenk a cood peeck oot a crew froom amoong th' *Shannon's* men who'd be pairfectly weelin' t' work her foor me." Sandy was red in the face.

"Y'd better try, then," was all he could say, and that came in a hoarse whisper. He couldn't speak.

"A wull," said Donald, "eef Captain Ashburn'll let me."

"Mr. Ferguson," I said, "what's your opinion?" —not that I valued it so much, for Ferguson never had much force.

"I wouldn't trust her to stay up long," he said, "if she makes much more water she'll be down to those breaks above the water-line in the forward compartments, and then she'll go from under us so quick that we can't get out of her."

" From which I'd infer that you would like to leave her too," I said.

" Not if there was any show for her floating," he said hurriedly, " but I don't believe there is."

" Don't explain," I said.   " I understand."

" Ma deear mon," smiled Donald, " eef y' knew the *Shannon's* strength and her engines as weel as y' shood,—bein' her first officer—y'd never talk sooch bleetherin' noonsense. A don' theenk y'r speerit foor adventure ees fery stroong.   Y' shood ha' been een th' navy, where y'd ha' been safe." Donald didn't know that he was hitting at me also, though perhaps the criticism wasn't far from true, as things are in these times.   Ferguson reddened and said nothing, probably chiefly because there was nothing to say.

" I can't take the responsibility of asking men to stay in a boat which they think will sink under them," I said; " so I shall take Donald's offer and let him ask for volunteer stokers and engineers. You'll act as chief, will you, Donald? "

" A wull," he said, " an' be prood t' ha' th' chance : 'n' a'll leave a document aboord th' *Leefey* t' th' effect thut eef a'm drooned een tryin' to breeng th' *Shannon* home, my heirs, executors, admeenistrators 'n' assigns sh'll pay t' Alexander MacKinnon, engineer—soometimes eereverently known as Saundy th' Miser—th' soom o' one thousan' dollars t' have 'n' t' hold teel death do them pairt,—they'll never pairt ony oother way." Sandy got red and white by turns and showed incipient symptoms of foaming at the mouth. I gave up the attempt to keep my face straight and laughed.

"Donald," I said, "if you go back to the old *Shannon* as chief I go back as captain, and together we'll pull her through." Sandy was hardly prepared for this.

"O' coorse," he began, "a deedn't refuse t' go een th' *Shannon:* a wiz merely tellin' y' what the' men sayed. A'll be quite weelin' t' go eef——"

"If you're asked," I said, perhaps a bit tartly, for the man had disgusted me. Sandy stopped short.

Donald pulled hard at the black pipe and looked at the sky during a thirty-second silence. Then he turned to Ferguson and Sandy, and with his sweetest smile and quietest voice said:

"Eet looks 's eef eet might be cloodin' oop for another squall o' snow." Ferguson stammered something about "a shift to the nor'east." Sandy was quiet for a second. Then he shook his fist in Donald's face and roared "Go t' *hell!* "—after which he walked aft, while Donald grinned his invincible grin.

I backed the *Liffey* up in her track and worked in alongside the *Shannon* until our deck lights shone

down on her battered deck and broken rail.   From
away down in her engine-room came the beat of the
Blake pumps and the throb of the big Bon Accord
centrifugals—the pumps that each throw three hundred tons of water an hour—and from all the discharges came heavy foaming streams.   Poor old
Shannon!   Her pram-bow was deep buried in the
ice and had lost the fierce look it had when roaring
up to the edge of a field.   I looked at her now and
remembered the day, a few weeks before, when, with
the white wave thundering at her bow, she went at
the pack that held the *Duncrieff,* and in the midst of
the gale, in driving snow and driving ice, stuck that
bow up in the air and saved the lives of sixty men
—and of MacMichael.

Just as Donald went aboard Wilson came up.
Captain Fraser would not be able to be about for a
day or two, he told me, so I had to give up taking
the *Shannon.*

"You will find that Hans will go," he said; "ask
him."   Hans was immensely pleased with the prospect, and especially pleased that he had been selected for such a responsible position.

"I vill haf endire sharge off her?" he asked.

"Entire charge," I said.

"Den I vill go, und I vill too my pest vit her."

Donald got practically the whole crew on deck.
I spoke to them from the bridge of the *Liffey.*

"Men," I said, "I understand that some of you

are afraid that the *Shannon* may go down and may take you with her. Your chief engineer, Mr. Mac-Kinnon, is of this opinion, and so is your first officer, Mr. Ferguson. I am afraid, from their reports, that your respect for their opinions must have affected the opinions of some of you, for I understand that a number of you wish to leave and come aboard the *Liffey*. Among those who think there is no danger now are Mr. Donald MacDonald and myself. I should have been glad to go back and take the *Shannon,* but I cannot leave here, so Hans Brun, who, next to Mr. Wilson himself, knows more about the ice and this part of the Gulf than any of us, has offered to take charge, and Mr. MacDonald wishes to act as chief engineer."

"Goot for Tonal 'n' Hans," came a voice from the deck.

"Now," I continued, "I do not want any man in the *Shannon* who doesn't want to stay in her. So any of you who are not willing to stay aboard, and help to work the boat to Caribou behind the *Liffey,* may come aboard the *Liffey* now. Of course it is stokers we especially want who are not afraid to do their best."

The men wavered between not admitting an implied cowardice and following the course suggested by their own sense of insecurity. Finally the latter triumphed in a good many cases, and even in the face of the *Liffey's* and the *Duncrieff's* men about

half the crew came silently over and climbed the
Liffey's rail. They were partly made up for, however, by some of the *Duncrieff's* stokers, who, of
their own accord, offered to go, because, as the
spokesman said to Donald, " It'd be a damned shame
to let the old boat go after she's saved the lot of us,
and all for the want of a little firin'."

When Hans and Donald went aboard, Ferguson
was nowhere to be seen, but Sandy was looking
moodily on. Donald smiled as he passed him.

" A hope y'll be feelin' better in th' mornin',
Meester McKinnon," he said. Sandy turned away
without answering, and Donald, winking at me as
he climbed down, said musingly and sympatheti-
cally:

" Poor mon! Poor mon! Eet's bad enough t' lose
y'r jedgment 'n' y'r temper wi'out bein' deeprived
o' y'r hearin' too."

Ten minutes later the *Liffey* was up and at it
again, but before I got away a great blast of smoke
started from the *Shannon's* funnel. Donald had
started the forced-draft fans. A little while afterward we ran into open water. Before, when Sandy
had her, when we would get into open water with
no ice to stop us, I would have to slow up a bit to
keep from running away from the old boat, but
now, in spite of the extra weight of water in her, in
spite of the steam used by the pumps, in spite of the
fact that the *Liffey* was actually faster, no matter

how hard the *Liffey* was driven, the *Shannon,* with
the little flagstaff on her stem trembling and shaking
with the vibration of the two thousand tons of steel
behind it, ploughed along doggedly at her heels.   I
had heard of the speed Donald used to get out of
the old *Dungeness,* but I had hardly believed it all,
for why a freighter should go much faster for one
man than another I did not see.   But now I was
willing to believe anything.   However, I would like
to have seen the *Shannon's* steam-gauge that day.
Not only did he get more out of her engines, but
he got more out of her pumps, for when daylight
came I could see that she was lighter, visibly lighter.
I could not resist the temptation to call Sandy up
and tell him what the *Shannon* had been doing in
the way of speed, and also that she was lighter and
getting higher in the water all the time.   He finally
had to admit that what I said was true, and you
should have seen his face when he did.   As we were
talking, Donald, with his arms bare to the elbow,
appeared on the *Shannon's* bridge to study progress.
The sight of him evidently stirred Sandy up.

"He's no engine-er!" he snarled, banging the
rail with his fist.   "He's a poor eemitation uv an
engine-er!   There's but one way he cood do 't, 'n'
that's by screwin' doon her pop-valves 'n' usin' the
foorced draft most ungodly har-rd; 'n' no engine-er
would do that, t' th' reesk o' th' lives o' hees men."

"And himself," I suggested.   Sandy ignored the
remark.

CHAPTER IX.

W ELL, it was about noon. It was a beautiful clear day, with the sun showing the strength of spring. We had been running almost free from ice with only an occasional clumpet, big enough to be called a berg, shining white in brilliant contrast to the water, which had that peculiar dark-blue appearance so characteristic in bright sunlight in winter. The old *Shannon* was doing splendidly. Hans had his wheel-house windows wide open and was enjoying the air. Once he had even succeeded in coming up alongside us. On the *Liffey* nearly everyone not at work below was on deck. Most of the *Duncrieff's* men were lying about on the forward deck, some smoking, some half asleep, with the warm sun beating down on their faces, some gathered in groups telling stories. Up in the wheel-house we had the windows and doors wide open and everyone was there—everyone meaning MacMichael and his daughter, Wilson, Cameron and I—all having an air and sun bath before the bugle sounded for dinner. Things were done a bit more elaborately on the *Liffey* than we used to do them on the *Shannon,* so we had a bugle instead of a gong.

Wilson had been watching all sorts of things with a glass, and taking notes most impartially on birds, and seals, and ice forms and distribution, and had been calculating the speed of drift and the effect of its pressure on coast lines, and twice as many other things that I don't remember anything about. The girl had been helping him, and out of the material at hand constructing some geological hypotheses of her own for the edification of us all,—hypotheses in which she brought within fighting distance of each other megatheriums and pterodactyls and plesiosauruses and rhamphorhynchuses in a way that would cause trouble both, at the time to the beasts themselves, and a million or so years later to Sir William Dawson. Cameron had been sing-songing some stories about when he " was in the China Sea with the *Duncrieff,*" and MacMichael had just told how, when before " Little Willie " had " quit whiskey " he went with a picnic to Antigonish, got gloriously full, wandered away, and had to be hunted up : how they found him leaning against a tree watching the big bucket-dredge *St. Lawrence,* and, with one hand stretched out, solemnly counting the buckets as they followed each other up on the chain ; and how, when they exhorted him to " coom awa hame," he'd said "he'd be damned eef he wud."—

that he'd " coonted fower hoondred 'n' seexty-
fower o' th' eenfairnel theengs, 'n' he wiz goin' t'
see th' last o' them eef he hed t' wait teel th'
fall."

At last the open water came to an end and we
saw the glistening peaks of a pack of heavy ice
stretching as far to starboard and port as we
could see.   In a little time we were up to it and
roaring into a lead between two exceptionally
heavy fields.   We stopped story-telling and
watched as the *Liffey* went for a flat cake a good
ten feet thick that closed the lead.   When the
crash came it was followed by the sharp metallic
grind that tells of hard ice.   Grind! grind! grind!
and the *Liffey* shook, and lurched, and heeled, and
finally stopped.   I backed her up and went at it
again.   This time we went through into a reach
of light ice and looked back at the *Shannon*.

Not a soul who saw it will forget a single detail
of the scene that followed—not if he lives a
thousand years.   We looked at the breach we had
just made and saw it closing up, and closing quickly too.   The fields on each side were moving together: no apparent reason as ever, but they were
moving.   The old *Shannon* was still back in almost
open water.   Everyone who saw it said the same
thing—that she seemed to be doing more of
everything just then than she had ever done before.   The truth of the matter is that she actually

was doing more of everything than ever before, and the reason of it all was that Donald was aboard. The smoke came out of her funnel in black woolly balls so thick that you could cut it. The water pouring from the pump discharges was spurting away from her sides with all the force of the whirling centrifugals behind it. Hans, the yellow-headed Swede, up in the wheel-house, saw the heavy ice closing in and headed her for the breach, and Donald, the wizard of the *Dungeness,* down in the engine-room, opened her wide. With Heaven knows how many pounds of steam on, her stern went down until the water and lolly ran over her counter, and her pram-bow went up like the nose of an American aristocrat. The pitiless sunlight showed every dint in her battered plates, every twist of the broken rail, and every long, yellow-red streak of rust, as, on a hissing cushion of boiling foam, she surged up at the barrier. Boom! Crash! Crash! She trembled with the shock, and the little flag-pole on the stem shook like a signal-staff in a gale. She came almost through into the light ice, then, wallowing, sank down to water again. She tried to back out: we could hear the throb of her big engine and see the water boiling over the ice at her stern, but she couldn't move, and the engine was stopped. The fields were still moving together and she was nipped between, as she had been that night she reached the *Duncrieff*.

The *Liffey* was caught too, and we watched the ice as it pressed in. Hard as it was, it groaned and cracked and broke up against the boat's sides. It piled up until I had to send a gang of men with slice-bars to keep it from smashing the rail. Finally it got well under us, and, still pressing in, forced the *Liffey* almost out of water. We watched it climb over the *Shannon's* port side half-way up her house. Then it stopped as mysteriously as it had begun, and we sank grinding down.

I was reaching for the telegraph to ring the engines ahead when Cameron seized my arm.

" Look," he said, " there's something wrong on the *Shannon*." She was not more than a hundred yards off our starboard quarter, and from her deck came excited yells. Half a dozen of her men ran to the rail, jumped down onto the ice, and tried to run over the broken pack. Four more burst from the stoke-hold door and followed the others over the side. Another man rolled over the stern into the slush and lolly, struggled through, climbed out on the ice, and ran like a deer. Hans rushed from the wheel-house, leaped clear from the bridge to the deck, and ran aft just as Donald stepped from the engine-room door. The Swede stuck his hands deep in his pockets and leaned against the house. Just then another man jumped

through the stoke-hold door and went over the
rail, Donald reaching for him as he went, but
missing him by a foot, and Hans just managing
to kick him hard enough to knock him end over
end on the pack below. The old engineer sur-
veyed the ice and the men struggling over clumpets and falling in holes in their efforts to get
away.

"Coom back!" he yelled, "y' poor meeserable
coowards, coom back an' help me close th' boolkhead. Coom back! a say." The *Shannon's* bow
dropped suddenly, perhaps a foot, and two more
men came round the forward end of the house,
slid down onto the ice, and started to flounder
over the pinnacled surface through the snow.

"Coom back!" roared Donald, "Och! y' eenfairnal coowards: lettin' a boat seenk lek thees.
Eef a had a goon heear a'd shoot y', so help me
God! a wud," and he and Hans ran toward the
bow and disappeared down the forward companion-way.

"There is a sliding door in the bulkhead between the number three compartment and the
stoke-hold," said Wlison, "the crush has broken
in the number three again, the door has been
open and it is flooding the stoke-hold. It can be
closed by a worm gear just under the forward
hatch." The boat was taking a list to starboard.

"See, the smoke is thinning," I said, "it has

reached one of the fires." Wilson looked anxiously in the direction of the *Shannon.*

"All the boilers are loose now; it may break
some of the steam connections," he said; "I'll
have to go—if I can get there,"—and he ran
out on the house, where the pike-poles were kept.
The first pole he seized broke into slivers as
he tried to tear it from the lashing. The second
was eighteen feet long and stout in proportion,
and the manilla lashing snapped with ends frayed
like the ends of a broken hawser. He ran forward with the pole and slid down it to the deck.
The girl leaned over the rail of the bridge:—

"Do be careful;" she said, half trying to conceal her anxiety and wholly failing, "even the
Shannon is not worth risking your life for."

"I shall be careful," was the answer, "though
if I would risk my life for anything inanimate the
Shannon is the thing," and I caught the glance
that flashed between them.

The men on the *Liffey's* deck were in a great
state of excitement, and when Wilson swung the
big pole down, jabbed its steel point into a little
rotten clumpet, and vaulted from the rail away
over on to a snow-covered pan, they rushed to
the side and howled encouragement; though what
they thought he could do alone toward saving the
Shannon I'm sure I don't know. He ran reck-
lessly over the small ice around the *Liffey,* jumping

from one piece to another without giving them time to sink under him. He reached the solid ice, and, throwing down the pole, started clambering toward the *Shannon,* now jumping from peak to peak and balancing himself on an ice point like a stream driver on a rolling log, now floundering waist-deep through snow and sometimes slush. Half a dozen more men jumped from the *Shannon's* deck, and when they saw him coming started away in another direction as though they were afraid he would drag them back to the ship.

In the few minutes that had elapsed the *Shannon's* bow had sunk still deeper. Donald and Hans appeared on deck again. The old engineer looked at the men on the ice and saw the last group struggling away toward the others.

"Booys," he roared, "foor th' Loord's sake, foor my sake, foor y'r own sakes don' he sooch poor meeserable coowards. Why, th're's a girrul oover on th' breedge o' th' *Leeffey* who, eef she cood get heere, wud go doon thees minute an' stoke unteel th' water floated her off her feet. We've got th' boolkhead door closed noo. Coom back, lads, an' stoke only foor feefteen meenites, 'n' eef a can't show y' thut y'r safe, then a'll ask y' t' do na moore. A only want two o' y' foor the engine-room an' seex o' y' foor the stoke-hold." Not a man among them moved. Donald's voice changed until the words snapped out hard and cold, like the singing, clicking clank of a quick-firing breech-mechanism. " Noo's y'r chance t' see an exhibeetion o' real coowards, joost tested, 'n' guaranteed genuine. Joost look 't each oother, noo, arrn't y' a pack o' beauties, standin' roon' on th' ice like a herd o' seals when y' ought t' be heear. Eeef a'd known y'd do thees a'd never 'a' stooped th' *Leeffey* t' wait foor us; then y'd a' worrked, y' damned coowards! " and the old Scotchman shook his fist at them. By this time Wilson had reached the *Shannon's* side and climbed aboard. I could see him talking hurriedly to Donald and Hans. Just then Malcolm Fraser, the *Liffey's* captain, who had heard the shouting, could stand the strain no longer, and in spite of his sore head came on the bridge.

" Do you feel well enough to take charge of the boat for a little while ? " I said.

" Yes," he answered.

" Quartermaster, have one of the starboard ice-boats lowered," I said. Then I shouted to Wilson.

" Go ahead and stoke. I'll go over and bring whoever will go. Now! " I shouted, to the men on deck, " who will go along and stoke with Mr. Wilson and me. I want three or four stokers and two engineers." Big Malcolm Macpherson, who had gone with the ice-boat to Gaspé, was the first man to step forward, and he was followed by

" Little Willie," the six-foot-six giant that was in the same crew. I almost fell off the bridge with surprise when the next man to step up was—— Sandy MacKinnon, looking contrite and shame-faced enough,—Sandy, who had been among the first to want to leave the *Shannon,* who had con-signed Donald to perdition, and who said that he was no engineer. Now he was willing to go back with Donald as his chief, and the boat in a far worse condition than when he left her. It was one of those incomprehensible and inconsistent reactions that men are subject to, but it told me one thing, and that was that Sandy was no coward, whatever other faults he might have. I was glad to have something to give me back my old opinion of him.

" A might be o' some use t' Tonal een th' engine-room," he said.

" He'll be very glad to have you," I replied; at which Sandy looked somewhat dubious. The *Liffey's* second engineer offered to go, and one of the stokers from the *Duncrieff's* crew made up the lot. We rushed the ice-boat across to the solid ice and left her there. Before we climbed up the *Shannon's* sloping side I saw that the streams from her pumps were getting feebler and feebler. What we did would have to be done quickly. As we reached the deck Donald stuck his head out of the engine-room door.

"A'm mooch obleeged t' y', booys," he said, addressing Sandy and the second engineer without a change in his voice or manner to indicate either late happenings or the least excitement or hurry; "coom doon,"—then, turning to us, "y'll find Meester Wilson 'n' Hans een th' stoke-hold, 'n' they're probably sights by thees time." Malcolm and "Little Willie" and the *Duncrieff* man and I went through the air-lock and down the greasy, black ladder into the stoke-hold. We could hear the buzzing whirr of the forced-draft fans, and the hiss and seethe and splash of the water, that still came in through the door in the bulkhead forward, which they had not been able to get tight closed. Hans, wading knee-deep in black water with coal dust and white ashes floating in a thick scum on its surface, was phlegmatically firing two of the boilers, and the fires were beginning to burn up pretty strong again. Wilson was on top of the wall using every ounce of his strength in shutting the two starboard boilers off from the rest. I looked below. The *Shannon* had a heavy list to starboard, and the water was deep in the starboard side of the stoke-hold. It couldn't be more than six inches from the fires. All the boilers had been shifted in the last crush and were loose, with the starboard ones the loosest of all. Even now the strain on the main steam pipes was so great that the steam was boiling out from the expansion boxes over the two starboard boilers.   If the *Shannon* made a little more water and listed further to starboard those steam pipes would go somewhere, as sure as day is day.

I wonder if you really know what that means. It is not the conventional go-off-with-a-bang type of boiler-explosion, in which you don't live long enough to know about it.   Instead there is a little crack, or perhaps a big crack, but enough, in any case, to let loose a hell of scalding water and scalding steam, and you're boiled alive.   Malcolm and " Little Willie " didn't know, and they might well be thankful they didn't, but the *Duncrieff* stoker knew and so did I.   I don't know what he thought and felt, but that was the narrowest escape I ever had from turning and running for my life.   I said a prayer through my clenched teeth and went on, and so did the stoker, though he was ashy white.

" Fire those two port boilers! " shouted Wilson. We dropped into the icy black water and went to work.   A moment later he had finished closing the valves and threw himself on the safety-valves of the starboard boilers, and the steam went roaring up the escape.   He jumped to the stoke-hold floor, seized a wrench, waded up to his arms in the water to starboard and opened the blow-off valves also.   It was barely in time, for when there was still a bit of steam left the *Shannon* listed still further, the main from the second boiler broke clear off and the steam, hot and wet, filled the stoke-hold for a time.   In the glaring reek we piled coal onto the white-hot fires while our feet and legs grew numb and cramped in the icy water. Donald had put one of the centrifugals to work pumping out the stoke-hold.   The water had lowered at first, but now was increasing again rapidly and came through the bulkhead with a more vicious hiss.

"Ashburn, go and tell Donald!" grunted Wilson between the heaves of his shovel.   I went up, and down into the engine-room.   Donald was working at a silent centrifugal and Sandy was trying to bully a Blake into doing what neither it nor any other pump could do.

"The stoke-hold is filling up," I said.

"A know eet ees;" was the reply, quietly, as ever, "an' so ees th' noomber three an' th' noomber seex.   Een a leetle while one o' th' greatest boats thut efer floated, an' one o' th' gran'est engines efer beelt, 'll be at th' boottom o' th' Goolf," and he looked about him sadly at the enormous cranks, and up at the mighty cylinders and the glistening piston-rods as big as the thrust-shaft of an ordinary steamer.   "Eet's a gran' job, a gran' job!" he said, with his voice thick, "but eet's no use tryin' noo.   The centreefugal a had on th' stoke-hold ees choked wi' ashes an' has loost a blade, and th' one a had oon th' noomber three is choked wi' ice. We'll ha' to geeve 't oop. Tell 'em all t' coom away 'n' leave her. Coom, Sandy; coom, Meester Carswell. Good Loord! but eet's a great peety; 'n' all oon accoont o' those coowards who ran when we cood ha' saved her." Donald turned and climbed the ladder, leaving the centrifugal circulating pump swishing away, the auxiliary feed groaning, and two big Blakes *boomp-boomp-boomping* to the solitude. I rushed through the air-lock and down into the stoke-hold again. " Little Willie " and the *Duncrieff* man were trimming in the port bunker. Hans, with his yellow hair ruffled and wet, was making over a fire with a long fire-rake, and Wilson and Malcolm were handling their big scoops full of coal with as little apparent effort as I would handle a snow-shovel. Wilson had taken the most starboard boiler himself and was in water above his knees.

" What's the trouble? " he asked as I waded over to where he was standing.

" The pumps are choked and some of them are broken," I replied, and I told him what Donald had said. He looked downward and swished his shovel slowly back and forward through the black water. He was silent for a few seconds and his lips were set, often the only visible sign of any emotion he felt.

" Well, well!" he said sadly at last, " if we have
to give her up I suppose we have to.   After all
I imagine it's nothing but sentiment, but Ashburn,
I love this boat more than I can tell you.   She's
——well, you know what she's done."

" You can call it sentiment or whatever you
like," I said, " but I wouldn't give this bunch of
waste for a man without it.   It's only loyalty to
a true friend; whether of flesh or steel makes but
little difference.   Yes, I know what she's done.
Done what's never been done before—in several
ways," and Wilson smiled a reminiscent smile and
thought for a second or two.   He looked up
quickly.

" The water is gaining fast," he said, looking
about him and up at the great boilers that seethed
above, " Malcolm, get Willie and that *Duncrieff*
man out of the bunker.   Men," he continued, as
Willie and the stoker came through the iron door,
" the pumps are choked and we have to leave the
Shannon after all.   You might give me a hand in
drawing those fires."   We started to rake out the
white-hot coals.   The hissing and spluttering as
they struck the cold water was deafening.   Wilson
started up to open the safety-valves.   The *Shannon's* starboard side dropped suddenly, and the
water surged to that side of the stoke-hold, almost
covering the extreme starboard boiler.   Wilson,
with nothing to hold to, fell from the boiler wall

into the water and disappeared under its ash-covered surface. " Little Willie " came swooping down past me and stopped himself by catching a standard. Hans, clutching at Willie, went past him and splashed into the water just as Wilson's head came up. The *Duncrieff* man hung to the ladder and stared up above the port boilers. They had shifted too, and the steam was screaming out from the expansion boxes and from a crack in one of the great pipes above. I never got a better illustration of Wilson's wonderful balance in an emergency than when he came to the surface of that mixture of iced bilge-water and coal-ashes.

" Boys," he said, as soon as he had wiped the streaked coal-dust away from his eyes and mouth sufficiently to see and talk, " it's a good thing we blew off those two starboard boilers. Now, with the boat over like this, the water will come in more quickly than it's come so far, so get out,"— and with all due credit to the spirit the " boys " had shown they got out with marvellous speed. I can still see " Little Willie's " long legs dangling out from the then overhanging ladder as he went up it hand over hand. I can hear Hans's " Yesus ! " as he struggled out of the water, with half an inch of wet ashes plastered over him, and crawled on his belly up that slippery wet iron floor. I can hear Malcolm's " Mye Go-od ! " as he sat down and slid at toboggan speed, catching

the ladder, as he went past, with a jerk that would
have dislocated the arm of another man.   The
Duncrieff stoker, accustomed to the stoke-hold,
went up the ladder like a Siamang ape.   Wilson
and I, clinging to the floor, worked our way to
the bottom rung.   I stood aside to let him go up.

" You may be the captain of the rest of the
Shannon," he spluttered, " but you're not captain
of the stoke-hold.   Get out."   He lifted me in
his hands as I would lift a child, and forced me up
the ladder ahead of him.   We climbed it for the
last time, and, leaving a steamy, watery, red-
glowing scene of destruction behind, · came out
on deck, black and wet and beaten.

I stopped long enough to take a cold chisel and
a fire-axe, and cut from the forward wall of the
house the crimson-lettered oval brass plate bear-
ing the words:—

SHANNON

————, ———— & CO.,

ELSWICK-ON-TYNE,

18—.

LONDON.

As I ran forward again I looked in through the
engine-room door.   Old Donald was standing on

the grating, hanging to the rail to keep from falling to starboard. He was gazing, motionless, down into the depths, where the auxiliary feed was still hissing and groaning, and the two Blakes still boomp-boomping to the polished glinting loneliness.

"Come on, Donald," I said, "we'll have to get out of this: the water is working up and we didn't get a chance to open the safety-valves."

"A'm coomin'," he said mournfully, "a'm coimin'. An' t' theenk thut they have t' go: th' gran'est set o' engines thut efer swung a wheel. An' all on accoont o' those damned coowards. A weel! A suppose a must go," and he turned slowly away and climbed out on deck.

The number six had filled rapidly, as well as the bow compartments, and the boat was down aft as well as forward. She now had such a list that her starboard rail was under water, and her port side—the side toward the *Liffey*—sloped so that you could almost walk down it to the ice. On board the *Liffey*, though there was no noise, everything was excitement. MacMichael and his daughter were standing close together on the bridge, gazing at the *Shannon*, the only motionless figures on the boat. Sandy and the other engineer were already out on the pack, and Donald, after standing for a second and looking from stem to stern, stepped through a breach in the broken

rail and slid down on to the ice. Malcolm and
" Little Willie " and the *Duncrieff* man were already struggling over the clumpets toward the
ice-boat. Wilson and I climbed down and followed them. The stokers who had deserted Donald, seeing no other visible way of getting back to
the *Liffey,* had collected around the ice-boat also.
They walked to the other side of the boat as we
came up, and talked among themselves, and tried
to look as if they had no connection with passing
events.

Wilson and I arrived at the ice-boat with
Donald, who leaned against the bow, watching the
Shannon and taking no notice of the men behind.
No one spoke. From behind us came the splash
of the constant stream of water from the *Liffey's*
condenser. Beside this there was no sound except
the faint muffled *boomp-boomp* from the indefatigable Blakes in the *Shannon's* engine-room.

" Eet's moornful hearin' those poomps goin',"
sighed Donald, half to himself, " a shood ha'
stooped 'em."

The *Liffey,* immaculate, a beautiful canoe-bowed
boat sitting stiff and upright, as though she were
conscious of her strength, without even a dint in
her plates and with everything trim and ship-
shape, by contrast made the *Shannon* look still
more battered. A crushing grind came from the
direction of the old boat, and every man on the

deck of the *Liffey* and on the ice became silent.
The *Shannon's* stern dropped slowly until the
counter disappeared beneath the pack, and she
slowly listed over still further.   Then for perhaps
ten minutes she was motionless.   She must be
filling, but the ice was holding her.   I looked at
the *Liffey* again.   MacMichael and his daughter,
on the bridge with Malcolm Fraser, and all the
men on deck, were leaning forward with eyes
fixed on the *Shannon,* low sunk now and hammered and crushed, with the snow and ice thick
on her rigging and deep-crusted on her scraped
sides, with the wheel-house door thrown open as
Hans had left it, and with the wheel-house empty,
but still the same ferocious, pram-bowed, big-fun-
neled, almighty-looking *Shannon,* that had seemed
to fight fearless and resistless, beyond the power
of the men that controlled her, as though she had
a soul of her own; the *Shannon* that had saved the
lives of most of us there and the happiness of us
all.   Do you wonder that the men were quiet as
they watched!

At last a cloud of steam came pouring silently
out the top of the funnel, mixed with the fading
smoke.   The water had reached the last of the
fires.   Then came a hissing sound that seemed far
away, and white wisps of steam floated from the
stoke-hold ventilators.

"The other steam pipes are going!" said Wil-

son, without taking his eyes from the boat. The
hiss increased. In five seconds it changed to a
scream, and ten seconds later the scream had
changed to a roar, a deep, thundering, shrieking,
vibrating roar. From the stoke-hold ventilators
a white cloud of steam boiled out over the *Shannon's* deck. From below came a muffled explosion, and the skylight over the stoke-hold blew
off onto the ice: then a sound, sharp and clear
and hard and deafening as the report of a six-inch
gun, then the rending burst of a steel house, and
then, amid the howl of steam, the clanging fall of
a big funnel. We could see the double curve of
the bow looming black through the white cloud,
and, with the exception of the spars, we could see
no more. In hardly a minute we could hear the
roar of the steam lessen, though it's marvellous
what a nest of boilers like those will hold at a
hundred and fifty pounds. Before another minute
was ended the roar had faded to a sigh, and the
sigh had died, as dies the last-drawn breath of a
child. A great snow-white dissolving cloud rolled
off to leeward in the sunlight and left the black
wreck of the *Shannon* still above water. Between
the engine-room aft and the saloon and wheel-
house was a torn gap with the funnel lying across
it, and on the ice alongside lay a couple of ventilators, the wrecks of three boats, and scrap steel
enough to make a stock for a junk-shop.

Again there was silence, with only the splash of the water from the *Liffey's* circulating pump. It lasted a few seconds, then a quick murmur came from the men, who had been paralysed by the scenes of the last few minutes.

"She's goin', sir!" said Malcolm. Yes! she was going this time. The ice creaked and groaned for a moment, and the masts leaned back as the stern sank, sank while the great curved bow rose slowly high in the air, as though preparing for one last crushing blow at its life-long enemy, the ice. She sank until only the bow and the wheel-house were visible, and she paused for a moment, while little clumpets and flecks of lolly moved in over the place where the stern had gone down. Then she slid slowly backward until the tip of the great pram-bow sank in among the clumpets. The last thing we saw was the truck of the fore-mast, and then the pack closed up, as though it were trying to hide the place.

"Poor old *Shannon!*" said Wilson, still gazing at the clumpets pushing in over the dark water where she had disappeared. For a little while not a man moved. We stood looking at the jagged, glistening, white pack, stretching away out of sight, with only a few tangled piles of débris to show where the *Shannon* had been.

Poor old *Shannon!* I looked down at the oval brass plate in my hand and thought of the even-

ings we had spent in the cottage at Percé working
out her design, of the winding Irish river that had
given her her name, and of the beautiful blue-
eyed girl that had lived on its bank: I thought of
the autumn afternoon when, with a couple of hundred flags fluttering from truck to water-line, she
had swept into Caribou harbour; of the day when
she went to work viciously at two feet of green
ice and silenced the critics; and finally of the great
fight she had made to save the men of the *Duncrieff* and MacMichael, and how she had won,
incidentally conquering the apparently impregnable heart of a girl, and, winning at too great cost,
was the sacrifice herself.

Poor old *Shannon!*   I suppose she had done her
appointed work, and her time had come.   Few
boats—or men—accomplish half as much.   Now
she could rest, with the Gulf weed clinging to her
in the dark, and each winter the murres and guillemots and black-backed gulls and seals could play
and fish, and the floes and clumpets could roar
and grind and crush each other into lolly far aloft,
away above her trucks.

I looked up quickly, out over the endless ice,
and around to where the *Liffey* towered black
and fearfully solitary.   Still no one moved and no
one spoke.   Wilson, grimy and wet, was sitting
on the gunwale of the boat, looking down into
the snow at his feet, noticing nothing around him.

One of the stokers—a fellow named Johnstone, who had been the first to run from the *Shannon*, a big, heavy-boned, round-shouldered man, with narrow eyes, thick lips, and a swagger about him that used to pain me a bit when I watched him— was the first to speak.   He was standing with the others behind the boat, and he looked toward Donald, who was still leaning against the bow, gazing over to where the truck of the *Shannon's* foremast had disappeared under the pack.   He took a step or two in Donald's direction.

"Well!   What did I tell y'!" he said.   Ain't the old pot down now!"

Donald half started, turned his head slowly, took the little black pipe from his mouth, looked into its cold bowl and then up at the stoker, who was grinning complacently at the thought of having saved his own skin.   The old engineer's glance travelled contemptuously from the man's head to his feet and back again.

"Aye!" he said, and his voice was as quiet as usual, and he spoke as deliberately.   "Aye!   On accoont o' y', an' th' like o' y', she's doon noo, doon foor efer.   Wi' regaird t' her bein' an' oold pot, y' may be eenterested t' know thut a wouldn' geeve one o' her foor all o' th' like o' y' th' devil 'd tur-rn oot een a yeear, wor-rkin' dooble sheefts night 'n' day, 'n' with an oonleemited supply o' dir-rt 'n' eegnorance, wheech 's th' kin' o' raw

mateerial he evidently uses,"—and Donald got
out a plug of tobacco and a jack-knife and grinned,
as did Malcolm and the *Duncrieff* stoker.   " Little
Willie " laughed outright,—a ponderous laugh,
which was too much for Johnstone's temper.

" See here ! " he roared, getting red in the face
and still speaking to Donald, " I ain't goin' t' take
any damned cheek from you, see ! You ain't my
chief, an'——"

" No, thenk Go-od ! a'm noot," interrupted
Donald, with his voice harder than I'd ever heard
it.   " When a peeck oot men, a don' choose them
oon accoont o' their bein' coowards.   Y'r a
cooward ; aye ! a beeger cooward th'n ony o' them,
foor a nootice y' got oop 'n' skeeped fir-rst.   O' !
Loord, th' way y' got oover those hummocks 'n'
cloompets wiz a gran' sight," and Donald smiled
and " Little Willie " laughed again.   This was
more than the big stoker could stand.   He roared
an oath and with clenched hands jumped at the
old engineer.   He struck at him with his right
fist, but slipped on a piece of ice buried under the
snow and half fell.   Donald tried to step aside,
but was prevented by the bow of the boat, so he
was probably saved a hard knock by Johnstone
falling.   As the stoker pitched forward against the
boat he caught the engineer's coat and forced him
backward.   I jumped, but was too late to be of
any use.   Wilson had been standing just across

the bow from where Donald was leaning. He vaulted over the boat and lit on the ice beside Johnstone just as he fell. With his feet braced well apart he bent and with both hands seized the stoker's shirt and coat collars at the back of the neck. Then his lips set hard, and with a mighty heave of those big shoulders he lifted the man from the ice as if he were a puppy, and hurled him clear away over the boat. He went past my head as though he had been fired out of a gun, and, going end over end, lit on the sloping side of a piece of snow-covered broken panice a good ten feet from the boat, and slid down into a hole full of slush,—a hole, as Donald would say, "communicatin' wi' th' Goolf o' St. Lawrence." Wilson was left with both hands full of torn woollen goods of various kinds, which he looked at with a pleased smile.

"That should teach him something," he laughed. But it didn't, at least for the moment. The man was evidently as tough as a wire nail. Besides, he had been lucky and had fallen easily, and was no more than dazed, and that only for a moment. Then, as he wallowed up to his middle in slush, with his legs waving around in the icy waters of the north end of Northumberland Strait, and with a good part of the back torn out of his coat and shirt, he realized the indignity that had been heaped upon him. His temper was not

helped by Donald asking in a sympathetic voice
the traditional question on such occasions: " Ees
th' water coold?" He climbed out of the hole
and came on again as mad as a wounded bull
moose, and swearing oaths that were new even
to me,—me with a sixteen-year experience of the
British Navy. He rushed for Donald again.   It
was my turn now.   Some recollections of the old
Centaur came up in a second, and made my nerves
tingle.   I stepped forward.

" Try a man a little younger," I said; " put up
your hands."   The man had evidently not been
accustomed to fighting with his captain, and he
was a bit taken aback; but it was only for a second.
He was fairly wild with rage, and I am not very
big,—that is compared with Wilson and some of
the others,—so he put up his hands and came on,
not very scientifically, perhaps, but he came.   I
had only to side-step.   I am afraid my temper got
a little the better of me, and I used my left a little
harder than I intended.   But then, you know,
when a big lout like that tries to strike an old
man like Donald,—well, it's difficult to feel for
him as you would for another man.   I know they
had to carry him aboard the *Liffey,* but he was
around all right the next day, though his jaw and
eye looked a bit swollen and discoloured.   It improved him in the end.   It appeared later that
Mr. Johnstone was considered a bit of a fighter

among the men, and I noticed a most marvellous increase in the respect with which they treated me; not that they hadn't been respectful before, but now they were unnecessarily so, as, by the way, was Mr. Johnstone himself. In fact, whenever the chance presented itself on the trip south he used to make a point of coming up to me and making some more or less irrelevant remark about something which usually neither he nor I knew anything about,—such as the probable type of weather for the following two days, or something of that sort. The conciliatory and truckling human being is indeed a marvel in his methods. I am digressing.

The little episode had been watched by all on the *Liffey* and had helped to break the spell which the almost unbelievably sudden loss of the old *Shannon* had thrown over every one. But still we went aboard quietly, so quietly that the rattle of the blocks as the ice-boat was hoisted to the davits sounded harsh and seemed to grate on my nerves. After getting on deck, one or two of the deserting stokers sidled up to Donald to have a talk. The old man waved them away with a sweep of the stem of the little pipe.

"Booys," he said, "a'm noot sayin' y' were noot right een goin' when y' deed. Thut wiz foor y' t' decide yersel's. But a wud noot a' doon eet mysel', an' a deedn', as y' know. But keep away

froom me. Keep away foor a few days ony way.
A don' want t' talk t' y',"—and keep away they
did. Poor Donald! he had gotten in love with
the *Shannon* as he never had with any vessel or
engine, and, do you know, for days he would
hardly say a word. He stayed on the *Liffey's*
bridge with us all, and smiled when we smiled,
and answered questions in monosyllables, but I
don't think I heard him speak more than a sentence or two at a time for a full week. Occasionally, when there was a stop in the conversation,
he would be silent, gazing out over the ice for a
minute or two, and then he would take the little
pipe from his lips, look into its bowl, and say
slowly and musingly, without any apparent refer-
ence to anyone:

"Wull, wull! Eet wiz a great shame. She wiz
a gran' good boat, the *Shannon*, wi' as gran' a set
o' engines as efer swung a wheel. Damn those
meeserable coowards!"—and he would hum to
himself and smoke.

About a week afterward he was leaning over
the rail of the bridge, and Johnstone was going
forward.

"Wull, Meester Johnstone," he said, "hoo d' y'
feel after y'r bath? Y' nefer toold me hoo y'
liked th' water!" Though Johnstone didn't answer, he had developed sufficient common sense
to grin and go on. After that Donald was more

like the Donald of old. Sandy McKinnon and
he became great friends and would sit and burr-r
stories at each other in the broadest of mixed
Highland and Lowland Scotch for an hour at a
time. That was the time to hear about glands
and throttles and cranks and shafts and extraordinary indicator diagrams—and some of Donald's would be extraordinary without doubt.

CHAPTER X.

FROM the moment we started once more, and left on the ice the little piles of wreckage that represented all that was left of the *Shannon,* the *Liffey* had troubles of her own, for the ice in the Strait was heavier than I had ever seen it before. However, the *Liffey* had been built for just such troubles, and, though it seemed like treason to an old friend to have to admit it, she went through places where the *Shannon* would have stuck. But hard times were not yet over, for we got one or two stiff storms from the southeast, storms that kept the *Liffey's* captain peering anxiously into the snow ahead for hours at a time. He had recovered from the results of his accident, and Wilson and I took turns with him in working the ship. Once the ice jammed hard into the Strait, and for three solid days the *Liffey* gave up and waited for a shift of wind, while Wilson used to go out and parade around the pack like a polar bear looking for seals. He was always the same, investigating everything as he went, with as much method as though he were out on a purely scientific expedition, and yet he always had all the human sentiment that so many scientists lack.

On that trip south I learned to know him better than ever before. The knowledge that he had at last won the love of Gertrude MacMichael seemed to come to him slowly, and, as it came, to hide more and more the iron in his character already so well cloaked by his wonderful control of his emotions and passions and by his infinite generosity. Whatever else he was, he was first of all a man, and the man in him controlled the marvellously precise machine that has made him the scientist most of you know so well. Think of the difference between him and the round-shouldered, spectacled, bloated, flabby, single-grooved recording-machines too often known as scientists. Do you think that the generalizations of such physically and mentally lopsided specimens can be balanced as they should? I am afraid that the majority of scientists—who should be the broadest men in the world before daring to deal with the questions they undertake—tire me with their jargon more than any other people I meet, more than the lady of Society when she's hot on the blood trail of a better woman,—and this is saying much. And the final stage of absurdity is reached when a biologist,—the limpet that clings to a rivet-head on the bottom of an onrushing battleship can tell you as much about her engines as the biologist from his science can tell you of the

Ultimate,—when a biologist, from his generalizations, tells you that there is no God.   David Wilson settled down to a talk one day and told me of
the doubts and the struggles that had come and
gone—gone when he learned the metaphysical im-
possibility of the human point of view being the
ultimate one—and left him with an intelligent faith
in all the influences that had so far tended for what
we call good,—a faith more intelligent but as simple as that of a child, and for which I loved him as
much as for other things.   The greater dangers
and troubles of the last few weeks were over, and
he could let himself free from the relentless control
and vigilance which had been guiding his every
impulse; and yet, while I knew the change, there
was hardly an outward sign to indicate it.   He was
the same methodical, alert, broad-shouldered, iron-
muscled, soft-voiced man, with the same frank, winning, almost womanly smile, the same gliding way
of walking that, wherever you saw it, always recalled the woods, and the same impressive way of
doing difficult things without much apparent effort
that was peculiar to him.

Yet, though there was but little outward evidence of it, I could see that the girl's entirely changed attitude with regard to him affected his every
thought; it could hardly be otherwise.   What a
change it was!   I thought of the evening after the
boat race, when a lithe, sun-browned, entrancing,

unapproachable girl used to laugh, half wearily, at each indication of his involuntary attraction. I smiled when I thought of how he settled down contentedly in competition with everything from bank clerks to Cabinet ministers, and for two years the only encouragement he got was in the fact that none of the others made any more progress than he.

Now, after having gone on his way with a profound disregard of its apparent lack of effect; after having risked his life a dozen times, each time belittling both the act and the motive,—the barriers had at last gone down, and MacMichael's daughter, impulsive as ever, had rushed to the opposite extreme, and now showed him that she loved him with all the love that a fearlessly frank, open-hearted, healthy young woman is capable of. I often watched them while we were talking—talking about things in general. Their eyes would meet, and the looks—they contained all the past and present and a good deal of the future—I shall remember for all time. They were both characteristically gay always, but now the girl was constantly riotously gay, a volcano of life, bubbling over. And of course it had its effect on him.

But there was something more; something that couldn't be accounted for by any influence of his own or Miss MacMichael's moods. One day he and I were in the wheel-house alone. We had been talking, and had stopped while the *Liffey* was forcing her way through a perfect wall of clumpets. Wilson had taken the wheel, and when I had worked into lighter ice again and looked back into the wheel-house he was gazing absently down at the binnacle and laughing to himself. It was an infectious sort of laugh, and I joined in.

"What's the trouble with you?" he asked, still laughing.

"Laughing at you," I said. "You'd laugh too if you saw a chap gazing down at what you'd always taken for an ordinary binnacle, and laughing as though it were a mutascope with an act by Dan Leno in it."

"Hmm!" he mused, "the binnacle didn't have much to do with it. But it's sometimes very funny when all sorts of complex situations have come up, and you've gotten through them all,—situations to which you have always held the key: it's funny to look back and see what might have happened; and then—though I know it's weak—one can't help deriving some pleasure from having fooled not only some of the people some of the time, but all the people all the time, and all on account of a principle which, in the end, the good sensible majority of humanity would probably classify as nothing more than a fad."

"You're a queer genius," I said; "but what under heaven you're talking about now I'm sure I don't know."

"I don't see any particular reason why you shouldn't know now," said Wilson thoughtfully, "unless——Oh! well," and he laughed again, "we'll just let you worry along in your ignorance for the present. Perhaps it wouldn't be fair to the others to tell you before I tell them. It looks as if it were going to clear up, doesn't it?"

"Yes," I said, "it does. But wait. Some day I shall have the chance to talk in inexplicable riddles to you."

"If you don't like it you should let people smile to themselves in peace, without asking questions," he laughed,—and that was as far as I got. A day or two later he turned to me suddenly and said:

"It's marvellous how things work out sometimes, isn't it!" I admitted that it was, and also that I hadn't the least idea in the world what he meant, at which he smiled drily and talked about the weather again. Now what did this all mean. The only thing in the least mysterious about David Wilson was that he had much more money than he was supposed to have——this he had virtually told me—— but how much I didn't know. However, if his father had left him money it could be no affair of mine, beyond the fact that we were great friends and that I therefore took a deep interest in his fortunes. I have already told you my surmise as to his reason for concealing the amount of money he possessed—that he wished to win as a poor man,

if at all, the love of the girl for which he had striven
so hard.   What there could be beyond this I hadn't
the faintest notion.   There was nothing on which
to found even theories, and as theories founded on
nothing are usually wrong I gave up the task and
awaited developments.

We had worked our way south slowly enough,
for the ice was unbelievably heavy, and it was near
the middle of March before we swung southeast
into Northumberland Strait.   Here the pack had
opened up, and the leads of open water ran in every
direction.   The first morning after getting into the
Strait I was up early and out on the forward deck.
The *Liffey* was roaring along beautifully, hammering her way east-southeast, up into the face of a
grand red-and-gold sunrise that turned every ice-
pinnacle into glittering fire and made the water in
the leads seem twice as dark.   Captain Fraser was
in the wheel-house.   I saw him come out and walk
to the front of the bridge, and with his hands on
the rail and his face screwed up stand for a full
minute gazing straight ahead.

"What is it?" I asked.

"If I weren't afraid of losing my reputation I'd
say it was a steamer," was the answer.

"A what!!" I said.

"A steamer.   Wait till I get the glasses."

"I thought we had exhausted about all the *Dun-
crieffs* in this Gulf," I replied, and ran up on the

bridge, wondering if we were in for another rescue of the crew of some boat that, for some mysterious reason, had come into the Gulf, perhaps on an errand similar to that of the *Duncrieff* herself.

Captain Fraser put up the glasses for a second or two, then put them down.

"Well, I'm blessed!" he ejaculated.

"What is it?" I asked.

"The *Walrus!*"

I took the glasses. Sure enough, there was the little old *Walrus,* frost-covered and shining in the red-gold light as though she were silver-plated, careening from side to side, and with her long, ugly ram knocking aside the clumpets in fine style. She was in her own particular pet kind of ice, loose, floating clumpets, and the way she went cavorting along was enough to make the big *Liffey* herself turn green with envy. I called up MacMichael and his daughter and Wilson. Donald came along at the same time.

"Look at that!" I said.

"A steamer!" said MacMichael.

"Aye!" said Donald. "Soom one's been following' th' example o' MacMichael 'n' Coompany, 'n' stairtin' a weenter sairvice between Gre't Breetain 'n' th' Goolf!"

Wilson put up the glasses.

"May I be hanged if it isn't the *Walrus!*" he laughed.

"Yes!" I said, "bound north to Gaspé to rescue the crew of the *Liffcy*. What do you think of that as an example of nerve?"

"I wonder what she would do if she were where we were yesterday!" mused Wilson. "They must have been fearfully worried about us; if they thought both the *Shannon* and *Liffey* were gone, I wonder what they thought they could do with the *Walrus!* I wonder who brought her up here!"

"I think I can answer the last question," said Miss MacMichael.

"Who?" I said.

"Mr. Henderson," said the girl, and I caught her expression. She knew he'd go to the ends of the earth for her, like all the rest.

"Very probably," said Wilson,—and so it turned out.

We shifted our course a point to the eastward, and half an hour later, with her little whistle coughing and spluttering, and squealing jubilantly, as though she'd rescued the three crews herself, the *Walrus* bumped triumphantly up alongside, went *crash bup* into a heavy pan, and stopped with a jerk that must have rattled the teeth of her crew. We stopped the *Liffey*, and the three crews gave a mighty cheer of greeting to the brave little boat that had been plodding along toward unknown dangers to their rescue. An ice-boat was lowered, and five minutes later Henderson, as dapper as ever, with his black moustache as carefully trimmed and himself as faultlessly groomed, climbed over the *Liffey's* rail and tried to shake hands with us all at once, though of course Miss MacMichael got more than her share of attention. A moment later, while everyone was talking, the girl found an excuse to turn away and wandered into the deserted saloon, where she sat down sideways on the piano-stool, ran through the first few bars of Mendelssohn's " Consolation "—with a method like a street piano —then swung round, leaned forward with her chin on her hands, and looked at the carpet. I had gone in to give some orders to the chief steward. I went over beside her and saw that she looked troubled—almost pained.

" He's a dear good fellow, isn't he ! " she said. " They're all dear good fellows to me, much better than I deserve." She was thinking of Henderson. She had felt the warmth in the grasp of his hand, and the look in his eyes that had told her what I very well knew, that apart from all duty he would rather try to go to Cape Gaspé in the *Walrus* for her sake than do anything else in the world for any other woman.

" Do you think," she went on, half-guiltily, " that when, on that night we left Caribou in the *Shannon,* I told him that I would know better how to thank him when we got back,—do you think he could have thought I meant any more than I did?

Often a very little thing will make a man—or a woman—have dreams, dreams that can never be realized." Here was a development,—a new kind of conscience for her: it's a pity there weren't more like her!—I was surprised.

"You dear, hypersensitive, tender-hearted girl," I said. "No, I dont. No sensible man could. But, by the way, you've changed. Three months ago you wouldn't have cared whether you broke the heart of every man alive; but I'm very glad to find that it was through ignorance, and that since you have learned new things you have sympathy for people that are in love as well as for those in other kinds of trouble."

"Trouble!" she said archly, blushing, but with her conscience evidently easier,—and we went on deck again. As we went up to the group about Henderson I caught the word *Aurora*.

"What about the *Aurora?*" I asked.

"The *Aurora!* Oh, she's out too," said Henderson. "She's gone outside, out around the east shore of the Island. She's trying to beat her way to Gaspé up through the open Gulf."

"She won't go far," said Wilson sententiously, "Who's in her,—Grahame [her captain] I suppose!"

"Yes!" said Henderson.

"Whose idea was it—going around the north side of the Island?" asked Wilson, smiling.

"It was suggested by the Honourable Edward Rose,—and he's in her too."

"What!" gasped MacMichael, "not only every boat of the Northumberland Steamship Company out, but the Minister of Marine and Fisheries on the trail too!"

"Have they sent t' Roosia foor th' *Ermak* yet?" queried Donald.

"No," laughed Henderson, "but Mr. Rose has got Irland in the *Amphitrite* circulating around somewhere between Cape Smoky and the Magdalen Islands, with orders to work his way into the Gulf as soon as the ice is sufficiently broken up."

"Well, well, well!" was all MacMichael could say, while Wilson roared with laughter.

"It isn't that I'm not duly appreciative," he said; "but it's funny to have the Canadian branch of Her Majesty's Navy out in search of you. Yes, and it's still funnier to think of the *Amphitrite,* hardly more than a good-sized yacht, going to the rescue of the *Liffey,*"—and he looked over at the armoured sides and up at the big funnel of the ice-crusher.

"I hope Mr. Rose won't get into any trouble," said Miss MacMichael, evidently feeling the responsibility of being sufficiently attractive to have Ministers of the Crown rushing around in steamers in the ice in the attempt to rescue her from supposed danger—though of course she was quite aware that the Department of Marine's interest in the welfare of the jeopardized steamer would be the official reason for the Minister's trip.

" He'll never get far enough to be in danger," said Wilson, " and, besides, the *Aurora* is a very staunch little boat."

Mr. MacMichael turned to Henderson.

" Mr. Henderson," he said, " I'm afraid I'm not enough of a talker to tell you how much I appreciate all this. No matter if I were; nothing I could say could ever tell you how I have felt through all the times when these wonderful boats have been working to save the poor old *Duncrieff,* and my men, and myself. The Northumberland Steamship Company has put me in a debt which all the resources of MacMichael and Company could never repay fully. But you'll not lose anything by it if I can help it."

" No," added the girl, with her arm round her father, " not if MacMichael and Company have to begin all over again."

" Wheech, coonsiderin' th' coomparitive health o' th' fir-rm, ees eemprobable," added Donald, with some truth. Henderson's face was a positive study. He was evidently seeing the humour of some situation keenly. He chewed his lip to keep from laughing, and got red in the face.

" I have already told your daughter," he began spasmodically, " that the Company——that if you

appreciate the services of the boats half as much
as the Company appreciates the chance to be of service to Miss MacMichael and yourself, the Company will be well——" and here he looked at Wilson, who was leaning against the rail studying the
various expressions of the group and with his mouth
screwed up at one corner, and went off into a fit of
uncontrollable laughter.

Wilson's smile broadened, and MacMichael looked from him to Henderson—who, in trying to
choke down a series of chuckles, was gurgling like
the half-fed suction of a bilge-pump—and his face
wore an expression of the most violent amazement
mingled with perhaps a little temper.

" By Heavens! " he said, a bit tartly, " you'd
think that losing a steamer like the *Shannon,* and
risking the lives of a hundred men or so was a big
joke with you." Then he softened down. " Oh!
I know it's some vagary of yours, Dave," he continued, " but what it is I'm damned if I know.
However, you've done the work and saved the lot
of us, so it's none of my business,"—but MacMichael looked puzzled, as he did, on occasions, for
some time afterward.

" Don't mind us," said Wilson, " you're perfectly
right. It's only a vagary, perhaps a foolish one,
but now its reason for being has gone for ever and
you'll know all there is to know about it soon
enough."

MacMichael didn't notice, but I saw a strange disappointed look come suddenly over Henderson's face as Wilson spoke, and to hide it he turned and asked me about some of the details of the sinking of the *Shannon*.

"You're coming aboard, aren't you?" asked Wilson. He had seen the change too, and his voice was more than usually low and with a ring of true sympathy in it.

"Yes!" said Henderson, and a minute later the ice-boat was on the way to the *Walrus* for his bag.

Miss MacMichael had watched him curiously and with a woman's perception, and had seen the change more quickly than any of us. She knitted her brows and looked absently over at the *Walrus*. Then her face cleared, as though a great light had broken over her mind, and I saw her cheeks redden while her eyelids snapped. She started vigorously humming Mendelssohn's "Wedding March" in a most triumphant way, viciously beating time with her foot on a glass deck-light. Her intuition had evidently led her further than I could see. She was beaming the most radiant smiles on me.

"Familiar tune," I ventured. The others had moved away.

"Very!" she laughed, with sparkling eyes that set off her gorgeous colouring in a way that made me gasp. Like MacMichael I was puzzled, and like MacMichael I remained so for some time.

Ten minutes later the throb of the *Liffey's* engine started, and with the *Walrus* following close we bore off southeast again on the way to Caribou. The ice was very open and we made splendid progress. The next day Cape Tormentine loomed up ahead, and what should we meet but the *Aurora*. She had failed to get north at all on the outside of the Island, and was bound up the Strait to help the *Walrus* rescue the *Liffey*. We took the Honourable Edward Rose aboard, and the *Aurora* swung in behind the *Walrus*. The *Liffey* was apparently engaged in making a collection of Miss Gertrude Mac-Michael's most violent admirers, and also gradually forming a most imposing procession. It was a sight now to see her parading down the Strait with the *Walrus* and *Aurora* following, ostensibly independently, but nevertheless sticking to the path of crushed clumpets and lolly left by the *Liffey's* resistless bows.

As the white tower of the Cape Tormentine lighthouse showed up, with the glasses we could see hundreds of people lining the banks, watching us pass down. Rose told us that the attempt to rescue the *Duncrieff* had become not only locally famous, but world-famous; that the newspapers were telling——but it's not so long ago but that you yourselves will remember what they said; so we felt quite notable and watched the moving specks on shore with peculiar interest. I can fully imag-

ine that the sight of three ice-crushers moving in
line down past Cape Traverse through the ice from
the north must have been an imposing spectacle in
its way, especially as two steamers that might be
in the procession, and one of them, a squat, pram-
bowed, big-funnelled boat that should be in it,—
the poor old *Shannon,*—were missing. The Cape
Tormentine light saluted, and the *Liffey's* red ensign was fished out of the locker and went whipping
down three times until it dragged in the boiling
slush under her trembling counter. We signalled
" All Well," and had the satisfaction of knowing
that twenty minutes later they would know it in
Caribou; then, with all of us feeling happier than
we had felt for many a day—for in the last week
or so it was the thought of the others that had worried us more than any thought for ourselves—the
red ensign was pulled down again and stowed.

The ensign was stowed, but not before it had had
its effect on me. I'd seen it hanging hot and limp
and dusty at Malta, hotter and limper and dustier
at Melbourne, still hotter, though clean, at Colombo
and at Bombay, reeking wet and clinging to the
staff at Esquimault, and just as wet but snapping
at the spanker-gaff of a barque in St. George's
Channel. With a red cross on a white field I'd
seen the same old jack floating out most quietly
and majestically over the *Centaur,* and again the
jack alone blowing out over the Thames from un-

der the golden crown above the Victoria Tower,—
yes, and floating lazily over Her Majesty's Theatre
and the Carlton. All this brought up thoughts of
the times that had been and of the ineradicable Miss
Kathleen Tyrrell,—and I winced.

That evening it came in a thick, white, March
mist, driving over the floes, and as the ice was fairly
heavy we got down well clear of Jourimain Shoal,
the *Walrus* and the *Aurora* drew in alongside, and
we stopped for the night.

Everybody aboard was hilarious,—everybody but
me. My thoughts ran along through the scenes
called up by the sight of the red ensign. The Honourable Edward Rose, and MacMichael, and Wilson, and Henderson stayed down in the saloon after
dinner. I went up in the wheel-house and sat in
the dark, and looked out through the open door
over to where the mist drove wet past the yellow
lights of the *Aurora,* and listened to the drip from
the overhanging edges of the floes, the occasional
sss-plup as a piece would break off a melting clumpet and slide into the still water, and the sleepy,
far-away, throbbing hum of the *Liffey's* dynamos.
Up from the forecastle companion-way came a
stream of light, the rasp of a forecastle fiddle, and
an exceeding great voice singing, " It was Friday
morning when we set sail,"—and then fifty voices,
" from a squeak to a roar," thundering the chorus:

" For the ocean waves may roll,
  And the stormy winds may blow,
  As we poor sailor lads go skippin' up aloft,
  And the land-lubbers lie down below, below, below,
  And the land-lubbers lie down belo-o-o-w."

Even the song brought things back stronger than ever, for I'd heard it almost everywhere I'd seen the red ensign. Everything that brought back those days brought back London. I could feel the sway of the coach, and the drag of the black four on the webs, as we rolled out to that Derby. I could hear the blatant song of the horn as we rumbled over Putney Bridge and out on the road to Epsom through the clouds of grey dust. I could see the crimson flush of the cheeks of the girl beside me, and the drooping lids showing only a line of the beautiful blue eyes under a white Panama grass hat,—with some crimson silk wound round it in some wonderful way,—and proud lips that I only looked at at the risk of running down a pony trap, or a tandem of mokes partly dressed in articles of female attire,—articles usually unseen in public except in London W. on very rainy days, and then only for a comparatively short time,—and dragging a coster family, two bottles of gin, and a union jack. Those were great days. Then I went back to the ship, thinking I was going to win; and later she told me she didn't love me and never could,— never could!—me! who'd had women, and beautiful women, good and bad, thrown at my head and feet until I'd grown perfectly indifferent; and she, the only one of the lot I'd cared for—and I'd have given my life for her, for she was worth all the rest of them put together—asked me to try to be sensible and not to talk about "love—idiocy:" and then, at the moment when I knew that her mood gave me no earthly chance, I lost all my balance— the balance that I used to talk about, to myself— and asked her to marry me, and she refused, of course. She wouldn't have accepted me then if she had loved me, which she didn't. At the same time I knew she didn't love anyone. Then I gave it up, along with everything else, and went out to Canada, to get educated,—educated!—I, who knew all kinds of women—but one.

Providence had been kind, and I'd had a good chance for education. I'd been thrown with a girl apparently so little affected by the love of men— and the best of their race—that Kitty Tyrrell's impregnability no more compared with hers than the armour of a protected cruiser does with that of a battleship. Yet she'd succumbed, and I'd seen the fight through from beginning to end.

Over from the *Aurora* came the *pink-a-pank* of a banjo, and I was gazing out into the mist and beginning to think I had made a mistake,—in fact was quite sure that I'd made a mistake,—when the rigging in front of me jerked, as with the weight of a man, the ratlines sagged and shook as someone's head appeared above the boat deck, and a moment later a young lady swung herself down by her hands and dropped with an elastic thud at the door of the wheel-house.

"That's one way of coming up!" I said.

"Extremely sensible and useful one!" was the answer; "but now tell me, what do you mean by sitting up here in the dark and moping. Just thinking! Oh, I gave you credit for that at least, if you were awake: but what were you thinking about?"

"Things that—well—things that I've seen and done."

"Quite so. Most people do,—often. I've no doubt that they were most extraordinary things, too, in this case. But there's no necessity for choosing this time and place. Now, see here, Captain Ashburn,"—the girl in the blanket suit sat down on the cover of a fire-bucket and rested her elbows on her knees and her chin on her hands, as was a habit of hers,—"I don't want any mysteries. I've known you for a long time now—years—and you think you know me well enough to assume a fatherly air, call me your 'dear girl,' and preach on various subjects: and, by the way, I'm always glad when you do, for you're always funny, and sometimes even interesting. But you've never told me very much about yourself; not that you didn't want to, but you thought I wouldn't be interested, or sympathetic, or useful. I would have been interested and perhaps even sympathetic at any time, but now I probably know enough even to be useful. I've watched you with most extraordinary care—you should feel honoured—ever since that night after the famous boat race two years ago, and I know, of course, that it is a woman, but even I couldn't tell what she is like without some further data. All I can say is that, with one exception, you've been the most marvellously constant individual I've ever seen—except once or twice, and then your inconstancy flattered me very much, and incidentally went in a perfectly safe direction,"—and as the girl laughed I could see her eyes sparkle even in the half-dark.

" Now," she went on, without giving me a chance to speak, " I'm going to sit here on this bucket, and out here in the Strait of Northumberland, in the ice, you're going to tell me all about it, immediately,— all! do you understand?—and if you don't acknowledge that I've been a help to you when we're through this little interview, I'll—let me see, what will I do—I'll eat the leather loop on that whistle-rope! Now, begin! and remember, everything! Every solitary thing! "

" That's an awful threat," I said, " and it must be a great thing to be gifted with intuition like yours; but my confession would only be one of weakness, though I didn't think it was weakness at the time. However, I know you better than any living woman, and if you command I suppose it's for me to obey," and I told her the whole story, and how the *Shannon* got her name. She was silent until I had finished, though once or twice she shifted with a jerk on her seat. Then she got up and came over and sat beside me.

"Well!" she said, "this is the most extraordinary thing that has ever happened to me in my life!"

"How? What do you mean?" I said, a bit surprised at the girl's manner.

"Was this Kathleen Tyrrell a niece of old Sir Bedford Tyrrell, who was killed in the Maori war?"

"Yes!" I said, almost paralysed with astonishment, "but how——"

"And did she live a good deal of the time with her aunt in a square house with a big stone portico in Belgrave Square?"

"Yes!" I said; "but how under heaven do you know?"

"Do you remember when we went to England last year?"

"Yes!"

"Well! old Sir Bedford's younger brother is the senior partner in the firm that builds all Dad's steamers in Belfast. They built the *Duncrieff*."

"What, Hansard and Blake?" I said. I remembered now having heard that one of Kitty's relatives had something to do with this firm. "But I didn't

think you would know anything of them personally."

"But I do. When I was in England the last
time I met Lady Tyrrell at the launch of the *Dunbar*,
and afterward was at her house in Belgrave Square
three or four times. She was a dear old lady. She
seemed to be impressed with me, for some reason,
and told me all about her beautiful niece, Kathleen;
how a captain in the Navy had fallen violently in
love with her at first sight—'excellent family, too,'
she said, 'one of the oldest in England'—had proposed to her after having known her five or six
weeks; how she had refused him through some
whim, though she really loved him; how he had
gone to 'the Colonies,' she wasn't quite sure where,
she thought the East Indies somewhere; and how
the girl, never hearing from him, and knowing no
way of explaining, even if she could find him, left
London, and, almost broken-hearted, went back to
live with her father in the little Irish village where
she was born and where she first met him. I remember at the time thinking it was a very romantic
and silly story, and that they were idiots, the pair
of them."

"Gertrude MacMichael," I gasped, "is that all
true?"

"Perfectly true!" she said. I sat fairly stunned
for a full minute, while over through the dark and
mist from the *Aurora* came the *pank-a-pank-a-pank-*

pank-pank! of the banjo, playing, quite irrelevantly, "The Water-melon Hanging on the Vine."

"Yes, they were a pair of idiots;" I at last managed to say, though with hot flushes running over me; "or, at least one of them was an idiot." There was silence again for a few minutes. The sound of the banjo on the *Aurora* was drowned by another chorus from the *Liffey's* forecastle. Then the girl spoke.

"Well," she said, "what about that leather loop on the whistle-rope? Will I have to eat it?"

"No, bless your dear heart, you won't," I said, jumping up; "the loop is perfectly safe."

"When I started," laughed the girl, "I hardly expected to win its safety in such a wonderful way. Come along! We shall go down to the saloon."

Even Wilson showed his surprise at the things I did and said that night. An hour after I had smiled a good-night at Miss MacMichael, when I was leaving to turn in, I heard Henderson explaining to Mr. Rose something to the effect that "Poor old Ashburn——couldn't——feeling well ——cleared out after dinner——never knew him to take a drop before."

I didn't sleep that night. To-morrow we would be in Caribou—if we had luck. I had visions. The mist cleared away and the stars came out, and a warm March wind came up. I couldn't stand my room; I had to have something big to look at; so I went out on deck and away up to the *Liffey's* bows, and, sheltering myself in the lee of a big badly stowed working jib, looked out over the pack, over to where the *Aurora* lay, with the *Walrus* a little astern of her, and back at the wheel-house and funnel of the *Liffey* looming black against the stars, and listened to the March wind, singing, singing, singing through the hawse-pipes. Now, I'm not very imaginative, but, as I said, that night I had visions, and the wind in the hawse-pipes and the hum of the dynamos got together and played tunes,—tunes that I used to hear in the old Savoy, and through the tunes I could hear the click-click-click-click-click of the hoofs of a horse in a rubber-tired brougham rolling down silent Pall Mall, and catch the swish of the water sluicing the day's dirt out of Trafalgar Square.

I took no count of the minutes or hours I stayed there, but I stayed until I saw the binnacle light turned on up in the wheel-house and heard Captain Fraser ring to stand by. I went on the bridge, and a couple of minutes later the *Liffey* started bumping and grinding off to the southeast, with the *Walrus* and *Aurora* following. I went in, took my morning bath, made a most elaborate and beautiful toilet, and went on deck again in time to see the big yellow flashes of Cape Tormentine light disappearing astern on the northern horizon, like a flying-away lightning-bug; and the sky to the southeast was getting grey.

CHAPTER XI.

A T breakfast I could see that the Honourable Edward Rose and Henderson had, probably not without some pain, arrived at a true knowledge of the situation, and had taken their definite passive positions in the new order of things in a way that showed they were diplomatists or had common sense enough to know that resistance was useless. During the meal Mr. David Wilson and Miss Gertrude MacMichael beamed—it was more on my account than their own, for I found afterward she had told him the little story. MacMichael would talk of getting home, and of the new *Duncrieff* that was to be, and then be silent and eat and look puzzled for five minutes or so, at the end of which time I'd hear him swearing softly under his breath, something to the effect that "he'd be damned if he saw——" and so forth. Mr. Henderson and Mr. Rose would talk agreeably to all of us about incidents of the trip, politics, the weather, and such unlike subjects, Mr. Rose descanting especially on the "interest he had always taken in the problem of Gulf navigation in winter, and the chagrin he

had felt that no one in Canada had sufficient
energy or ingenuity to develop such a line as
these Northumberland Company's boats, but had
to leave the credit in English hands." All I can
remember about what I did is that I sat and ate,
said " yes " or " no " or whatever I thought fitted
the conversation best or would give me the least
trouble in the end.

It was a day to be remembered. There was not
a patch of cloud in the whole sky. The sun shone
with a dazzling white glare, the water in the leads,
which stretched in every direction shimmered
as blue as on a summer afternoon. The pans
and clumpets, white and green, were melting fast,
the latter in all sorts of queer hour glass shapes,
with tops like the tops of big mushrooms, breaking off, coming down with a crush and sliding
plup into the water. Little lone clumpets were
navigating around by themselves, with the ripples
insulting them by washing clear over their peaks,
—peaks which used to be so high that the big
black ice-crusher, that now roared over them
without even feeling the shock, would turn aside
when they showed up ahead and try another path.
The breeze blew in from the southwest warm and
moist, and the damp, hot air, seething up over
the reeking floes, distorted everything out of all
resemblance to itself or anything else, making the
Walrus and *Aurora,* wallowing along astern, by

turns loom up big and fierce, and look for all the world like the *Powerful* and the *Terrible,* then like a pair of mogul locomotives with masts, and again, as if they might be a couple of little volcanic islands being dragged through the ice by the devil. The lanes were full of seals, velvet ducks, cockawees, and golden-eyes, and everywhere were black-backed gulls, burgomasters, kittiwakes, and herring-gulls, watching the mergansers fishing, and robbing them when it seemed fit and profitable. Up and down the Strait went big V's of Canada geese, honking in a way to give a sportsman chills, with here and there a long swinging pr-r-r-r-uping line of brant, and a bunch of dusky ducks, with their white undercoverts flashing in the sun as they wheeled and thundered away at seventy miles an hour, away from the three big black smoke-vomiting machines that were swimming along below them. It was spring; the typical shining, crashing, dripping, reeking, honking, quacking spring day of the beautiful Gulf, when the sound of whistling wings is constant, and the weird cry of the cockawee comes always from the Lord knows where.

The ice was getting more and more open, and noon saw us well past Point Prim. When we came on deck after lunch the red banks of MacDonald's Head were in sight, with the Roaring Bull beyond, and by twenty minutes to three the

Liffey, leaving the *Walrus* and the *Aurora* to work their way in alone, put on such a final burst of speed that the water and lolly were washing over her deck astern, and with her syren howling an acknowledgment of the red table-cloth waved at us from a window of the quarantine hospital, and flying every flag we could find in the lockers, steamed in past Caribou Light and went hissing through the rotten board-ice stretching up the three miles to the Northumberland Company's wharf.

Mrs. Wilson told me about it afterwards.

"I didn't think people could get in such a state of excitement," she said. "After the *Shannon* had proved what she could do in the Straits they got to put implicit faith in her; to believe that she could stand anything that ice could do. When they heard that she was too badly crushed to get home alone, and that the *Liffey* had to go to her assistance, they made up their minds that the *Liffey* would be no more likely to get back than the *Shannon,* and when the weeks went by with no sign of her, and the *Walrus* and the *Aurora* started out on what all felt must be a hopeless task, Caribou was almost in mourning. There was hardly a working family in the town that didn't have a relative or a friend on either the *Duncrieff,* the *Shannon,* the *Liffey,* the *Walrus,* or the *Aurora.* When the telegram '*Steamers*

Liffey, Aurora, and Walrus passed Cape Tormentine bound south at four o'clock this afternoon. Report all well,' was posted in the door of the Western Union office, every man, woman, and child in Caribou had to read it for him or herself. We felt thankful enough too, you may be sure, though we never had any doubt that you would get back safely. People began to gather about the wharves at daylight in the morning, and one or two of the younger men drove over to the north shore to be able to report you first. They drove in about noon, wild with excitement, and saying they could see your smoke somewhere off Point Prim. Then every soul in Caribou crowded about the Company's pier, so that Mrs. Mac-Michael and I could hardly get through. The crowd finally picked us up and literally carried us to the end of the wharf. They began to shout as soon as the *Liffey's* bow came in sight around the point, and really, from that moment they never stopped. You know the rest."

Yes, we knew the rest. Mr. MacMichael and his daughter, Wilson, Mr. Rose, Henderson, Donald, and I,—yes, and Betsie—I mustn't forget Betsie, who had condescended to come among us this once,—were on the bridge. Every man of the three crews not needed below was on deck, of course. Ashore the snow had gone, except in a few patches, and the sloping town with its nest of church steeples stood out against the cloudless sky, beautiful as ever. As we came opposite the east end we could see that the streets were perfectly deserted; there was not even a dog or a horse in sight. When we swung around the Government pier, and looked up at the Company's wharf it was really a great sight,—a sight I can see now almost as plainly as at the time. The wharf and all the adjoining wharves were covered with a densely packed, swaying crowd, rocking with one continuous roar of cheering. As the *Liffey* ran slowly up to the end of the pier the cheering lessened, and when the boat came near enough for faces to be seen it ceased entirely and there was a dead silence broken only by the grind of breaking ice. I knew what it meant. That " All Well " in the telegram might not necessarily be all inclusive. Each man, woman, and child in the crowd was looking for someone, some particular one, and as we drew nearer the wharf it was easy to see that they were finding them.

" Hi! Jimmy, lad, ees that you? Och! Thank God y're safe! " would come the voice of an old man. Then a fat woman would dance up and down, waving a baby in her enthusiasm, and screaming " Henery! Hullo! Henery, how are y'? " and " Henery," a stoker from the *Duncrieff,* would wave his oil-soaked cap and yell, " All right, mother." Another voice would inquire facetious-

ly of " Little Willie " how many polar-bear skins
he had brought home, and so it went until the
rattling steam-smothered winches had dragged the
Liffey to the coping of the pier.

Donald smoked the little black pipe and took
in the scene in silence.

" Eet's too bad," he said finally, " thut th' poor
old *Shannon* eesn' here. She desairves all th'
credit foor thees after all." Then his mood
changed, and he smiled, and took the little pipe
from his lips as the crowd cheered again.

" Thees ees better th'n beein' alive t' read y'r
own obeetuary notice," he said, " a've na doot
thut plainty o' those stokers neyver knew hoo
mooch value they were t' th'r families teel noo!"

" Is everyone safe? " came a voice from the
crowd, and suddenly there was a deep silence
again, the peculiar rustling silence of many people.

" Every soul! " shouted Wilson. Both the purport and source of the answer set them cheering
again. The gangway was run aboard, and we
left Captain Fraser leaning over the rail of the
bridge, beaming down on the crowd,—it was the
proudest day of his life,—and filed ashore to meet
Mrs. MacMichael and Mrs. Wilson on the pier.
Hands to be shaken were thrust in from every
direction, and I, though I didn't deserve it especially, was patted on the back,—patted much as a
bear pats an ox. Wilson and Henderson were

carried backward and forward until the former got his back against the warehouse, and even then he had to use all his strength to shield his mother and Mrs. MacMichael and her daughter and Betsie from the crush of good-natured men and laughing, crying women.

But the crowning scene of all was just after Wilson and Mr. MacMichael and I had worked our way to the warehouse and formed a sort of breastwork in front of the four women. Without looking for gangways the men of the three crews climbed over the *Liffey's* rail and poured down onto the pier. Groups of the particular friends of each man would surround him and try to force their way toward the town. One of these groups has made me laugh every time I've thought of it since. The friends of Malcolm and " Little Willie " had surrounded those worthies, and Donald, Henderson and the Honourable Edward Rose had gotten involved in the group and were rushed struggling along on the top of the human wave. Henderson was light and kept on top beautifully, and the Honourable Edward would disappear, and turn up again a few seconds later with another dint in the Derby hat he had put on before coming ashore, until at last the hat was a pulp, and the Minister threw it away and laughed with ʰhe rest as he fought his way through bare-headed. Malcolm and " Little Willie " pursued two entirely different systems in dealing with their difficulties. When the six-foot-six giant would find that he was being carried off his feet and down, he would glance about him for two solid-looking heads and on each of these he would place a big hairy hand and bear down like a man climbing out of deep snow, until he had regained his position, head and shoulders above the crowd. Above the noise we could hear the owners of the heads, without being able to look up to see who it was, ask " who th' hell he thought he wuz shovin'," or something to that effect; and then, without ever learning the answer, or even to whom the question was addressed, they would succumb to the pressure and go down under the rush, down into the tangle of legs and feet. Malcolm had to adopt different tactics. He wasn't tall enough to use Willie's system. His big fuzzy tam-o'-shanter would disappear, and then, a moment later, near the spot where he was last seen, there would be a great upheaval of the crowd, a halo of legs, red faces, and reaching hands, as though the ground beneath had burst, and in the centre of the disturbance the fuzzy tam-o'-shanter would appear again, followed by Malcolm's big shoulders. Now Donald, not having either Malcolm's strength or " Little Willie's " length, could pursue neither of these methods. It was one of the rare occasions in this life when keeping perfectly cool, as such, was

of no avail in accomplishing one's salvation.
Three times Donald went down, each time studying the situation more thoroughly. At last, after
noting "Little Willie's" ingenious, ingenuous,
and impartial method of abasing others that he
himself might be exalted, and seeing the great
success of its practical operation, he evidently
came to regard him as the most comfortable and
safest man to rely on. In a way that rather surprised me, considering that Donald was not as
young as some of us, he climbed up Willie's long
back and wound his legs round his waist and his
arms round his neck. The black pipe was, as ever,
clenched tightly between his teeth. He grinned
and hung on.

"Noo, Wullie," he said, "a'm quite coomfortable. Y' can go on 'n' a'll keep th' beggars away
froom y'r back," and Willie accepted the charge
and went on. Johnstone was near. He looked
up at Donald and laughed.

"Now's yer chance, ladies an' gentlemen," he
thundered, "come right along, now's yer chance
t' see a real live gorilla just imported from the
wilds of Africa, climbin' on the hairy neck of the
spotted giraffe," and the crowd roared—because
it was a crowd. Donald, with one arm around
Willie's forehead, took the black pipe from his
mouth and waved it aloft with a commanding
gesture. There was silence again.

" Ladies 'n' gentlemen," he began, turning
Willie around by twisting his head.   " Eef y' look
carefully at th' back o' thut mon's coat "—pointing at Johnstone and grinning—" y'll see a beeg
squayre patch aboot th' nape o' th' neck."   Every
eye was turned on the stoker, who saw his mistake
and tried to work his way back into the crowd:
but there was no room for manœuvers of this sort.
" Wull," continued Donald placidly, with a com-
prehensive sweep of his eyes over the sea of heads,
and another wave of the pipe to command attention, " Woonce upon a time th're wiz a steamer
called th' *Shannon*—she wud 'a' been here noo
but foor a lot o' coowards"—there was a rustle
and murmur of interest and excitement at this,
and Donald saw and realized his power.   Would
he use it?—" 'n' one day——" Donald looked at
Johnstone's red face triumphantly.   " A'll tell y'
th' story soom other time," he said, " a' mus' be
movin' aloong noo," and Willie started struggling
up the wharf, leaving the circle wondering, and
probably filling in the rest of the tale for themselves.

" He's a queer Donald! " I said.

" He's surely that! " said MacMichael, laughing
until the tears came.

A few minutes later the pressure became a bit
lighter and we started up the pier.   MacMichael
and his wife and daughter walked ahead, closely

followed by Betsie with the bundle in the patchwork quilt. The crowd gave way before them,
cheering and shaking hands. A jubilant group of
Miss MacMichael's girl friends struggled up,
flushed and hot and dishevelled, and each of them,
of course, had to be kissed. I remember thinking
at the time that she'd save herself a lot of trouble
and work and give the girls and me a great deal
more pleasure if she'd depute me to do that part
of it. Conceit? Oh, no!—a mere statement of
fact; knowledge based on experience.

Then one or two of MacMichael's captains who
happened to be in Caribou worked their way
through, followed by the greater part of the office
staff, and the last trace of the worry that had
shown in his face in the last few weeks faded away,
and the old smile came back, as kindly as ever.
A moment later I saw the tears running down his
cheeks, as on that night when he left the *Duncrieff*.

Jim MacIntyre lurched up and banged me on
the back in a way that made me think I'd been
eating something I shouldn't have eaten.

" Hi! " I said, " stop that, I'm all right," and I
reached out my left hand and tapped him on the
chest hard enough to send him back into the
crowd.

" Aye ! " he laughed, "yoo're a' recht. Wheyre's
Tonal? "

" The last I saw of him he was riding straddled

on 'Little Willie's' neck to keep from being trampled to death by the crowd. You make a great success of giving people a welcome."

"Aye! they're doin' fery goot. Why deed y' no breeng th' *Shannon?*" he went on, turning to Wilson, who looked solemn as he answered:

"There's no *Shannon* now, Jim, she's at the bottom of the Gulf up off Bay Chaleur—more's the pity!"

"Mye Loord!" was the surprised reply, "d'ye tell me, noo. A'm fery sorry. She wiz a gran' boat. Ah! theyre's Tonal!"—and the big Scotchman went off, waving his arms in the direction of the old engineer, who was still riding along on "Little Willie's" back and placidly smoking.

With the crowd giving way in front and cheering MacMichael on either side, and with an ever-increasing train, we soon formed quite a triumphal procession, that sauntered, talking and laughing, up the hill, until we came to the big iron gates and smooth spruce hedges in front of Mac-Michael's house. We stood and looked down at the pier, still black with the crowd, and heard the rattle of coal down the iron chutes as they coaled the *Liffey*,—a sound that called up the crisp, clear winter night, nearly two months before, when the *Shannon*—God bless her!—was preparing, in the fearful uncertainty, to go to the saw-toothed cape in search of the *Duncrieff*.

MacMichael took Wilson's hand.

"Well, Dave," he said, "thanks to Heaven and you we're home again, though there were times when I wasn't quite sure we would be." The three of us were standing apart from the others. "I know " he went on, "that nothing I could do, nothing that anyone could do, could repay a man, even a young man, for a service of this kind, a service in which you have risked your life over and over again, I can't tell you how I feel. Ashburn knows. But if you were only in the firm; if you were only my own son, so that I could do something practical to show, even in a small way, how much I appreciate the whole thing—though, as I've said often enough already, nothing I can ever do can show that. Don't you think you'd better change your mind and come in with the firm?"

Whether it was only the dark flush from the months of winter and spring winds and sunshine, or whether Wilson was actually blushing, I couldn't tell.

"Mr. MacMichael," he said, "you very well know, as does Ashburn, that any thing I did was only my duty, as it would have been the duty of any other man who knew that part of the Gulf in winter as well as I did. How I, in my turn, appreciate your offer as to the firm I can't very well tell you, but I am afraid it would be impos-

sible for me to do as you suggest. But with regard to my being your son," he laughed, " I'm
not so sure that that might not be accomplished
if you and Mrs. MacMichael were willing. Perhaps you might ask Miss MacMichael about it!"

MacMichael knew, of course, but only then did
he seem to realize that the impossible had come
to pass. I went over and spoke to Mrs. Mac-
Michael and Mrs. Wilson, so I don't know what
he said, but a little later, as we separated, Mac-
Michael was telling Wilson that he thought he
was being adequately rewarded, after all; with
which Wilson seemed to agree.

I walked up with him and his mother, and then
to the telegraph office, where I sent to Kathleen
Tyrrell, Nosmoht, London, a cablegram which
left me a poorer man by some thirty-five dollars.
When I started for home the lower streets were
still jammed with people, each telling his or her
story of the loss of the *Shannon* and of other
events of the trip, and coming to me for verifica-
tion, which, having a conscience, I couldn't always give. As I got nearer the Company's wharf
the crowd got thicker, as did their speech, for
some of them had been celebrating the return
by a few " sneefters o' Scootch." I got more and
more vigorously congratulated for my part in the
affair, until I tried to escape by taking the back
streets and getting home over the hill. It was

no use, however, for the crowd decided, evidently, that an attempt to get away proved that I was doubly deserving of recognition, so they picked me up, and I tried to look dignified while being carried home on the shoulders of two men—one six foot three and the other five foot nine—and followed by a mob of fifteen hundred men and women and Academy students singing—each in-dependently—" *For he's a jolly good fellow,*" and such-like songs, and finishing with " *We won't go home till morning;* " and as far as I know they didn't,—not one of them. Yes, it was a great time in Caribou when the *Liffey* got home with MacMichael.   Nowadays when you go into Johns-ton Hendrie's store, or into Vail's blacksmith shop, or into the fire station where Donald and the black pipe and the black cocker spaniel pre-side, all the stories of things that happened at that time or thereabout begin " Aboot thr-ree weeks afore th' *Leeffey* got back," or " D'ye mind th' beeg gale th' fortnight after th' *Leeffey* got back?   Well——" and so forth.   Yes, it was a great time in Caribou.

After I was thrown in through my own front door, and my old housekeeper had gotten through her preliminary greetings,—I had a narrow escape from being kissed,—she stopped talking so sud-denly, while I was taking my boots off, that I looked up to see what had happened.   She was very seldom troubled by any stoppage of speech. She was evidently thinking, though I don't know that I ever remember a time before when she couldn't think as fast as she could talk. She saw me look up and probably saw the inquiry in the look.

"I don't see that Mr. Wilson has much money t' marry Gertie MacMichael on!" she said, in a challenging tone.

"Who said he was going to marry her?" I gasped.

"Oh, everybody!"

"The deuce they do!"

"Oh, yes! Well, it'll be a good thing for him in the end. He's a fine young man an' plenty of brains, and she's a rare girl, an' I suppose she'll have plenty o' money some day." The old lady was evidently seeking for further information, but there the conversation stayed. It is a marvel how news travels in a town the size of Caribou, no matter where—but then Caribou had the "gang," as Wilson used to call the gossiping sisterhood.

The next morning I got up just in time to see the *Liffey,* making a great cloud of black smoke, and with a wisp of steam floating around the top of her safety-valve escape, go boiling out toward the rising sun and "the Island," where enough freight for a dozen steamers of her size was waiting, as it had been for many weeks.

By half-past eight Miss Gertrude MacMichael came galloping down the street on a big bay horse, and gave me fifteen minutes to get ready to go with her for a ride. On that ride, over muddy slushy roads in the glaring March sunlight and wind, were formed various plans by which a blue-eyed Irish girl would visit Nova Scotia. Before I left her at her own gate she told me that her father had asked Mr. Henderson to come in that evening, so that he could get at least some preliminary information that would help him in arranging to reimburse the Northumberland Company for the loss of the *Shannon,* and for the time and expenses of the other three steamers, and that Henderson had asked that Wilson and I should be present also. Of course I said I would be on hand, but when I left the girl and watched her as she went bouncing up the avenue in clouds of flying gravel I had no idea in the world that that evening would give me one of the surprises of my life. Of course I have known all about it while I've been telling you this story, and I may have told you more than I knew myself at the time, and as a consequence you may have already guessed what I never dreamed of guessing.

After I took the horse home I found a cablegram which read:

"Understand perfectly. Cannot tell you by cable. Depends on yourself. Yes. Writing.   KATHLEEN."

—and this apparently incoherent message set me dancing around the room like a small boy, until I heard my housekeeper coming to see what the trouble was about. Then I seized a pair of iron dumb-bells and tried to save my reputation for sanity. After she'd gone, apparently satisfied with my explanation, I looked in the glass—as I used to look when I was watching for my moustache to sprout—and hunted for grey hairs, and I found them, too; not many, but a few, sprinkled over my ears and about my temples. After all, I don't know that they were all due to age. The girl that wrote that cablegram—well, perhaps she could take them away too.

All the afternoon I wrote; dreamed and thought and wrote, and sent to some of the dear chaps I used to call my friends copies of newspapers with headlines such as these:—" Remarkable rescue. James MacMichael, the principal in the famous Nova Scotia shipping firm, MacMichael & Co., and the crew of the MacMichael liner *Duncrieff* saved by Northumberland Steamship Co.'s ice-crushers *Shannon* and *Liffey*. The *Shannon*, badly injured by the heavy ice, lost in the attempt to return to Caribou. Company will probably claim heavy salvage," etc. Heavy salvage! Yes, and as it turned out, they got it, too.

CHAPTER XII.

THE evening came, and I went up to the MacMichaels'. The night was sharp enough, and I found MacMichael sitting in his big dark library alone by a snapping wood fire that roared in an old-fashioned stone fireplace. There was no other light in the room, and he was stretched out comfortably, gazing into the flames. He looked up with an expression of contentment as I went in.

"Good evening, Ashburn," he said, "it's all very well to be up off Gaspé; but, after all, this is a good thing to get back to." I was beginning to think so myself, more than I would have once thought possible. Going over all the world is right enough for a time, but it palls,—palls most fearfully,—and you begin to want a resting-place, if it's only a log house. In a little while Miss MacMichael came in. It was a great transformation: from a hooded girl in a loose blanket suit to a girl in a dark-crimson velvet dress, a dress with that indescribable low hiss, a dress that showed every curve, that instead of being a steel mould was nothing more than an appendage to the lithe-limbed girl; a dress that clung and swung into every motion of her supple figure and waved into the flexing throw of her accurately poised elastic-muscled step; a simple, sweeping, beautiful dress with a V-shaped low-cut throat, showing through and beneath the intricate design of a froth of white Irish lace the infinite sweep of rounded neck and wide, strong-balanced shoulders, —shoulders on which the muscles behind—I've watched them when she was dancing—showed in waves and dips beneath the warm, glowing skin; a dress that showed to glorious advantage the deep, crimson-brown flush of her cheeks, bred of the winds that roared and hissed across the floes and clumpets, and of the sun that glared into the white northern spring. The girl finished the picture by throwing herself down in a big oak chair almost hidden by a great creamy-white polar-bear skin.

" Good evening, Captain Ashburn," she laughed, " I see by the *Globe* that ' Captain Frederic Ashburn, who was in command of the lost Northumberland Company's steamer *Shannon* in her heroic and successful attempt to rescue the crew of the *Duncrieff,* was bourne triumphantly to his home on the shoulders of some of his enthusiastic and appreciative fellow citizens of Caribou.' It's a grand thing to be famous, isn't it! "

" Yes," I said, rubbing myself on the black and blue spots.

" Now," continued the girl, " I propose being present at this solemn conclave." She clapped her brown fingers over her father's mouth. " No!" she went on, " I own part of the *Dungeness* and the *Duncannon,* and I'm just as much a part of MacMichael and Company as you are. I feel that I should be present to safeguard my own interests and those of the firm. I am afraid," she continued with mock gravity, " I am deeply afraid that certain complications are going to arise, complications so grave as possibly to affect by their stunning unexpectedness the usually keen business instincts of the head of MacMichael and Company, and therefore I feel that some other member of the firm should be present to——" MacMichael captured the brown hand.

" What under Heaven are you vapouring about now? " he asked jocularly, " has Henderson been giving you some original ideas? "

" Neither Mr. Henderson nor anybody else has been giving me directly any ideas. But you needn't think that I'm dependent on Mr. Henderson or anybody for ideas," she went on, banteringly, " I'm capable of producing original ones for myself. I've just been using what Captain Ashburn chooses to call my ' unerring intuition,' and it has led me to believe that complications exist, and whether they are disclosed or not it is as well for me to be present. Of course I may be wrong, but remember that the captain says my intuition is unerring, and so I suppose there is no appeal: it must be."

"Don't be too hard on me," I laughed.

"Hard on you! I'm not. I'm in earnest."

"Thank you!" I said.

MacMichael looked puzzled, as if trying to connect things of the past with things of the present, and the girl stood up by the fire, assumed a tragic air, and said:—"Behold! He is thinking." He looked up.

"Are you talking nonsense, Gertrude, or are you trying to convince your poor old dad that you know things that he doesn't know?" The girl laughed again.

"Perhaps I only wanted an excuse to stay in the room and hear the sages talk business," she replied; "women are always wanting to hear about things far above their comprehension, you know,"—and she adroitly turned the subject to the night when the *Shannon* was fighting through the big pack toward the *Duncrieff*.

A few minutes later Wilson came in, and the girl's face lit up in the same entrancing way I had seen so often of late. He drew an arm-chair in close to the fire by Miss MacMichael's side, and we still talked of things that had happened during the trip. Each had his or her own particular pet scene. MacMichael said that the sight of his life was the moment when Wilson reached the *Duncrieff* with the ice-boat. The girl's favourite, quite naturally, was the time when her father climbed over the rail of the *Shannon,* and stood half-stupefied at the roars of the cheering men around. " And you cried, you dear old thing, didn't you! " she said, throwing her arms round his neck at the recollection. Wilson and I agreed that the sight of sights was when old Donald stood by the stoke-hold door with the *Shannon* sinking under his feet, and while the stokers were fleeing over the broken pack calling them all the names he knew, and cursing them as " eenfairnal coowards."

At last Henderson came in. The first thing he did was to congratulate Wilson and Miss Mac-Michael, and, considering everything, he did it with marvellous heartiness. Then he joined the circle around the fire. I shall remember that circle a long time. On the left Wilson, in a grey reefer-coated suit, very much the same David Wilson I had met on the wilderness island in beautiful Nictor Lake two and a half years before; perhaps a little heavier, and if possible a shade more sun-tanned than ever. Then the girl in the velvet dress; not the same girl altogether: just as uncon-ventional, just as kind-hearted and frank and true,

just as plucky as on the day she sailed the *Osprey*
or taught the biting horse a lesson, just as strong
as when she " shinned " up the *Osprey's* mast with
a steel throat-block in her teeth, and more beautiful than ever.   But she had learned how to love,
and wit' the knowledge had come a world of new
sympathies.   Now she was all that she had been
and withal much more of a woman.   In the centre
was MacMichael, ruddy-complexioned, with a skin
almost as smooth and velvety as his daughter's,
his hair and moustache pure white long before
their time, with his keen, alert eyes roving about,
and now wearing a distinctly puzzled expression.
Henderson was exactly as I first saw him ; scrupu-
lously neat, almost ostentatiously clean,—if you
know what I mean,—with the ends of his peculiarly silky black moustache trained far down below
the corners of his mouth.   His expression, always
easily read, showed that he had something on his
mind which evidently caused him to feel as many
mixed emotions as it is well for one man to feel at
one time.   Through all I could see that he felt
deeply the fading away of his last chance—if he
ever had one—for winning the love of Mac-
Michael's daughter.   Then to the right of the fire
sat I, I who had come into the circle as an entire
stranger ; I who had been educated, and learned
many things.   I had been miserable enough when
I came in—being one of those none-too-common

mortals who finds that one woman and only one
is all in all to him, as she always must be; but
now, when I let my thoughts run in certain directions, I could feel hot flushes run over me, and my
heart would beat faster, even if I had a few grey
hairs.   I was happy, but I, too, was changed.   The
Navy had lost its charm for me: adventure, yes,
always, and sport of any kind wherever it was to
be found, but no more roving over the world.
London at its best and gayest could never have
the same indefinable charm it has for a younger
man.   The lights could glint across the wet pave-
ments, but never lure as they used to do.   London
would do to visit, but now, God willing, I would
make my home by the shimmering waters of the
beautiful Gulf in the bracing cool climate of all
climates.   You who haven't seen a summer on
the Gulf shore of Nova Scotia have yet to live.
I'm digressing.

MacMichael had heard good news.   Three of
his boats had been chartered by the Home Government for transport work, and he would make
a good deal out of it.   He wandered along, talking of charters he was making from everywhere
to everywhere, and how the line was prospering,
then he suddenly squared up with a business-like
air.

"Well, Mr. Henderson," he said, "I have already told you how much I have appreciated all

that your Company has done for me, and all you have done personally; but I asked you to come in this evening especially to get some idea of how we are to come to a basis for settlement. I suppose you will act entirely on your own initiative on behalf of the Northumberland Steamship Company."

" I hardly feel that I should like to undertake that responsibility," said Henderson, apparently highly amused at something, and trying to hide his amusement, " I am afraid that you had better arrange this matter with the Company directly. I haven't full jurisdiction over such important things." MacMichael noted Henderson's efforts to keep his face straight, and looked bewildered and a little nettled. Still, what could he do!

" You seemed to be able to send all four steamers off in search of us without having to consult your principals!" he said, rather stiffly, for when MacMichael talked business he wished to talk business and be business-like.

" I received permission from the firm in each case. They were exceedingly glad to give the permission. In fact, in this case, if they had lost the four steamers, and it would have done any good, I'm sure they would have willingly bought other ice-crushers from the Russian Government and sent them also, even if it ruined them,"—and

Henderson half drowned the laugh which Mac-
Michael pretended not to see.

"I'm sure," he said, "I don't understand you.
Why should your firm be so careful about my
safety as to do that?" Henderson smiled again.

"Partly," he said, "because the Company is a
close personal friend of yours and Mrs. Mac-
Michael's, and partly because it is a still closer
personal friend of your daughter's." MacMichael
turned and gazed at Henderson as you'd gaze at
a lunatic. The girl's foot was tapping the big
andirons, and Wilson was apparently studying the
foot.

"But, my dear man," said MacMichael, as soon
as he could speak, "I never even saw a member of
your firm!"

"Oh! yes, you have. You've seen the whole
Company more times than you can remember.
There is the Northumberland Steamship Company
entire, hulls, spars, boilers and engines, bonds,
notes, liabilities and assets," and he jerked his
thumb in the direction of Wilson.

I've often sat since and thought of MacMichael's
expression in that minute,—yes, and mine. The
two of us sat there open-mouthed, like a couple
of Bechuanas seeing their first steam pinnace. I
don't believe a word was said for a good two
minutes. Wilson was smiling in much the same
amused way I had noted as peculiar to him when

I first saw him. He shielded himself behind Miss MacMichael.

" Don't let your father look at me in that way," he laughed, " I'm really quite innocent, you know! I haven't done anything wrong." The girl smiled, put a protecting arm around him, and was about to speak when MacMichael found his voice.

" Wilson!" he said, " You—don't—mean—to —tell—me——and all this time——. Damn it all!" he thundered, " then why did you register in London? Why did you make such a secret of it? Nobody could think any the worse of you for owning the boats. Why did——Wilson, you're a crank! you're an inexplicable character. No! you're a genius! For anybody that can lie to us all like that——" and MacMichael stopped and shook his head.

" I never found it necessary to lie!" said Wlison, " you seemed to have as much idea that I owned the Northumberland boats as that Donald owned the MacMichael boats. I found it convenient for business reasons to register in London, but my real reason was that I didn't wish people in this country to know that I owned the boats. I suppose," he continued musingly, " that they'll have to know now. Oh! well, it doesn't make any difference."

" But why didn't you want people to know?"

asked MacMichael, looking as puzzled as ever. Wilson hesitated for a second.

"Why," he said, speaking very slowly, "I knew that if my own connection with the line were known, people would wish to come to me direct in certain dealings and would ask a good many impossible things of the service,—things they would never think of asking of the company in London," and he laughed.

"It would take a gread deal of time from my zoölogical work," he went on, "and besides I wanted to see if I could accomplish a number of things independent of any influence the ownership of the Northumberland boats might possibly give me. This was my real reason for keeping the secret, after all."

"Yes! you brute!" laughed the girl, "and one of those things was getting me to promise to marry you. You thought if I knew that, instead of being a young man with a fortune consisting of face and brains and prospects, you were the sole owner of a steamship line paying fifty per cent. or some such ridiculous dividend, that I might think more of you."

"I thought nothing of the sort," was the reply; "but I thought that my own belief in your common sense—and some of your other attributes— might be the result of my judgment being warped by outward things, and now I've proved that it

wasn't: that's all.   You see, it wasn't a disbelief
in you; it was only a distrust of my own judgment
in an important matter."   The girl blushed and
took an interest in the fire.   MacMichael was beginning to see the humour of the situation, and
was chuckling to himself and remarking under his
breath, as he not infrequently did, that " he'd be
damned," and so forth.   He turned to Wilson.

   " Ashburn remembers the day that you beat
Oldham in the sculling race," he said, reminiscent-
ly,—" yes, and you remember it too.   We stood
on the Market Wharf, and we watched the old
Walrus come in loaded to the hatches—and above.
I remember seeing you smile in a way that used
to nettle me a little.   By Heavens! you had reason to smile!   I was telling Ashburn about the
boats and how they were paying, and then I said
I thought I could bring one of our boats into the
Gulf in winter, and I remember you said the ice
would crush in her sides as I'd crush an eggshell
between my fingers.   Hmm!   Well that was a
pretty good description, but the real thing made
a deal more noise than breaking an eggshell! "—
and MacMichael paused for a moment and
thought.   " Then you went up the wharf with
Gertie, and I told Ashburn that you were a pretty
fine chap, but that it was a shame you didn't have
some business at which you could make some
money: and you were making a hundred and fifty

per cent. more than I was and probably planning the *Shannon* and the *Liffey* in your head at that very moment! Well! I'm glad you got them in commission as soon as you did. If you hadn't I wouldn't be here, that's all!"—and MacMichael laughed and chuckled to himself for full five minutes. "Well, well!" he said, a few minutes later, still chuckling, "I've been fooled a few times before in my life, but never so badly—or so pleasantly. Dave,"—MacMichael got suddenly serious,—"I knew before that I owed you a great deal, but now—besides what you've done personally you've taken your own magnificent boats out, and lost one of them, and lost any amount of business, to save the boat and crew of what, from a business point of view, was a firm that was trying to become a rival." Wilson looked pained.

"Mr. MacMichael, please don't say any more about it in that way," he said, "for, as you very well know, there was no business point of view involved. To make your mind easier I can only say once more that anything I was able to do was nothing more than my duty, and I hope I would do as much for any other firm's boat that might be in the same predicament."

"Well, well!" said MacMichael, "then I suppose you and I settle it between us. You won't lose anything if I can help it."

"I haven't lost anything so far," was the reply,

and Wilson's eyes met the sparkling eyes of the girl.

MacMichael looked at his daughter.

" Well, Gertie," he said, " what do you think of all this." The girl laughed.

" This is the complication I told you about," she said.

" It is, is it! and how did you know? "

" Oh! intuition," she laughed. " I put two and two together and made five, when you would have made four. I added one of my own, you see, and in this case five happened to be right."

" You weren't told? " he asked, looking suspiciously at Wilson.

" No! on my honour! " and the girl thumped the place over her heart with a sonorous bump.

" How long, please, has what you call your intuition been good enough to let you know about this business? "

" I didn't know; I only suspected."

" How long have you suspected."

" Oh! two or three days, that is all.   Only since we met the *Walrus*."

" Hmm! " grunted MacMichael, " women are a queer lot.   There are times and things at which the best and sharpest of them are remarkable for nothing but their thundering stupidity, and then again, sometimes they know things, and you don't know how they find them out.   They're a queer lot, but

they're not a bad lot after all!"—and he got up and
walked up and down the dark room with his hands
under his coat-tails, chuckling and humming to himself.

"Well, well, well!" he said finally, "and to think
that David Wilson owns the Northumberland boats,
the boats that I've been envying for the last two
years. I don't know what you'll come to," he went
on, turning sharply on Wilson; "here you're not
thirty-one yet, and you've got all sorts of F. R. G.
S.'s and things after your name, and you own a
line of steamers, the best in the country,"—and
MacMichael drove in the switch with a bang and
flooded the room with electric light. His eye caught
something through the window; he turned off the
light again and looked out.

"Come over and see one of your boats coming
in!" he said, and we all looked down to the harbour, where we could see the lights of the *Liffey,*
getting back from her first trip.

When MacMichael turned the switch again I saw
tears on the girl's cheeks. I didn't blame her.

For an hour more MacMichael kept recalling
things and freely calling himself a "damned idiot"
—in his usual forcible way—for not having known
before.

"I sat for two solid hours," he said, banging his
fist on the big shining walnut table, "and wondered
why the devil the Northumberland Steamship Com-

pany of London, England, wanted to give a hundred pounds toward the maintenance of the cottage hospital in Caribou, Nova Scotia. Hmm! Pfff!" and he snorted at what he now looked on as his own stupidity. Wilson and he had one grand point in common: the only person either of them never forgave for a wrong act, or a real or apparent mistake, was himself.

For a long time the girl had been perfectly silent. Her father had been monopolizing the whole conversation. Finally, just as we were leaving, he turned to her.

"What's the trouble with you, young lady," he said; "you're looking fearfully quiet and fearfully solemn!"

"Am I!" she said quietly. She got up, gathered up her skirt in one hand and pirouetted out toward the window. She crouched, ran at an old-fashioned high-backed sofa in the middle of the room, went clear over the top of it as clean as a Virginia deer clears a railway fence, and landed as lightly as a cat.

"I'm past talking, dad," she said, and kissed his forehead. "You have been doing it very well for me." Then the five of us sat down and laughed until Mrs. MacMichael came in and asked if this was the "business" she was being shut out from. The girl had expressed her feeling better than if she had talked for hours, and in a way that was characteristic of herself and of no one else that I had ever had the good fortune to know. We left MacMichael still humming to himself and calling himself various things for not having guessed the true state of affairs, but at the same time I could see that he was mightily pleased with himself and all the world, and especially with his prospective son-in-law.

"Well," I said, after we had left Henderson, " of all the things that ever happened to me or I ever heard of I think that for sheer novelty this has first place. Of all the ridiculous things in the world there could be but few more unlikely situations than to have an apparently comparatively poor man live in a small town for years without a soul in the place guessing that he was the owner of a line of steamers which ran under their very noses every day of their lives. Nothing but the unbelievable audacity of the plan ever saved you." Wilson laughed.

"And the funny part of it," he said, " was that I took no especial pains to conceal it. I often said things that really could only be explained in two ways; either by supposing that I owned the Northumberland boats, or that I was a lunatic. When this is generally known, 'the gang' "—his irreverent soubriquet for the extraordinarily ignorant and viperish Caribou branch of the international society of old-women gossips and scandal-mongers—" 'the gang' will be able to remember at least fifty things I've said in the presence of its members which might have led them to the truth. Like MacMichael, they'll curse themselves for stupidity,"—and Wilson laughed again at the thought. Then he became serious and said:

"Ashburn, if you think enough of the line to invest some of your capital in it, I should like you to come in with me."

"My dear boy," I replied, pleased more than I can tell you, "it's really too good of you to offer; but if you are in earnest I'll accept." So thus I became a part of the Northumberland Steamship Company, and to-day I've got over six hundred thousand dollars in the business.

In June of that year there was a wedding in the Church of England in Caribou, a wedding such as Caribou had never seen. Not that it was in the least different from other unostentatious weddings, for to me weddings look a good deal alike; but the remarkable part of it was the crowd. There were more people about the church than were about the Northumberland Company's wharf "the day the *Liffey* got back." Donald smoked in the church porch and when remonstrated with by the sexton told him to "go t' blazes," that he'd "smooke een th' chair-rch eef he wanted to." I had to rake a frock coat and a silk hat out of a trunk—I hadn't had the brutes on since I'd left London—and be best man, and when the organ began to roll out Mendelssohn's "Wedding March" I leaned over toward the bride and groom and said: "I suppose you remember where you heard that before!" The girl gave me a smile and looked far away. I suppose she was thinking of the ice floes, and the stars, and the quivering Northern Light, and the great silence broken by the whistle of unseen wings and the cry of the dog seal. I shall have to be like the society journals on such occasions, and say that the bride looked radiantly lovely; but between my belief in what I say and their belief in what they say there is as much difference as between the old *Benbow's* sixteen inchers and a Krag-Jörgensen. Three of the MacMichael boats were in, and, with the *Aurora* and *Liffey* and most of the other craft in the harbour, were dressed from truck to water-line. It was a glorious sunshiny day, with the cool heart-lightening Nova Scotia air breezing in over the shimmering blue waters of the beautiful Gulf. We could hardly get the carriages through the crowd. Through all the triumphant progress, under the newly leaved trees and between the dark-green spruce hedges from the church to the big stone house on the hill, above the clanging of the bells came the howls of every steamer whistle in the harbour, and above all we could hear the ungodly shrieks from the *Liffey's* syren. We could look down and see her lying motionless and black and ferocious below the pier, with a cloud of white steam drifting off to leeward. Her voice sounded as if she fully realized the important part she had taken in bringing these things to pass, and was duly pleased. MacMichael had gotten together an exceeding great lunch, with delicacies from all the ends of the earth, and there were present to partake of it, among all sorts of the bride's old admirers from St. John and Halifax and further afield, the Honourable Edward Rose, and Irland, and even Billings, all of whom bore their parts nobly. Bless their hearts, but how they must have cut expenses for a month or so!—most of them—for the wedding presents they brought her were a sight. The station platform was like the floor of a rice warehouse, and when the train pulled out with the two of them, setting off signal torpedoes until it sounded for all the world like the old *Centaur* in one-pounder target work, Kitty looked at me in a suggestive way and laughed.

Oh! I forgot to tell you about Kitty. Miss Mac-Michael had arranged in some mysterious manner that she was to spend the summer with them in Caribou. She did.

Donald, the imperturbable, still sits around a good deal on the big coal-bin near the whitewashed stove in the fire station, and under the bin lies the black spaniel, now getting extraordinarily fat. The old engineer has forgiven all the men that deserted him on the *Shannon*, admitting that " na doot there wiz soom leetle danger o' gettin' par-rboiled eef they'd not used soom caution een stayin' een th' stoke-hold," and the deserters, or as many of them as are in Caribou, turn up at the engine-house and tell yarns every wet night in summer and every night in winter. When I said he had forgiven all, I left out Johnstone. Jim MacIntyre told me of the first time that worthy undertook to join the circle in front of the coal-bin. " Y' may be all right," he said, with the usual dry smile, "but a woodn' troost y' heere. Y' know y' tek queer feets o' fly-in' thro' th' air, goin' end over end 's eef y'd been blown oop wi' an explosion. Eet's all right oot on th' ice, but eef y' tr-ried 't heere y' might brek th' bar-roometer, or fall on th' doog, so y'd better keep away." Mr. Johnstone kept away.

I saw Donald only a day or two ago. He handed me a slip of paper covered with figures. " A bin caalculatin' the coombined ice pressure aloong th' entire length o' th' *Shannon* the night when th' beeg crush smashed een the noomber seex," he said, " Eet amoonted approoximately t' th' extraoordinar' soom o' foorty-seven thoosan' ton. Ah! she wiz a gran' good boat, wiz th' *Shannon*. 'Twas a gret peety she coold not 'a' coom home. Damn those coowards! " and the old man walked on toward the Northumberland pier to see Sandy.

A good many times through the long, clear, glorious Nova Scotia summer, on days when the breeze swings hissing through the rattling leafy tree-tops in the town, bends the asters and dahlias in the old-fashioned gardens, and works up a decent little chop on the shimmering deep-blue water, Caribou's grand harbour is dotted with white boat sails —including some extraordinary rigs and extraordinary sized spinnakers; and the *Osprey* and the *Glooscap,* and some others, fight it out, and both are sailed by their old skippers and with the same inflexible pluck.   But never since has there been anything like what they now speak of as " the big race."

It's useless to say anything about MacMichael, for the majority of people know what he has been doing, and nobody, including me, knows what he is going to do next.   It's generally supposed that he's made one or two fortunes out of this South African war alone.

Up on the hill top, not far from MacMichael's house or each other, and buried in spruces, pines, beeches, and lindens, are two comparatively new grey stone houses owned by the partners in the Northumberland Steamship Company.   In front of one of the houses, half grown over with vines, is a big, rough-hewn grey granite boulder.   On its one polished face is the inscription :— *To the memory of the SHANNON, the first of the ice-crushers. She saved a hundred lives and accomplished other things.*   The three stone houses are great centres for the type of outdoor and indoor gaiety that lacks every element of social formalism, and makes the

life of eastern Canada the most normal and health-
ful and happy in the wide world. In summer it's
boat-sailing and sculling and canoeing and golf and
tennis, and unlimited steam yacht picnics to the islands in the Strait outside. And what picnics they
are! At midnight you'll see the boats come boiling
home, racing all the way up in the moonlight.
Only a week ago at full moon we were outside with
the three boats, MacMichael's and Wilson's—the
old *Scoter*—and mine. I can see them now, the
three of them abreast, throbbing in toward Caribou
Light, swishing through the warm, glittering, phos-
phorescent water, and swinging on the low, long,
calm-surfaced swells, the same swells that had silently washed up against the cliffs at Cape North
or thundered down on the long beach at the Race as
they swung in from the North Atlantic a little while
before. The boats looked for all the world like
three destroyers making in for a hostile port, though
the crews of destroyers on duty don't send songs
rolling across the water the way they rolled that
night. In winter it's ski and snowshoeing and skat-
ing and informal parties afterward, and the result
of it all is that the young people of this part of the
world are healthy, and never morbid or blasé, which
is a good deal in itself in adding the final charm to
living.

About Wilson it is useless for me to say anything
more at present. His later scientific work is too

well known and of too much general interest to
necessitate my even speaking of it.   The peculiar
adventures in the Labrador Peninsula, and the particularly peculiar relations he came to bear to two
Governments and some great commercial forces I
may tell you about later, when it would be safe.
He is still a good deal the same; quiet, resourceful,
and kind to the point of self-sacrifice.   His wife
commands her friends with the same imperious
sway—and her friends are legion; the charm of her
impetuous unconventionality is as strong as ever,
and she keeps the now grovelling " gang " in a
reign of terror, for they know that what she does,
that must they do, and they never know what she
is going to do next.   They've become quite os-
tentatious in giving Christmas trees, and boat-sails,
and drives, and such unlike entertainments to the
poorer children of the town, and all to the tune set
by Mrs. David Wilson.   All sorts of distinguished
people, which Caribou has before only read about,
come and visit at the Wilson's, and indicate that
they are pretty thoroughly human by going in—as
far as they may be able—for everything that the
younger Mrs. Wilson goes in for.   Needless to say
they are kept busy.

Henderson is still, as he is likely to be, the man-
ager of the Northumberland boats.   He spends a
good many evenings in some one of the three stone
houses on the hill.   He is still single, and the only

time we miss him altogether is when any new and really interesting girl visits Caribou. He has a few permanent stand-bys who seem to receive a certain amount of attention as a matter of course, but he rushes at each newcomer apparently in an investigating spirit, and not infrequently drops her within a week, as if disappointed at the result. He seems to have set up an ideal, and to be looking for it; but if, as I suspect, the ideal is modelled pretty closely after a Miss Gertrude MacMichael that once existed, he might as well give up the search. This world could only produce one of that kind, at least in one generation.

As for me, I'm living the happiest days of my life; at least, of as much of it as I've seen. It's useless for a man to describe his wife to anyone, either man or woman. This moment she is just Kathleen Tyrrell, as I first saw her: a tall, stately, blue-eyed girl, with golden-brown hair and a wonderful thrilling rich Irish voice. Perhaps she hasn't the iron nerve that seems peculiar among women to Wilson's wife, and perhaps she is a bit more conventional—more of a woman and less of a girl —but, there! there! it's useless to make comparisons. They're both perfect enough. We've been in London together again, and renewed old acquaintances, and driven home after dances when the grey light was sifting up through St. James's Park from the east, and the big cartloads of green stuff

were creaking in to Covent Garden from Wimble-
don way : and we've come home content.   I've got
a big, low, oak-ceilinged library-den, and in it are
all sorts of things reminiscent of other days in the
old life.   But over the big stone fireplace, with the
whole space above the mantel to itself, a space on
which nothing else is allowed to encroach, is a
souvenir which I wouldn't give for all the rest.   It's
a polished oval brass plate showing the marks of
having been pried from a steamer's house, and on
it, in crimson letters, are the words :—

There's a new *Shannon* now,—a new *Shannon*
beside which the *Liffey* in her strength has to bow
down : near on to four thousand tons of steel driven
by two wicked screws swung by triple-expansion
engines of eleven thousand horse-power.   That's an
ice-crusher in earnest.   She hasn't a pram-bow like
the old boat, but her stem is straight above like the
Liffey's.   With all her strength and her big funnels
—she has two of them—her model is as pretty as

that of a canoe. In the ice she's a perfect marvel, and it's really a grand sight to see her boiling through a six-foot field, or riding over packs and clumpets twenty feet thick, absented-minded like, as if she hadn't noticed they were there. And all the time such a grinding of ice and swishing of water you never heard. The old *Aurora* and the *Walrus* have given up ice work, have retired from active life, as it were, and for the sake of amusement in their old age go pottering round the coast in summer picking up odd jobs, and incidentally a good deal more than paying their way: and besides, over on the dirty, smoky, hammer-clanging Tyne, there's another Northumberland boat on the ways, a sister to the *Shannon* of to-day.

All through the long clear days in summer, Northumberland Strait, as ever, shimmers and sparkles in the sunlight; and occasionally, when the wind comes down hard from the northwest, gets up a great chop of its own, boils itself into green and white streaks, and rips the spars out of the lobster-boats. Away across, you can see the red banks and green fields of the " Garden of the Gulf." But some day in late January, long after Caribou's spruce hedges are buried under the snow, some day when the wind is northeast and has been for a time, and the Gulf looks grey-blue and rough and cold, if you're lucky enough to be out on MacDonald's Point or the Roaring Bull you'll see, perhaps, a solitary big clumpet with a high peak, moving along silently to the south, not two hundred yards from the shore. Suddenly you'll see it stop, while the water swirls past, as its green bottom, away down among the gulf-weed, grounds on a reef and rests; and looking away to seaward you'll see, coming down from the north, a great, white, jagged, glistening line, stretching out of sight in both directions, coming silently as ever: the ice, the queer, fantastic-formed, irresistible northern ice driving into the southern bight of the great Gulf of St. Lawrence. It comes with a few big pinnacled clumpets navigating along ahead by themselves, and with it come the seals and kittiwakes and burgomasters and murres and auks and puffins and grebes and mergansers,—yes, and the cockawees in all the glory of their winter plumage. It piles up over the reefs, up into great grounded hummocks as high as a house, it grinds on the shore and roars and crashes as it lands, and drives in until it fills the whole bight, and stretches away to the north and east clear to the horizon and beyond, far up to where the old *Shannon* hears it grinding away above her trucks, and remains undisturbed and peaceful down below.

THE END.